SPIRITS & SIRENS

What Reviewers Say About
Kelly & Tana Fireside's Work

Whiskey and Wine

"Lovely! Really enjoyed Lace and Tessa's story. I love the community feel surrounding the story. Lovely story that had my heart melting and just hoping there will be more from Lace and Tessa in future stories."—*LesBeReviewed*

Vintage and Vogue

"Smart. Sexy. Unputdownable. *Vintage & Vogue* hooked me on page one."—Tessa Layne, USA Today best-selling romance author

"Lots of great humor. There are some fantastic lines in this book. There are also some funny and interesting characters. Vintage and Vogue definitely feels like the set up for a longer series based in Owen Station."—*TBR Reviews*

"So lovely and heartfelt! A great story with a lovely contrast between the past and modern times. Really enjoyed this story and Mango the cat really stole my heart. Stories with cats are always a winner! Excited for what Kelly and Tana Fireside's next story will be!"—*LesBeReviewed*

By the Authors

Vintage & Vogue

Whiskey & Wine

Spirits & Sirens

SPIRITS & SIRENS

by

Kelly & Tana Fireside

2024

SPIRITS & SIRENS

ISBN 13: 978-1-63679-607-9

This Trade Paperback Original Is Published By
Bold Strokes Books, Inc.
P.O. Box 249
Valley Falls, NY 12185

First Edition: May 2024

CREDITS
Editor: Cindy Cresap
Production Design: Susan Ramundo
Cover Design By Inkspiral Design

Acknowledgments

Thanks to all the trailblazing women, many of whom are way younger than we are, who have inspired and encouraged us over the years. We love writing stories that honor you and the courageous choices you make in your personal and professional lives.

Thanks, especially, to Chief Cheryl for being a role model to so many—and for giving us insight into what it's like to be a woman in the firehouse. You helped bring Assistant Fire Chief Al Jones to life and now we can't imagine never having met her.

Thanks to our son-in-law for coming up with the title for this book, even though we know you won't read it. More importantly, thanks for helping raise our granddaughters to be brave and strong. They inspire us, too.

Thanks to the whole team at Bold Strokes Books, especially Radclyffe, whose vision and persistence both inspires authors like us to share our stories and creates a platform for getting those stories into the hands of our readers.

And that brings us to you, dear friend. Thank you for coming with us as we journey back to Owen Station. We hope you fall in love with this quirky little town and with Al and Elena and all their friends. We know it's not a perfect story but we told it with love and an unshakeable belief that everyone deserves a happy ending.

That means you, most of all.

Dedication

To our family and friends—
your encouragement is everything.

PROLOGUE

San Francisco, 1975

"Wake up, honey, you're dreaming."

Margaret's eyes fluttered open and she saw Betty beside her, her eyes filled with worry. Margaret was disoriented, still smelling smoke in her nose and alcohol on his breath. She was thankful the nightmares didn't come as often as they used to.

Sunlight had begun peeking through the window, and sounds from the street below told her the city was waking up to another day.

"I'll go make coffee. Take your time getting up." Betty kissed her and then headed to their small kitchen in the third-story walk-up that had been their home for more than twenty years.

Margaret still expected that, any day, he would come looking for them. It was hard to believe, even after all this time, that they had made it out. But she would do anything to protect her family.

Anything.

She stretched and put her feet on the floor, finding her slippers. Then, just like she did every morning, she got up, made her way to her desk, pulled out a sheet of paper, and grabbed a pen.

Dearest Sis,

I have written you countless letters. I hope you are doing well. Not a day goes by that I do not think of you, and long to see you again, to assure you that I am alive and that all of my dreams have come true.

We made it to the city. It's wonderful here. Love and understanding surround us. People like us live openly, without fear. We have become good friends with the two women who live in the apartment above us. We have established ourselves here. We have jobs. And we are doing important work, providing hope for other women, and giving them a place to stay here in our home, women who have been through the same nightmare I escaped. I couldn't have done that without your help. I will be forever grateful to you for that.

I tell the women who come to us that it can be a long road, but there is hope and healing and acceptance along the way. Convincing them that it is not their fault is the hardest. But when I see them walk in, sometimes years later, with their shoulders straight and smiles on their faces, it makes all the risks that we took—and all that we gave up to be here—worth it.

I wish I could talk to you, Sister. My heart aches to see you and hold you again. That you and I have had to sacrifice being together, in order for B and I to live in peace, remains my only regret.

Margaret's tears stained the paper. She wiped them off her cheeks and stopped writing. She knew she would never mail this letter, either. It was just too dangerous.

Betty came in carrying a mug of coffee, and kissed Margaret on top of her head.

"Are you okay?"

"I'll be fine, my love. The dreams make it feel like it was just yesterday. They remind me why we can never go back. But I miss her so. It is like part of me is missing. I can't explain it. I have to believe she knows I am alive and well, but I wish I could talk to her, just to be sure. I wish she could see the gift she has given us."

Betty smiled softly. "She would be so proud of you, dear. Of all that you have done with your life. I know she would be your biggest champion. Why don't you go ahead and finish that letter. It always makes you feel better."

Betty went back into the kitchen to make breakfast, and Margaret picked up her pen.

We have managed to save up some money, Sis. It's now ten times the amount you sent me off with. I have wanted to send it to you, to thank you. But I know that is not possible. So we have decided to use it to make a bigger difference, to start something that will help dozens, maybe even hundreds of women. One day I hope you will know just how much of a difference you made in my life and in so many others.

You are always in my heart.
M.L.

Margaret folded the page, opened the drawer, and placed it with all the others. She hoped beyond hope that her sister, across all the years and miles, could somehow hear her heart beating in time with her own.

Chapter One

It was, in fact, a pretty impressive hole. And assistant fire chief Allison Jones had seen her share of them.

At least a dozen people were already there, looking at it.

"Dammit." She flipped off the siren and leaped out of her department-issued SUV. It wasn't her style—she'd rather be on her Harley than stuck driving a cage any day of the week—but it came with the job.

"Everybody, stand back." She managed not to roll her eyes. Or at least she hoped so.

Al had just jumped out of the shower—looking forward to a much-needed day off, canyon carving her way through the Chiricahua Mountains on an early spring day—when the call came. Still, she managed to be the first one on the scene. The first member of the Owen Station Fire Department, anyway. And so far, the only first responder. Somehow, though, news of the hole had spread through town fast enough to have drawn a crowd of civilians.

"I said...*stand back*!"

That got their attention. They kept one eye on the mysterious hole and one eye on Al as they backed up, opening a path down the middle.

"Sorry, Chief."

"No problem, Chief."

"Right away, Chief."

The murmurs were loud enough for Al to hear as she passed through.

It was one hundred percent not fair that she was forced to walk that narrow line between being commanding and being called aggressive. Or angry. Her male colleagues never had to worry about that, but a lot of them wouldn't think twice about tagging a Black woman that way.

That being said, she had to admit to herself that she had sounded a bit of an asshole.

Pausing mid-stride, Al looked around at the crowd, making eye contact with at least a dozen of them, flashed a huge smile, and tipped her chin at them like they were all good buds, having the same big adventure. "We just don't know what we're dealing with yet, you know? And I wouldn't want any of you beautiful people getting hurt out here today."

They all grinned back and nodded their heads.

Al gave herself a mental high five. She had been turning groups of strangers into fans, if not friends, for almost three decades. Ever since she got yanked out of her grandparents' cozy East End row house and dropped across an ocean into the middle of an Illinois cornfield. She knew how to win a room. And it never got old.

A kid who looked like she—or they—were maybe eight years old was standing next to a guy old enough to be their granddad. The kid had Band-Aids on both knees and their freckles were freaking adorable.

"Thank you, Chief Jones." They smiled from underneath a Phoenix Suns cap.

Al was about that age when her parents packed up again and dragged her from Illinois to the base outside of San Antonio. She shook her head, remembering what it was like to be that age—and different from most everyone else she knew—and went in for a fist bump.

"No problem, kid. That's my job."

The kid looked up at their Grandpa with wide eyes, a shocked smile lighting up their face, shaking their hand out like they had just fist-bumped a superhero.

Al grinned and threw her shoulders back.

Since becoming an officer, she spent most of her time schmoozing electeds, dreaming up ways to make the department run better, and showing up in classrooms trying to make fire safety exciting for ten-year-olds. But there was nothing better than being on location, at the heart of the action. And as she was learning, a big hole in the middle of a sleepy street qualified as major league action in a town like Owen Station. Located three-plus hours south of Phoenix, fifteen minutes north of the Mexican border, at an altitude of six thousand feet, the population could swell to twenty or thirty thousand during festivals and three-day weekends. But fewer than six thousand people actually called the former mining town home.

And apparently, quite a few of them had nothing better to do on a Sunday morning than stand around looking at a hole.

Sirens blared in the distance. The crowd had nearly doubled in size since Al jumped out of her truck, and people were snapping photos. A couple of teens scrambled up a nearby Arizona ash to get an aerial view. And two women were setting up to sell what smelled like burritos and coffee out of an old van. But the crowd was respecting Al's authority and the invisible barrier she had thrown up. They were keeping their distance.

Because she was first on the scene, Al did an initial size-up. The hole had taken out a good portion of the road and part of the sidewalk. It was deep, although hard to tell exactly how far down it went, and oblong in shape. The length of an engine, maybe. The width of an ambulance. An older model compact car had just missed being swallowed. Its right front tire hung precariously over the edge. The car was empty. Al inched as close as she dared to the hole, which may or may not have finished eating pavement.

It was nothing like the ground fissures Al was used to seeing. Those were more natural looking, ragged where the earth gave way, mostly caused by too much groundwater pumping. They would show up now and then in the fancy new neighborhoods being built on former farmland on the outskirts of Phoenix. Al had responded to more than a few calls from frantic homeowners back when she first joined the fire service.

Al shook her head. It wasn't her job to figure out what caused the hole everyone was staring at that spring Sunday morning. She would leave that to the engineers, who would come later.

The most important fact in that moment was that it didn't appear anything—or anyone—had fallen in.

Al pivoted toward the crowd, turning on that smile. "Okay, everybody, listen up. I need your help now. Who saw what happened?" Most people shook their heads, but one woman stepped forward. Silently, Al did a quick witness ID—the woman was white, sandy brown hair, mid-forties maybe, wearing scrubs. Al thought she recognized her from the ER.

"I was on my way to the hospital." The woman's voice sounded shaky. "I'm here on a six-month contract. Renting that house right there." She pointed to a small bungalow across the street. "I saw the street open up just as I was stepping off the sidewalk. That's my car. In the hole. Three minutes later and I would have been sitting in it."

Which meant one minute earlier and she might have been buried.

"That must have been scary." Al empathized, knowing her response was being watched by the crowd and it was important to hit the right tone, in order to ensure everyone's cooperation. "Are you alright?"

The woman nodded.

"Okay. That's good. Did you see anything else? Was anyone—besides you—nearby when it happened?"

The woman shook her head. "Just me."

"She's right." An older man—late seventies or early eighties, Hispanic, wearing pajamas and slippers—volunteered info from the back of the crowd. "I saw it all happen from my window." He pointed to the house next to the one the scrubs-wearing woman was renting. "Nobody else was out here. And nothing else went in."

"Thank you, sir. That's very helpful. And also, very good news."

Al threw a thumb toward the house behind her, on the hole side of the street, and addressed the crowd. "Does anybody here live in that house?"

There was no obvious sign of damage or immediate threat to the property but it was closest to the hole, not more than fifty feet from the edge. Close enough to be concerned.

There was a lot of looking around, shrugging, and head shaking in the crowd.

"The owner left for work an hour ago," pajama-man said. "She works at the funeral home. Takes pictures. Talks to ghosts. Her name is Elena."

That would have been a lot to unpack, if Al didn't immediately know who he was talking about. The house had to belong to Elena Murphy. No one else in town could possibly fit that description. Al didn't really know her, but she knew of her, and had seen her around town. Her exhibit of black-and-white photos at the new tasting room last summer was bomb.

"Does she live alone? Is anyone else in there?"

The man shook his head. "No. No one else lives there. Just her cat."

Al would double-check that information, but she had what she needed to call in. "Owen Station 2 is on scene at 185 Old Mine Road. We have a sinkhole with no injuries. We'll need extraction equipment for a small vehicle. Have all responding units slow their response and stage at Old Mine Road and Hummingbird Lane."

The sirens immediately went silent, as she expected they would. Al knew her crew was still on their way but given her initial report, there was no reason they needed to raise the alarm as they drove through town.

There wasn't much more she could do at that point. Those burritos were smelling really good, and her stomach grumbled in agreement. She had planned to follow that shower with breakfast.

"Hey, Chief." Bobby Garcia sidled up next to her. He was a young guy. Ambitious. And good. He had just made captain, which wasn't at all surprising. Police Chief Dana Garcia was Bobby's mom.

Dana was Al's best friend in town. Her family had been in the area for generations, since before the border existed, and way before the wall. Dana had worked her way up the ranks to become the town's first female chief. Making friends was one of Al's superpowers—but being at the top created a whole different dynamic inside the firehouse. Dana was one of the few people in town Al could totally be herself with. She was a damn good drummer, too. Dana's husband came up with the name for their all-female, first responder band. The Fireballs had been playing gigs around town for the past year or so.

Bobby kicked a rock and watched it fly over the edge. "That's a big hole."

Al cocked her head and gave Bobby side-eye. "I can see why you got that promotion."

Bobby grinned. "That and my good looks."

Al laughed and slapped him on the back. "'Bout time you got here, by the way. What happened? Did I interrupt a video game?"

"We were here in under five and you know it. You only beat us 'cause you live like a block away."

"Ah, is that it?" Bobby was so competitive it was easy to push his buttons. And fun.

Bobby glanced sideways at Al. "Folks are already starting rumors. About the hole."

He knew how to push Al's buttons, too. Rampant conspiracy theories, especially in recent years, as they battled crises on multiple fronts, made public service even more difficult than it already was. Bobby knew it made Al's head spin.

"Of course they are. What's the best one so far?"

Bobby shrugged. "That hole is actually Big Foot's footprint."

Al snorted. "Yeah, let's go with that."

"So, what's next?" Bobby was itching to get to work.

"Tape it off—make sure nobody who shouldn't be in there gets within two hundred feet. That means you're going to have to move the burrito van—and get those kids down out of the tree. We don't know if the hole is still hungry. And make sure that tow is on its way." Al shook a thumb at the man in pajamas and the scrub-wearing woman. "Those two saw what happened. Take their statements. And do a sweep of this property." Al nodded in the direction of Elena Murphy's house. "Double-check to make sure no one is inside.

The city's gonna need to do a structural assessment before it can be cleared for occupancy."

The fire department's job at a scene like this one was simple. Make sure people were safe and property was secure. The city would have to deal with the hole—and the homeowner.

"I'm on it, Chief."

"Alright then, I'm going to go take that day off I've got coming. You're in command." Al slapped him on the back again, and Bobby snapped into action.

He was one of the few guys in the department who had never given Al some kind of shit, not even during the hazing period, when everyone was still testing Al to see what she was made of. Dana would have kicked her son's ass, but Al appreciated his refusal to participate, anyway. It was mostly just stupid games, like filling her desk drawers with Cap'n Crunch. She had experienced worse in her first job after the academy, although nothing as bad as what previous generations of women in the service had been through—and what some, in other departments across the country, were still experiencing. For being a small town, both the fire and police departments in Owen Station seemed surprisingly committed to building a more inclusive culture, even before the town had its own wakeup call a few years ago. Dana, of course, was a big part of that. But so was Al's boss, the chief.

It had been a little more than two years since he had called Al to offer her the job. The first thing she did was break it off with Maria. Maria was chef-de-cuisine in one of those high-end resorts on the edge of the desert, a place with linen tablecloths and two-hundred-dollar bottles of wine and pretty food that never actually filled you up. The rich and famous showed up there every once in a while with an entourage. Maria was never going to follow Al to a small town like Owen Station, and they were six months past their expiration date, anyway. At first, it had been exciting to feel needed—nobody loved responding to emergencies more than Al. But everything was an emergency with Maria—up to and including burnt out lightbulbs in her bathroom—and Al was over it. So, within a month of getting that call, she bought out of her lease in Tempe, packed up her clothes, and moved to Owen Station to become their first ever female assistant fire chief.

Given that like five percent of all smoke-eaters in the country were women, and there had only been maybe a dozen women of color in the top spots, Al knew exactly what she was walking into. Which was a big part of the reason she wanted the gig.

Her parents thought she had lost her mind. She told them about the offer the day after she got the call, when she went to their house for Mum's birthday dinner.

"Do they even have people like you down there, Allison?" Her father scowled as he squeezed hamburger into patties, a little more forcefully than usual.

"What do you mean *people like me,* Dad? Top of my class at the academy? Rock star level vocalist? Elite mountain biker? Funny as hell after two shots of tequila?" She paused, as if deciding whether or not to toss an accelerant into the mix. But what the hell. He started it.

"Or do you mean *queer?*"

Dad had gotten used to the idea that Al was never going to have a Cinderella wedding, where he'd walk her down the aisle to Prince Charming. But Al knew he hated it when she used that word.

That was alright.

Al hated it when he called her Allison.

Dad slapped the last patty on the counter and stormed off silently to light the grill, and then Mum did what she always did when the two of them would get into it. She tried to contain the fire with excuses.

"He's just worried about you, Al."

Al shrugged, grabbed a sweet pickle off the relish tray—carefully avoiding the piccalilli Mum insisted on putting on her burgers—and popped it into her mouth. "Whatever, Mum."

"Now, honey, you shouldn't be so hard on him. You know, his work kept him away from home for so many years. Now that he's retiring, he's been looking forward to seeing more of you. I think it just feels like bad timing, to have you moving so far away."

Al rolled her eyes, knowing they were all being overly dramatic. "It's only three hours."

"It's almost four, dear."

"Okay, fine. Three and a half."

Al took a swig of the sun tea Mum had learned to make because it was Dad's favorite. It was Al's, too. "Besides, Mum. It's not my fault his buddies and his career were always more important than me. Or you, for that matter. I'm not the one who dragged us all over the US, from one base to another, forcing us to start over and over again, with new friends, new routines, new everything. He did that. It's not my fault that he was never home, either. Even after you moved halfway around the world to be with him."

Mum had been in the Royal Air Force when she met Al's dad on a joint training exercise just before Desert Storm. He was an airman. The relationship—and the pregnancy—was complicated, and Al spent the first five and a half years of her life with her white grandparents in the East End of London.

That was the last bit of stability Al ever experienced.

As soon as she was able, Al's mum picked up her life, packed up her daughter, and moved across the pond to be with him. You would have thought Dad would want to settle down, get a regular job somewhere nice, somewhere a British wife and a biracial-binational daughter with surprisingly blue eyes, tousled sprigs of dark brown hair, and a strange accent wouldn't feel so out of place all the time.

"He had years to focus on his family, Mum. Decades. But no. So, it's not my responsibility to try to build a relationship with him just because he now all of a sudden has time for it. I have my own life."

And her own path.

A path that had brought her here.

To this one-stoplight town in the middle of nowhere.

And this hole.

Al looked around, double-checking to make sure she wasn't needed any further, and then headed toward her SUV, fist-bumping every member of the crew along the way. She was about twenty feet away from her truck—and twenty minutes away from that ride she was looking forward to—when an older model, mid-sized hybrid slipped right past the guys setting up a perimeter and sped toward the hole.

Al didn't think twice.

She quickly stepped in front of the oncoming car and held up both hands in a stop-right-there, don't-you-fucking-dare-come-any-further motion. Not the smartest move, probably. But it worked.

The car stopped about a foot in front of Al. The driver's side door flew open, and a woman leaped out—white, dark brown hair, early thirties. Elena Murphy. She might have turned heads in Phoenix or LA, even. In Owen Station, she was in a league of her own. Wearing all black, her designer pants had a dropped crotch, those open-toed wedge shoes looked European, and her sleeveless vest, worn without a shirt underneath, showed off nicely toned arms. All five-foot-four of her marched toward Al, her dark wavy hair pulled tight into a low ponytail, and it was waving wildly behind her. She looked more ferocious than her size should have allowed.

She definitely looked like she could handle changing her own freaking lightbulbs.

Al smiled, but not as big as she was grinning on the inside. "Thanks for not running me over."

Elena did not smile back. She planted herself in front of Al, hands on her hips, legs spread slightly, looking completely unintimidated by Al's badge or her five-foot, ten-and-a-half-inch frame. In fact, she just tilted her head back to look Al in the eye and squinted as if she didn't understand what she was seeing. "What is *wrong* with you, anyway—jumping in front of me like that?"

"Hello, Ms. Murphy." Al kept her voice steady. "I'm Al Jones, assistant fire chief. I don't think we've formally met." Al stuck out her hand.

Elena did not take it. "I know who you are. And you are clearly *new* here. That is my house over there. The one by the hole. It's been in my family for four generations. The hill it's built on is literally named for my family. I need to make sure everything is okay. And you are in my way."

"Well, I can appreciate that, Elena—may I call you Elena?"

"No, you may not."

"Okay, Ms. Murphy." Al kept smiling. She was used to dealing with the public and had de-escalated more situations than she could count. Plus, she was enjoying watching this petite but powerful woman hold her ground. "I understand that you're concerned. But it's actually our job to make sure everything is okay, and to keep you safe. And right now, we need all civilians to stay back so that we can do our job as quickly and efficiently as possible."

"I am not a civilian, Chief Jones." Elena snapped her head back so hard, her ponytail flipped in front and then back again. "In my line of work, I've seen just about everything."

"Of course. My apologies, Ms. Murphy. I'm sure you have. Fortunately, though, right now there aren't any dead bodies to deal with. There is just a big hole in the ground. We don't know what caused it, how deep it is, or—and this is the most important point—whether or not it is done collapsing."

"Fine." Elena kept her chin up defiantly. "But I need to know when I am going to be able to get into my house, which is also my studio, and obviously it is very important to me."

Al nodded. That was a good question. And Elena Murphy didn't seem like she was in the mood for anything other than a good answer.

"We're going to get you back into your house as soon as possible, I promise. Our first priority is getting that car out of there, though, and making sure the hole doesn't have expansion plans. Then, we need to make sure there is no structural damage to your home. As you can see from here, the hole isn't on your property, but it's close enough for us to be concerned. The assessment shouldn't take long. It can probably be done sometime tomorrow."

"Tomorrow?" Elena's voice jumped an octave.

"I know this is a terrible inconvenience, Ms. Murphy. And I'm sorry about that. But the last thing I want is for you to be in any danger."

Al was on a full charm offensive, but she braced herself for another blast.

Instead, Elena looked from Al to the hole, from the hole to her house, and then back at Al. Twice. She seemed to be working hard to process what was happening. A multitude of emotions crossed her face. Finally, after a long minute, Elena closed her eyes and took a deep breath.

When she swung her eyes up toward Al, the icy glare was gone. "I'm sorry, Assistant Chief Jones. I don't mean to sound like an entitled brat." Elena glanced down at the ground, her cheeks flushing a little, as if embarrassed. "And I'm sorry I almost ran you over."

Al shoulders relaxed and she grinned. "I'm pretty sure I was never in danger of being run over."

A smile slowly emerged onto Elena's face. "You're *probably* right. But you shouldn't make a habit of jumping in front of moving cars."

"I do make a living running into burning buildings, Ms. Murphy. So, I can't promise anything."

Elena raised an eyebrow. "Yes, of course, Chief." Then, after a beat, she stuck out her hand. "Please, call me Elena."

Al took Elena's hand, which felt tiny, soft, and warm. But she had a firm grip. "It's nice to officially meet you, Elena," she said in her best Cockney. "And you can call me Al."

"Now I'm going to have that old Paul Simon song stuck in my head for days. Also, is that an Adele accent you're doing?"

Al chuckled. "It is. Although millions of others have it, too. Including my grandparents and my mum. I've been away from the UK so long, and moved around the US so much growing up, that my own accent is chameleon-like. I can pretty much adapt to wherever I am. But I don't think I'll ever completely shake East London. Nor do I want to."

Elena's eyes lingered on Al's, and it was quick, but they flicked down to Al's mouth and then back up again. "I love Adele. I wouldn't mind if you used that accent all the time, Al."

A warmth that started below Al's waist rose up through her chest. And she was in no hurry to let go of Elena's hand. Also, she was adorable.

"I think you have the longest eyelashes I've ever seen."

Elena blinked, her eyebrows popped to the top of her head, and her cheeks exploded in three shades of pink. "Oh, my goodness."

"I'm sorry," Al said, giving Elena's hand a little squeeze. "I didn't mean to embarrass you."

"Not at all." Elena smiled. "You just startled me. I *do* have long eyelashes. When I was little, they would get stuck together. Sometimes they still do. I used to cry and scream to my mother. 'Cut them off. Cut them off!'"

"Oh my God. I'm glad she didn't."

Elena gave Al's hand a quick squeeze. "Me, too."

All around them, crews were busy executing Al's instructions. Bobby was clearly doing a good job. Local police had blocked the street off on both ends, and the crowd was being herded farther away from the action. But somehow a bubble had formed, and Al was inside of it, holding Elena's hand.

Finally, because it couldn't last forever, the bubble broke.

Elena let go of Al's hand and scanned the scene around them taking it all in. "I'm going to have to find someplace to stay tonight, aren't I?"

Al nodded. "You have lots of family in town, though, right?"

Elena nodded. "My great-grandparents started the business more than a hundred years ago. Almost everybody except me has stayed."

"Except you...?"

"I left right after school. Was gone for more than a decade. I only came back because my dad asked me to." Elena frowned and folded her arms across her chest. "Not long after that, my grandfather got himself into some serious trouble. He was court-ordered into a nursing home—"

"The incident at the library. About a year and a half ago. I remember."

"I figured you would." Elena nodded. "After that, my grandmother moved in with my parents, which left the old family house vacant. Now, I'm managing the people part of Murphy's Funeral Home and Mortuary and living here."

"In a house on the edge of a hole." Al tipped her chin in the direction of Elena's house.

"That's the one."

It was hard not to feel sorry for Elena, especially now that she had calmed down. And she was, without question, strikingly beautiful.

"Do you think it would be safe for me to get into my house, just long enough to grab an overnight bag? And check on Casper?"

"Casper?" Al laughed. "I thought the story about you being a ghost whisperer was just another Owen Station rumor."

Elena's eyes narrowed and little lines formed between her eyebrows. "Casper is my cat."

"Of course." Al smiled. "Way to lean into it. Give the people what they want. I get it. When my dad got transferred for the third time in six years, I let the kids in my middle school, back in Philly, believe I was the queen's cousin for two years."

"What happened when they found out you weren't?"

"They never did. My dad got transferred to Arizona a few years later. He retired from the Air Force here and joined the Guard. I spent high school in Chandler."

"And you're *not* the queen's cousin." Elena's eyes sparkled.

"If you say so…" Al grinned.

She really needed breakfast. And the mountains were calling. But all that could wait. Freckles were dancing across Elena's nose, and the sun glistened off her shoulders. There was something paradoxical about her, too. Like a teddy bear cholla, a cactus that looks soft on the outside but is covered with sharp spines. Or a stone fireplace. Inviting, but also a little dangerous. Al was intrigued.

"So…what do you think? Is it safe to go inside?" Elena was talking to Al but looking at her house.

Al paused, but only for a second, and then nodded. "Only for a few minutes. I think that would be fine. But I should come with you. Just to be safe."

Elena tilted her head, with half a smile, eyes searching Al's face for something. "Okay, great. Yeah. Come with me, then."

Al let Elena lead the way, and waved off Bobby when he came over to intervene. "She's just going to grab some things that she'll need for the night and check on her cat," Al explained.

Bobby raised his brows. "Aren't you trying to get out of here and get that day off started? I hear a mountain road somewhere calling your name."

Al grinned. "Duty before pleasure, Captain."

"Uh-huh." Bobby smiled and winked. "Whatever you say, Chief."

"What's that supposed to mean?" Al laughed.

"Nothing, Chief. Nothing at all."

But it wasn't nothing.

It was definitely something.

Al just wasn't quite sure what. Yet.

Chapter Two

Elena was on the sidewalk in front of her house when her fingers started tingling, like they were on the end of a live wire. She was waiting to be escorted into her own home by Owen Station's very handsome assistant fire chief, who had stopped to talk to a young man in uniform, but suddenly she was in no rush to get inside.

Although it looked like the house was too far from the hole to have been damaged, and Al made it seem like the inspection was just going to be a formality, the closer Elena got to the house, the more certain she was that something was terribly wrong. And she was in no hurry to find out she was right.

It wasn't even noon and the day had already gone sideways six times.

Casper had been up chasing a bug or maybe a ghost around the house before six. He knocked over a floor lamp and sent pieces of lightbulb scattering across the old pine floor. At that point, Elena was wide-awake and in serious need of a cup of tea. And although there were three boxes of tea bags in the pantry, each box was completely empty. Then the water heater went out. Or at least she thought it was the water heater. It was always something with that old house. Elena didn't have the time or patience at seven a.m. to figure it out or fix it. But that did mean she couldn't clean up the kitchen, which she had promised herself the night before she would absolutely do before leaving for work, because it was a disaster and maybe even a health hazard.

Okay, to be honest, she didn't mind the not-being-able-to-wash-the-dishes part.

She did mind having to take a cold shower.

But she didn't even mind that nearly as much as she minded having to clean up after her brothers. Figuratively speaking. Again.

The Truman family was in the parking lot waiting for her when she got to work.

Connor and Sean had gone to collect Mr. Truman the night before. He had been in hospice following complications from surgery, after he accidentally hit himself with his own drone, and died prematurely, but peacefully, at home. Well, it was peaceful until the arrival of the Pasty Pair. Her unnaturally pale, extraordinarily odd brothers had picked up that nickname in high school. It was unkind, but it wasn't untrue.

Mr. Truman's oldest daughter was raging before they even got into Elena's office.

"Let's start with, your brothers didn't say hello when they came in. They were just like *where's the body?*" The daughter spread her arms out dramatically, as if to illustrate the enormity of her brothers' stupidity. "My father isn't just a body, Elena."

"Of course not. I'm so sorry." Elena ushered them all into chairs, and then took the seat behind her desk.

The daughter didn't skip a beat.

"We showed your brothers where Dad was, but we didn't go in there with them—we couldn't bear to watch. But we could hear them. One of your brothers said, *I forgot how big this guy was.* And the other said, *Yeah, no wonder he couldn't outrun the drone.* And then they laughed. Maybe they thought we couldn't hear them, Elena. But we did. Every word. Then they made a big deal out of having to bring in a lift to carry Dad out. It was horrible. All my mother could do was cry."

The mother was still crying.

Elena's stream of apologies and promises they wouldn't have to deal with the boys again, because Elena would handle all the details herself from that point on, managed to calm the family down. She helped them select the package they wanted, which included a beer-can-shaped coffin and a motorcycle rally to the cemetery. Everyone except the daughter looked sad but relieved—the daughter still just looked sad and angry—but they all seemed happy to be doing something that would give Mr. Truman a send-off he would have loved.

Just as they were wrapping up, Elena's phone started vibrating all over the desk. It was Mr. Martinez, who lived across the street, was mostly homebound, and kept an eye on the neighborhood.

"I'm so sorry, Mrs. Truman, but I need to return this call." Elena stood up and helped Mrs. Truman to her feet. "I promise we will take good care of Mr. Truman."

The daughter huffed her lack of confidence, throwing her chin in the air as she headed out of Elena's office. But Mrs. Truman held back, sniffling into a tissue. "Thank you, my dear."

Then she turned and grabbed Elena's hand. "You'll tell me if you see him, won't you?"

Elena nodded. "Of course, Mrs. Truman."

"And if you do see him, you tell him I am good and mad at him for dying on me. But I still love him."

Elena put her hand on Mrs. Truman's and kept her moving toward the door. "Yes, of course. If I see him, I will tell him, but I'm sure he already knows that."

"I'm going to get a tattoo in his honor. An orange road sign that says *Watch for flying objects*. You tell him that, okay?"

Elena smiled. "I will. Of course. That sounds perfect, Mrs. Truman. I think he will love that."

Elena hurried back to her desk as soon as the Trumans left, thinking she ought to tack a communications fee onto Murphy Funeral Home services. Requests to deliver messages to loved ones happened more often than not with their clients.

She listened to all six messages Mr. Martinez left on her phone, double-checked her schedule to make sure she didn't have another appointment anytime soon, stuck her head into the prep room to let the boys know she was leaving, and hurried out to her car.

Mr. Martinez had not been exaggerating.

The hole in her front yard looked big enough to swallow one of the fire trucks that responded to the call.

Now Elena was doing her best to ignore whatever her tingling fingers were trying to say.

She looked over at Al, who was still talking to that young man. Garcia.

That was his name.

Elena tried to remember his first name, too. Bobby, maybe? He had been seven or eight years behind Elena in school, and she knew his older sisters. But they hadn't been friends. Elena hadn't really had any of those back then.

Finally, with a couple of long strides across her yard, Al caught up with her.

"Let's go through the back door," Al said. "It's farther away from the hole."

Elena snapped her head up to search Al's face. She was already feeling anxious about going into the house. This didn't help. "Do you really think that's necessary?"

"I'm sure everything is fine, Elena. But let's go around back. Just to be safe." Al smiled softly. "Why don't you let me go in first?"

Elena took a deep breath and stepped aside so Al could take the lead. It actually felt good, for a change, to have someone else calling the shots.

The chief was in uniform cargo pants and a short-sleeve, white polo with the department logo on it. She wasn't as tall as Elena's brothers, five-ten, maybe. But she walked taller. Like she knew exactly where her feet were and exactly where she was going at all times, totally in control. She took the steps up to Elena's back door two at a time.

At the top of the stairs, Al stopped and turned toward Elena with one hand out. "Keys?"

Al's eyes were shaded by the brim of her cap, which also deepened the sepia tones in her face. The photogenic smile she flashed was absolutely luminous in contrast. Elena couldn't help but think about what it would be like to have her on the other side of a camera lens.

"Do you have keys?" Al asked again, enunciating each word, as if Elena was hard of hearing, her smile still bright. "Also, are you okay? You seem very distracted."

"Oh, um." Elena pulled herself away from Al's smile, back into the moment. "I don't have keys."

Al gave her side-eye. "You mean you left them in the car?"

Elena shook her head.

"You lost them?"

"No, I mean, I don't have keys. Just go on in."

"You. Don't. Have. Keys. Does that mean you don't lock your doors?"

"Not that one. It's broken."

"So, you lock *other* doors—"

"Sometimes I lock the front door. I don't know why. I mean, I always locked all my doors when I lived in LA, of course. But most people here don't bother."

Al dropped her open hand, which she had been holding out, as if unable to believe that a set of keys was not going to magically appear. "Okay. Let me get this straight. *Sometimes* you lock the *front* door, but not *this* one because it's broken."

Elena nodded. "My family has been in this house for over a century and no one ever locked that door. Honestly, I don't think anyone could find keys for it, even if it worked."

Al took off her cap and, with her free hand, rubbed the top of her head, as if trying to massage this nonsensical bit of information into her brain. "This seems like a very bad plan."

"I'm assuming you met my neighbors this morning. Did you find out what time I left for work?"

Al raised an eyebrow.

"Did you get a blow-by-blow account of what happened with that hole out there?"

"Maybe..." Al drawled, some kind of light appearing to come on.

"Did you find out what I was wearing? Maybe even what I had for breakfast?"

"Okay, I get it. You have very attentive neighbors."

"Nosy, you mean."

"Sure." Al raised that eyebrow again. "But that doesn't mean you shouldn't be locking your doors."

"You've never lived in a small town, have you? There's not much privacy. My neighbors know my every move. They are probably already talking about us right now. How you're following me in here. They're coming up with all kinds of stories about why. On the other hand..." Elena shrugged. "Everybody is looking out for me. It kind of makes a lock seem unnecessary."

Besides, the only things Elena might be scared of couldn't be kept away with locks and keys. But that wasn't something she felt like saying.

She rubbed her hands together, noting that the tingling wasn't as bad as it had been when she was closer to the hole. But she was still feeling uneasy about going inside.

Al cleared her throat and shoved her hat back on. "I think we need to agree to disagree here. So, let's get moving, shall we? I don't want to give your neighbors more to talk about." She winked at Elena, then turned, pushed open the door, and stepped into Elena's kitchen. Which, of course, had not managed to clean itself since morning.

"Wow. It looks like I missed the party."

Elena glanced sideways, her eyes suddenly drawn to the sharp creases in Al's pants. It even looked like that polo shirt had been ironed. If she got close enough, she could probably have seen her reflection in Al's boots.

She looked up to find Al's surprisingly blue eyes looking down at her, amusement just behind the surface.

"What can I say?" Elena shrugged. "I don't like doing dishes."

"I can see that."

Elena flipped her hair back. "When you said the house was going to need an inspection, I didn't know you meant the clean patrol was coming through."

"I didn't. But on second thought, we might need to send the health inspector through here."

Elena rolled her eyes. Al clearly thought she was funny. And she was. But Elena didn't need to encourage her.

"Which way are we going?" Al asked.

Elena pointed through the door that led to the living room. "That way. I need to get some things from my bedroom."

As soon as the words came out of her mouth, Elena's stomach dropped. She was about to take Al Jones—handsome, five-ten, funny, even if Elena didn't want to admit it, Al Jones—who did a great accent and had a killer smile, into her bedroom. And just like that, Elena was sixteen again. A missile shot out of her hypothalamus, straight down the middle of her body, and when it made contact, everything below her waist was suddenly wide-awake.

"Um...you can just stay out here, can't you?" Her voice sounded a little squeaky in her own ears.

Al shook her head. "I need to at least do a quick walk-through to make sure there are no obvious signs of danger."

"Of course." It made sense, but that didn't make Elena's heart stop racing.

"Follow me. But stay at least six feet behind me." Al straightened her back, turned toward the living room, and took one step through the door—where she stopped short.

"Um..." Al looked over her shoulder. "You should rethink the not-locking-your-doors thing, Elena. You've been robbed."

"What?" Elena screamed and thrust her way through the door into the living room. Al, however, grabbed her by the shoulders, preventing her from going any further.

Elena quickly scanned the room, looking for signs of forced entry, a violation of her privacy, missing belongings, anything at all to indicate that she had, in fact, been the victim of a robbery.

But everything was just as she had left it.

Elena turned around, which wasn't easy because Al was still restraining her, and looked up into Al's eyes. "What is *wrong* with you? You scared—" Elena paused, her unexpected proximity to the chief causing her to lose speech function.

They weren't more than six inches apart. Saying nothing, Al searched her eyes. Her hands were strong, holding Elena in place, and heat radiated from her body. She smelled clean, fresh, like bergamot and ginger, like she had just come from the shower. Elena could hear her own heart thumping. Thankfully, finally, Al took a deep breath, tore her eyes away from Elena's face, and gave the room a second good look.

"You mean, you *haven't* been robbed?" Al's face scrunched up like she had just eaten a Brussels sprout.

"No!" Elena pushed herself off, using Al's rock-hard belly as leverage, which made Al let go of her shoulders. "No, I have not been robbed. What would even make you think that?" Elena's heart was still racing, and not just because Al had scared the hell out of her.

Al continued looking around. "Well, I mean—"

Elena followed Al's eyes and saw what Al was seeing. Photos, some framed and some not. Frames, art catalogs, mat samples, camera bags, half-empty shipping boxes. A studio-worth of equipment, all of her supplies, and so much of her work filled the room—every table, every chair, the couch, and every inch of the floor. In the middle of it all, a broken floor lamp lay in pieces, and bits of lightbulb were strewn everywhere.

Elena sighed. "Well, okay. I guess it does look a little messy."

"*Messy?*"

Al's snort snapped Elena out of her momentary embarrassment. She spun around and stood as tall as she could. "Excuse me, Chief. I don't have to answer to you. But just so you know…this is my creative space. And until I find the right location for a gallery, it's my studio. Works in progress are stacked right over there. This pile is my complete retrospective of Owen Station. The catalogs on the table are current exhibits happening around the country. Mats and frames for new works in progress are over there. These are pieces of my debut show, the one I want to open my gallery with. Everything in this room is one hundred percent organized and completely accessible."

"And the smashed glass?"

"*That* was an accident. Casper—"

"The ghost?"

"My *cat*. He had the zoomies this morning and knocked over the lamp. It woke me up, if you must know. I was late for work after a series of unfortunate events and didn't have time to clean it up."

"Sounds like it's been quite a day." Al's voice warmed. "I'm sorry to be giving you such a hard time."

Al's apology and sudden bout of empathy were startling.

"Thank you."

"Of course. Okay, point the way. Let's get your things and get you out of here."

Elena gestured toward the door to her bedroom. Nodding, Al carefully picked her way through the obstacle course in the living room. Elena followed, trying not to picture how she left her bedroom that morning, not wanting to think about what she was going to have to explain next.

Get in. Fill a bag. Get out.

That was the goal.

Al led the way into the bedroom, but Elena zipped right past her, into her bathroom, as if wearing blinders, trying not to notice the unmade bed or the dirty clothes in a pile on the floor. She grabbed her toothbrush, cosmetic bag, a couple of hair ties, a hairbrush, and her supersonic hair dryer—she had bought the bedazzled thing on a whim and never went anywhere without it. It was ridiculous but it made her smile.

Elena popped back into the bedroom and headed straight for the bed without even a glance in Al's direction. She pulled out the overnight bag stored underneath and threw it on the bed. Normally she wouldn't bother with pajamas, but she was spending the night at her parents' so she grabbed a set out of the dresser and shoved them in the bag.

Then, Elena slid open her closet door, took a half step back, and took a cleansing breath. The shelves and hanging rods were neatly organized by color—black, white, gray—clothes, shoes, boots, accessories, everything. Each carefully curated piece had a purpose. Nothing extraneous. Nothing that wasn't regularly used or worn. Not a single sock or scarf out of place. She closed her eyes and took another deep breath. In the midst of her creative, chaotic life, that closet was her Zen. Plus, every morning she could grab any pair of pants, any tunic, asymmetrical skirt, vest, or jacket without even having to think about whether or not they would work together. It meant one less step and ten more minutes of sleep.

Her moment of peace was interrupted by a soft whistle from behind.

"That is *impressive*."

Elena opened her eyes with a sigh. Of course, Chief Shiny Boots would have something to say. She tried to not think about it while she pulled some of her favorite pieces out. But when she turned around, to put the clothes in her bag, Al wasn't looking at her or her closet. Al's eyes were fixed on the nightstand. Elena's latest Frisky Business purchase—a rainbow-colored, unicorn-horn-shaped vibrator—was standing at attention. And it was blinking. Apparently, it was at full charge.

Now would have been a good time for that hole to open wide and swallow her—perfectly organized closet and all.

Fire raced from Elena's belly to her cheeks.

"Um…"

What else was she supposed to say?

Al's eyes flicked toward the sound of Elena's voice, and her head slowly followed. It looked like a smirk was lingering just behind her lips. "Um?"

"Um, I'm *ready*." Elena's cheeks were burning, but she straightened her back. Nothing to see here. Nothing at all.

Al glanced over Elena's shoulder toward the closet and then back toward the nightstand. "You sure you have everything you need?"

Elena was certain she saw a smirtle lurking beneath the surface of Al's otherwise composed face—that's what Grandma called the expression Elena or her brothers would have when they got caught doing something mischievously fun.

"Yes, I have everything I need," Elena said crisply. It felt like the room was a hundred and twenty degrees.

"Well, I think it's best if we scoot on out of here, don't you?" Now Al was wearing a full-on grin. "I'm not sure it's safe in here, if you know what I mean."

"I'm sure I don't." Elena huffed, flipping her ponytail. The chief had a lot of nerve, marching through her house, judging her. And now this. It's not safe in *here*? In the bedroom? As *if.*

"What I mean is, we can't be sure the house is undamaged. Just because we can't *see* it, doesn't mean it's not there. Also, we should get out before anyone comes looking and finds us in *here*."

Al gestured around the room. "You said it yourself. People in small towns like to talk."

Al found herself way funnier than Elena did.

Elena threw her shoulders back. "I'm ready when you are."

She followed Al back through the living room, which Al was navigating dramatically, as if the floor was lava.

Suddenly, Elena stopped. "Wait."

Al flipped around. "What?"

"I almost forgot. Casper."

"The ghost?"

Elena squeezed her eyes shut, shaking her head. When she opened them, Al was wearing a shit-eating grin.

"My *cat*."

"I know. I'm just teasing you."

"Well, now is not a good time."

Al quickly wiped the grin off. "Where is he?"

"I don't know. He always comes to meet me at the door when I get home."

"Maybe he's freaked out by all the commotion outside. Where does he hide when he gets scared?"

"Check under the couch. I'm going to look under the bed."

Elena hurried into the bedroom. No sign of Casper.

"He's not under the couch," Al yelled.

"Oh my God. Casper!" Elena called out. "Casper, where are you?"

Elena raced down the hallway, searching the guest bedroom and closets. Nothing. She tore back into the living room and skidded to a stop.

Al was sitting on the floor in the middle of the mess with Casper in her lap.

"I don't know where he was hiding. He came out of the kitchen and just started head-butting me. He's purring now."

Elena dropped to her knees and started petting him. Al wasn't lying. Casper sounded like he had an old motor inside his chest. "Everything's okay now, Casper."

Elena kept scratching Casper's head while she glanced up at Al. "He likes you."

Al grinned. "No one can resist my charms."

"Is that so?" Elena huffed, but she was a little afraid Al might be right. "I'm going to get his carrier."

Casper didn't love his carrier, but when Al lifted him in, he didn't hesitate to crawl inside. Elena took the carrier and Al picked up Elena's bag.

"Anything else you need?" Al asked, looking around the living room. "You okay leaving all this stuff here?"

Elena nodded. "I have my camera bag in my car. These things can wait until I get back home. Which I am expecting will be *tomorrow*."

"Understood."

Al led the way into the kitchen and out the back door.

From the sound of it, the crowd had continued to grow. That wasn't at all surprising. Three years ago, after Mrs. Dixon saw the face of Jesus on the bottom of her old chest freezer, dozens of people stopped by every day for a month to look at it, until finally Mr. Dixon cleaned it out and chased them all out of his shed and off his property. Mom told Elena all about it during a Sunday afternoon call. It was mold. Not Jesus. But it was all kinds of entertainment for locals while it lasted.

When Elena and Al came around the front of the house, they could see the tow truck, which had finally made its way up the street and was moving into position to pull the car up and out. The hole, at least, didn't seem to be growing like the crowd.

Of course, there were no guarantees the ground would hold.

But as they got closer to the action, that wasn't what made the hair on the back of Elena's neck start waving. The tingling in her fingers had disappeared as soon as she stepped inside her house, but it was back. In a big way. And that was never a good sign.

Elena put Casper's carrying case on the ground and started shaking her hands, trying to force blood into her fingertips, hoping to make the tingling stop.

"Are you okay?" Al was squinting at her from beneath the brim of her fire cap. She was frowning.

She was also glowing. And pulsing with a reddish tint. Just like everything else.

"Elena." Al's voice was sharp but sounded far away. "Elena, *look* at me."

But Elena was focused on the hole, which was hissing angrily. A few seconds later, it erupted in flames.

She wanted to run in the opposite direction. But that car. The firefighters. The tow truck guy, whose name she couldn't remember. People in the crowd. A young kid in a Suns cap. Old Mr. Martinez.

They were all just standing there.

She waved her hands, trying to tell them to get back. Trying to warn them. Trying to scream. But she couldn't move, and she couldn't make a sound.

The smoke was suffocating.

She covered her mouth and nose with the crook of one arm, still waving with the other, and tried to move closer, to reach them and pull them away out of danger. But the heat from the fire pushed her back. It was unbearable. Her skin was burning. It was impossible to breathe.

The smoke was so thick, it stung her eyes, so she closed them. She couldn't see anything, anyway.

And then there was silence.

When she woke up, she was on the ground. Al was kneeling beside her, cradling her head and shoulders. Three firefighters were standing right behind her. They were all staring.

The smoke was gone. So was the heat. And the fire.

"Elena! Are you okay?"

Elena looked up into Al's eyes, which were deep with worry. "What…what happened?"

"I don't know. You just started waving your hands around. And then it sounded like you were having trouble breathing. And then it looked like you were going to faint. I caught you just in time."

Elena closed her eyes again and took a deep breath. When she opened them, the air was still clear. The pulsing red light was gone. She pushed herself up into a sitting position.

"You tell *me* what happened." Al put her hand on Elena's back. "Are you okay?"

"Yes, I'm fine."

"You want me to call a bus, Chief?" Bobby asked.

"A bus? Why do we need a bus?" Elena frowned. Nothing was making sense.

"He means an ambulance," Al said. She turned back toward Bobby. "I think we're okay, here. Thanks."

Bobby and the other two firefighters stepped away, but didn't go far.

"Can you stand?" Al was still rubbing her back.

Elena nodded and Al stood up, extending a hand. Elena took it. The tingling sensation was gone. Her legs were a little wobbly, but she could move again. Al put an arm around her, which helped her steady herself.

Then she looked around. Everyone near the hole was gaping at her. So was everyone in the crowd. Some people were taking pictures.

Elena dropped her head. "Shit."

"What did you see, Elena?" A middle-aged woman called from the edge of the crowd.

"Yeah! What did you see?"

"Did you see a ghost?"

"Are there spirits in that hole?"

"Or something worse?"

"What caused the hole, Elena?"

"Should we be afraid?"

"Come on, Elena…tell us what's going on?"

A dozen people, at least, were all shouting at the same time.

Bobby shot over to them, his hands upraised. "Alright, everybody. That's enough. Show's over. Y'all shouldn't be here, anyway. Don'tcha have jobs or somewhere to be? How about y'all go home?"

That was unlikely. But his voice did seem to shake his crew, at least, out of whatever stupor they were in. The tow truck guy went back to work and the crew refocused on the hole.

"You sure you're okay?" Al asked, a little sharply.

"I said I'm *fine*." Elena scooted sideways to get out from under Al's arm.

"Good. I'm glad. Now, I suggest you take yourself and Casper home." Al paused. "Urr. I mean, back to work. Or wherever you're staying until you get the all clear on your house."

Elena cocked her head. "Excuse me. Is there a problem?"

Al scoffed. "Well, yeah. Actually, there *is* a problem. I'm supposed to be flying through the mountains on my bike right now because it's my day off. That burrito van is reminding me that I haven't had breakfast, and I'm starving. I have a big *hole* in the middle of the street, with a car stuck in it. And now I have a town full of people who think the hole is haunted. Just what I need. More wacky theories in a town that feeds on them."

"Okay. But none of that is *my* fault.*"*

"The burritos, no. But the haunted hole? That is all you, Elena." Al crossed her arms, glowering. "What the hell was that, anyway?"

"What was *what*?"

"That show you put on."

"That wasn't a show, *Chief Jones*. I just—"

"You just *what*?"

"I just couldn't...breathe for a moment."

"You couldn't *breathe*? Do you have asthma? Allergies? Long Covid? A lung condition of some kind? Any sort of explanation at *all*?"

"You know what?" Elena crossed her arms, a mirror image of the chief. "I don't have to explain myself to you. And frankly, I am tired of the constant interrogation. Just take care of this hole and get me back in my house as soon as possible. Thank you and good *day*."

Elena snatched her bag away from Al, picked up Casper, and stormed toward her car, ignoring the handful of people who were still taking pictures and begging her to tell them what was in the hole.

The burritos did smell amazing. But Elena wasn't hungry.

She was angry with the chief—and with herself for being even a little attracted to someone so annoying.

And she was worried about whatever was in that hole.

CHAPTER THREE

Al sauntered into Banter & Brew—the only microroaster and the fastest place for a sit-down meal in town—ten minutes late for her regular weekly lunch with Dana. The twenty-minute walk from her office had taken thirty-five because everyone she passed had a greeting or a question or a bit of town gossip they wanted to pass along. Most wanted an update on the hole. She needed to remember to give herself more time when she was on foot.

Tessa Williams, owner of Mujer Fuerte Vineyard, and her new wife, Lace Valenti, were just heading out when Al came through the door. She couldn't not say hello. The Fireballs had played for their wedding earlier in the year.

"How are my favorite newlyweds?"

Tessa, looking fresh and natural, like she just walked out of a wine country magazine, squeezed Lace's hand, beaming. "So good, Chief."

"How many times do I have to ask you to call me Al?"

"I think she has a thing for uniforms." Lace grinned. "We're great, Al. How are you doing? Everyone is still talking about what a great party it was."

"I was just the wedding singer. That party was all you two. And I gotta say, marriage looks good on you."

Tessa blushed. "You have no idea. For one thing," she dropped the volume by half a step, "there are serious benefits to marrying someone who owns an adult toy shop—"

"Frisky Business was voted best sex toy shop in the state last year." Lace announced proudly, smoothing her pompadour like a swaggering Elvis impersonator.

Al laughed. "Yes, we all know, Lace. Congratulations, again. Also, Tessa—oversharing."

Tessa gave Al a hug. "I can't wait to have the band back at Mujer Fuerte."

"We're looking forward to that, too."

After listening to the G-rated details of their honeymoon, Al slapped Lace on the back, gave Tessa another hug, and the two headed out.

Dana had already grabbed a table and was slurping an iced coffee, scrolling through her phone. On her way across the room to meet her, Al fist-bumped a table of guys from Station Three and said a quick hello to a pair of ER nurses sitting at the counter, one of whom had been flirting with Al for a year. She nodded to at least a dozen people who greeted her as she crossed through the café.

"You literally know everyone," Dana said without looking up.

"Not *everyone*." Al grinned, unzipping her department-issued bomber, and then hanging it over the back of her chair.

Dana's dark brown hair was pulled back in a tight bun, and she was in her blue short-sleeved Owen Station Police Department uniform.

"Feeling the heat today, Chief? It's still jacket weather. At least it is today. You look like you're dressed for June."

"Menopause sucks, Al." Dana laughed and put her phone down. "I'm always so hot. Ricardo says sleeping with me is like sleeping with a furnace."

Al took a seat. "It's not a bad thing to have a husband who thinks you're hot."

"Very funny." Dana grinned.

"Seriously. You two are like the original hashtag #relationship goals."

Dana leaned forward, wide-eyed. "Well, that's new. Are you telling me you have hashtag #relationship goals all of a sudden?"

Al laughed. "I didn't mean *my* relationship goals."

Dana sat back and crossed her arms. "Still too focused on making your next career move, huh? No room in your life for love?"

"Don't look so disapproving, Dana. You know I'm not built like you. Your family has been here forever. You married your high school sweetheart and you're still madly in love, after more than twenty-five years. That's not me. I've never lived anywhere for more than three or four years at a time. Never had a relationship that lasted half that long. And I'm not necessarily looking for it, either."

Dana raised an eyebrow. "Everyone needs a someone, Al. Even you."

Al shook her head and flashed a smile. "I can't be a mover and a shaker if I'm anchored down, Dana. And there aren't too many women out there who would want to follow my ambitious ass all over the country."

"Pobrecita." Dana grinned. "You poor thing. You just need to meet the right girl. My cousin in Hatch has a sister-in-law in Albuquerque who has a niece in El Paso who would be a perfect—"

"Okay, that's enough." Al laughed. "I'm *good.*"

Al turned and waved at Knox Reynolds, Banter & Brew's owner, who was behind the counter. He waved back, and Al knew he'd be over to take her order as soon as he was able.

Banter & Brew was the first place her boss, the fire chief, brought her when she came to town to interview for the job. "If you want to know what's happening in Owen Station, this is the place to be," he said.

Today, it was packed.

"On a different subject—everybody's talking about that hole." Dana looked at Al over the top of her frosty glass.

Al sighed. "Don't I know it. What are the latest rumors *you're* hearing? Have you heard anything that can beat a *ghost*? Because that one is about as weird as it gets."

Dana raised an eyebrow. "I don't think a ghost caused that hole, my friend. But you could at least try to be more open-minded. Just because *you* can't see something, doesn't mean it's not there. And just because you don't believe in something, doesn't mean it's not real.

"Don't tell me you believe in ghosts." Al scoffed.

"I wouldn't call them that, no. But on Día de los Muertos, when my family builds an altar to honor and welcome our loved ones who have passed on, the veil between here and there feels very thin."

Al cringed. "I didn't mean to—"

"Insult my culture?" Dana smiled. "I know."

"It's just all the rumors that are flying around—"

"I know, I know. I hear them, too. Have you heard the one about how the government is testing a secret energy-directed weapon in the desert?"

Al dropped her head. "Oh my God."

"No, seriously. I actually think they may be on to something with this. The weapon is super powerful. It causes weather incidents and mind control and—guess what else? Earthquakes. The latest test took place just west of here. Guess when? *Three days ago.* On Sunday. And apparently, the blast shook the ground hard enough to open up a giant hole over on Old Mine Road."

Dana managed to deliver this routine with a totally straight face.

"You don't say?" Al answered just as seriously, which made Dana snort-laugh.

Al shook her head, shrugging. "Honest to God, Dana. How do you manage it?"

"Manage what?" Knox was suddenly at Al's side, menus in hand.

Al looked up at him. He was a good-looking guy. White, light brown hair, taller than her, she guessed maybe six-two. Probably about her age, on the other side of thirty-five.

She took the menu he offered. "The ridiculousness."

Knox cocked his head and raised his eyebrows. "The what, now?"

"Our new assistant fire chief is discovering the joys and sorrows of small-town gossip," Dana explained.

"No joys. Just sorrow." Al scowled. "And it's not just a small-town thing. I dealt with this at my last post, big time. More than half the department was refusing to get vaccinated, even after we lost two good men. There were protests outside our stations, people upset because they thought the city was going to issue mandates. As if that was ever going to happen. Honest to God, I almost left the service after that."

Dana grimaced. "Well, you wouldn't want to let the gubbermint implant microchips in your brain, would you?" She gave the phone sitting on the table a poke. "As if our every move isn't already being tracked through one of these."

"Right?" Al said. "People hear things on those so-called news shows. The pundits don't even believe a word they're saying, but people get caught up in it."

Knox nodded. "You wouldn't believe some of the stuff I hear from behind that counter, conspiracy theories people have found online. By the way..." He winked. "You don't think Big Foot caused that hole, do you?"

Al used her menu to smack him on the arm. "Ha ha. Funny. *Not* funny. Also, by the way, I'm not *that* new. I've been here almost two years now."

Dana blinked. "Has it really been that long?"

"Two years is nothing," Knox said. "I've been here since I was in grade school, and the old-timers still talk to and about me like I'm a newcomer."

Al shook her head, half-smiling. There were things to like about this small town. There were some good people, present company included. The mountain biking was world-class and the weather was pretty great year-round. But she was already keeping her eye open for which departments around the country would be hiring a new chief in the next few years. She was determined to land the top spot somewhere before she was forty. Owen Station was just a step in that direction. That didn't just make Al a newcomer. It made her a transient. She was just passing through.

"So, what'll it be?" Knox had his order pad and pen ready.

"What's the special?" Dana asked.

Knox raised an eyebrow. "Well, it's *Wednesday*. So it's *quiche.*"

"Just kidding." Dana handed her menu back. "I already knew that. I'll take it."

"Me, too."

"Two quiche specials coming right up." He didn't bother to write it down.

"Bring a piece of that rhubarb pie, too, while you're at it," Dana yelled at him as he walked away. She looked at Al and shrugged. "It's the best I've ever had."

Al made a note to try it sometime. "So, I saw Tessa as I was coming in here. Did you talk to her?"

Dana nodded. "She reminded me that we have a gig in her tasting room coming up."

"Exactly. That means we only have a few practices left. And somebody needs to rein in our bass player. I wanted to kill Sam last week. She needs to know she is not the most important person on stage."

Dana laughed. "Of course not, Al. We all know that's you."

"That is not what I mean." Even though, as the band's lead vocalist, she kind of was. "I just mean we all have a role to play. But if it was up to Sam, her bass line is all anyone would hear."

"Okay, okay. I'll talk to her."

"You know it's awkward for me. I'm her boss at work. I don't want to be her boss in the band."

"Got it."

Al shifted on her chair. "It's hard enough navigating the firehouse. They all want me to be their best friend. Hell, I want to be friends, too. But I can't be."

"I feel you."

"I'm still getting used to the whole dynamic."

"I know."

"So you'll talk to her?"

"Yes."

"Use your mom voice on her."

"Let me tell you something, my friend. My mom voice comes in very handy."

"I am aware. You use it on me all the time."

Dana chuckled, but then leaned forward. "Seriously, though." She lowered her voice. Ears were everywhere. "What is happening with that hole? It's been three days. My guys have blocked off the road in both directions, and we're starting to get complaints from the folks who live there—it's hard finding parking, and they have to carry their groceries more than a few steps, so, yeah. They're not happy."

Al shrugged. "Everything moves slow here. You know that better than me."

"Have they figured out what happened? What caused it?"

"It was Big Foot. Didn't you hear?"

Dana sniffed. "I'm being serious."

"I know, I know." Al laughed. "But before we go too far down that hole, have you given any more thought to coming with me to Camp Fury next year? We're already putting the team together for the Tucson camp."

"You want me to spend a weekend teaching teenaged girls about life as a police officer?"

"And fire fighters."

"I had a teenage girl once. Hell, I *was* a teenage girl once. You can't teach them anything."

Al laughed. "You're not wrong. But Camp Fury is different. You should see the girls, Dana. Climbing ladder trucks. Rappelling over the edge of a building. Really pushing themselves. Getting a taste of what it's like to make a difference. Learning how strong they are. And every girl gets a mentor—I'm still in touch with the kid I met at the first camp I did, eight years ago. It's the highlight of my year."

"Paving the way for the next generation, eh?"

Al nodded. "Something like that."

"Who did that for you, Al?" Dana asked quietly.

A half dozen faces flashed through her mind. Teachers. Coaches. Mum. She didn't know where she would be without them. She sure as hell didn't get much encouragement from her father—he was never home.

Al looked at Dana and grinned. "You do that for me, amiga."

"Me?"

"You."

"I guess you did look like a lost puppy when you first got to town."

"I did not."

"You did."

"Okay, maybe a little." Al felt shy saying it, but it was true. "You've been a good friend, Dana. And a good mentor." She paused dramatically, knowing she had Dana right where she wanted her. "Just think how great it'll be to do that for a whole bunch of girls at camp next year."

Dana threw her head back and cackled. "Alright, already. You got me. I'm in."

Al pounded the table. "Yes!"

Dana shook her head, still smiling. "Now that you have what you want, give me something in return. What in the hell is going on with that hole?"

Al cleared her throat and tried not to look too smug. "Okay. Right. The hole. The engineer the city brought in has some more work to do. But she thinks it was an old mine tunnel. It's her guess that the snow melt, followed by that big storm a few months ago, created enough pressure that it weakened the pavement. Since the road was built above a tunnel, which could be as much as a hundred and fifty years old, there wasn't much there to support it. So, at some point, the pavement just gave way. And boom."

"Boom. So that's it, then? What are they going to do?"

"Reinforce it and fill it in, so they can fix the street, I guess."

Dana put her glass down. "Why do you sound like there's more to this story?"

"I don't know. It just seems a little strange. I asked where the tunnel went, how long it is, are there more in the area. You know, I'm thinking we would want to know if we should expect other incidents like this. Can we alert homeowners whose properties might be impacted? Is there something we can do to prevent a tragedy? We were lucky this time. Someone, like that ER nurse, could have gotten hurt. Or killed."

"Makes sense. Track down the tunnel. See where it goes. Figure out if there are any threats."

Al nodded. "Exactly. But—"

"Lemme guess." Elena Murphy, in all of her pixie power, seemed to materialize out of thin air, carrying a voice that was three times bigger than she was. "They're *not* going to investigate, are they? They're going to close that hole in front of my house and just pretend like it never happened."

Elena had appeared beside the table with Hazel Butler, the town librarian and local historian. Knox was right behind them, plates in hand.

Al looked at Elena, not sure what to say. She really did not want to like this woman, and did not like this intrusion. Elena was emotional. Dramatic. Her life was a mess. Or at least her house was. The last time Al saw her, she was storming away, an overnight bag in one hand and a cat carrier in the other.

As if *Al* had done something wrong.

As if she hadn't just ignited the second biggest rumor-filled dumpster fire Al had ever seen.

The town could not stop talking about the ghosts who caused the hole. Or came out of the hole. Or both. It was absurd.

Managing the crowds who were still showing up every day to catch a glimpse of the hole was creating a logistical nightmare for the city, and using resources that could be used elsewhere. The city manager ordered the fire department to keep a bus on site at all times, in case of medical emergencies.

Al was in charge of her department's budget.

She was seeing the impact of Elena's little episode on a spreadsheet every day.

So, no. Al did not want to like her.

But here she was. In a sleeveless gray, asymmetrical vest that hit her mid-thigh, with a black turtleneck beneath it, black leggings, and mid-calf boots. Elena's shimmering brown hair hung in long waves over her shoulders. Freckles were sprinkled across her smooth fair skin, like they were on their way to a party. She really had been put in an inconvenient situation, through no fault of her own. And she was understandably frustrated. Elena jutted out her chin and crossed her arms over her chest in the kind of pose accident lawyers use on billboards to say they'll fight for you. Scary if you're the bad guy. Comforting if they're on your side.

Al couldn't look away.

"Chief...?" Dana squinted, a question mark in her eyes. When Al didn't answer—because the sight of Elena had inexplicably sucked the air out of her lungs and made her feel a little dizzy—Dana's head swiveled toward the trio beside their table. "Hi, Elena. Hi, Hazel. How are y'all doing? Knox, that quiche looks great, as always."

"I'm doing well, Chief." Hazel smiled, putting one hand over her belly—she had just started showing. "Thanks for asking. How are—"

"To be honest, I am not doing well at all," Elena said, interrupting. "I've had to sleep in my childhood bedroom for the past three nights, with my father snoring down the hall, and my mother telling me to eat something every five minutes. I would like to sleep in my *own* bed, in my *own* house tonight. But that's probably not going to happen...is it, Chief?"

Everyone was looking at Al, waiting for her to say something. Why couldn't she think of anything to say?

"You did promise you would move as quickly as possible to get me back in my house. You said that would happen *days* ago."

Knox quietly deposited the plates onto the table and backed away slowly, his eyes darting around the table from woman to powerful woman. Then he spun around and ducked back into his kitchen.

Dana kicked Al under the table, which made Al sit up straighter and find some words. "I can understand why you're frustrated, Elena. I didn't *guarantee* you'd get the all clear right away. But I can see how I got your hopes up. I'm sorry about that. I didn't find out until Monday morning that the town's building inspector is gone for a few days."

"Oh, that's right." Hazel jumped in. "I heard he was at a pickle ball tournament in Mesa this week."

Hazel got a point for trying to be helpful, but it didn't do much to lower the temperature.

Elena was still zeroed in on Al. "So Inspector Bill is gone. And no one else in this town can take care of this?"

This had to be a rhetorical question. Elena had been away for a long time, but she grew up here. She knew how things worked. The lack of redundancy in local government services was intentional. One building inspector. One guy in planning and zoning. One person in code compliance. It saved the town money. The problem was that, when that one person wasn't available, *no one* was.

"That's right." Al tried to regain control of the situation. "No one else can do it. Inspections are Bill's department. He's supposed to be back tomorrow."

"Tomorrow, again." Elena sighed heavily.

"Tomorrow. And I will make sure this is the first thing he sees when he gets back to his desk."

"I appreciate that, Chief. But it doesn't answer the question about what comes after that. If I'm understanding things correctly, no one is going to do anything to make sure there isn't another collapse." Elena still had her arms crossed, as if daring Al to confirm her assumption.

Al had easily been able to catch her when she fell. She was tiny.

But she was fierce.

And she clearly wasn't going to let this go.

Everyone looked at Al again.

Why was she on the hot seat, anyway? It's not like she created the hole. Or had any authority over making sure it got fixed. Or could prevent another one from popping open somewhere else. She was a first responder. She ran into burning buildings. She pulled people out of upside-down cars. Now that she was an officer, she gave orders the toughest guys in town followed.

But she wasn't a goddamn magician.

And as much as she would like to see another collapse avoided, this hole wasn't her problem.

"Elena. I wish I had answers for you. I really do. I don't know what the city is going to do, if anything, beyond just closing up that hole and fixing the street. It's not my job. Frankly, even if it was my job, I'm not sure I would have time to do it. Because my crew and

I are being inundated by 'I saw a ghost' calls, which have tripled in the past seventy-two hours. Apparently, in this town, the answer to 'who you gonna call?' is your local firefighters. Who knew? It is a total waste of department resources. It is distracting us from the real work we have to do. And it wouldn't have happened without your—"

"My *what*?"

Al's heart raced. The look on Elena's face dared her to respond. Dare accepted.

"Your *what*? You mean you don't know? You can't be serious. I'm talking about the scene you made by the hole on Sunday morning. Passing out. Then getting up and letting everyone think we were all in the middle of *Nightmare on Mine Street*."

Elena turned five shades of pink. "The *scene* I made? I told you, I suddenly had trouble breathing. I don't know, maybe you would too if your house almost got swallowed by a hole. And as for all the weird things people in this town think, I learned a long time ago that I am not responsible for that."

Al was loading the next round, but Dana kicked her under the table again and scowled at her like the mom she was. She stopped and looked up at Elena, whose blue eyes, which were framed by those impossibly long lashes, were still fixated on her.

Al took a breath and tried to see things from Elena's perspective. "That is a fair point. You are not responsible for what other people think. It makes sense that you're feeling unhappy about all of this. You can't move back into your house. You have a big hole in front of it. And you're wondering where the next hole might open up. Honestly, I feel a little frustrated, too. We got lucky this time…and it would be great to make sure we avoid a next time by tracking down the origin of that tunnel and doing some research into any others that might be beneath this town. Unfortunately, that is not my call."

"She's right, Elena." Hazel intervened again, putting her hand on Elena's arm. "There's not much the chief can do, beyond what she's already done."

Elena looked at Hazel and sighed. Her shoulders relaxed and her face softened. And dammit if that didn't make Al want to put *her* arm around her, to feel Elena's head resting against her chest again.

Those couple of minutes after Elena fainted had been scary. But it wasn't fear that Al remembered when she thought about having Elena in her arms.

"I wish I could say this situation with the tunnel was unusual," Hazel said, arching backwards, her hands on the small of her back.

"What do you mean?"

At which point, Dana kicked Al under the table again, which freaking hurt.

"Hey, everyone." Dana glowered at Al and then looked at Hazel and Elena standing beside the table. "Before we get into an even *longer* conversation...do you girls want to sit down? One of you, especially, looks like you could use a seat."

Hazel looked relieved, immediately pulled out a chair, and groaned as she sat down. "Thanks, Chief. How'd you know?"

"Um...been there, done that," Dana laughed, pointing at Hazel's belly. "A few times."

Al looked up at Elena, who hadn't made a move to sit down. She just stood there staring at the empty chair.

"Elena? Are you going to sit?"

Elena's eyes shifted toward Al.

"I don't bite." Al raised her eyebrows, knowing that she sounded like she, in fact, might.

Elena finally flipped her hair over a shoulder and tipped her chin up. "Of course you don't. And if you did, I would bite you back."

Al's mouth dropped open and nothing came out.

Then everyone started laughing.

And having reset the vibe, just like that, Elena took a seat. Both corners of her mouth tipped upward just a hair, but her eyes were sparkling.

Al waved at Knox to make sure he knew their table of two just turned into a table of four, and he fired off a quick salute.

"Okay, now that we're all comfy. And no one is biting anyone—" Al shot Elena a little side-eye with half a smile. "Tell us what you meant, Hazel. About the tunnels?"

"Well, the state is full of abandoned mines. Some estimates say there could be as many as a hundred thousand of them, more than any other state in the country. And a lot of them are here in the south."

Al shook her head. "That's not possible—is it?"

"It is. Many of these mines date to the late eighteen hundreds. And it's not like there was a lot of regulation back then. Somebody would see something that made them think there was copper or silver or gold under there, and start blasting away. Most of those old mines were never registered anywhere, and many were never closed up properly."

Dana nodded, frowning. "We don't know where they are until someone falls in. Most rural counties have volunteer rescue teams. They pull at least a couple of people—hikers, mostly—out of old mine shafts every year."

Knox stopped by to drop off two more quiche specials, which no one had actually ordered, and put them down in front of Elena and Hazel. Al cocked her head at him. "How'd you know?"

He laughed. "Hazel is the reason quiche is the Wednesday special in the first place. It ought to be named after her."

Hazel huffed dramatically. "Excuse me, but for as much elbow grease as I put into this place before you even opened, you ought to name the whole place after me. Besides, I don't *always* order the quiche on Wednesdays, anymore."

"That's true." Knox put his hands on his hips. "You've become a lot more adventurous since Sena swept you off your feet. Do you want something besides quiche today?"

"Um, no." Hazel looked a little sheepish.

Knox laughed. "I didn't think so."

After he left, Hazel dug in like she was eating for four, not two.

Elena just moved the food around on her plate. "I don't understand why no one is doing something about these abandoned mines."

Hazel shrugged, swallowing a big bite. "There's no money in the state budget for it."

"Actually, there would be plenty of money for it...and for our schools, and our roads, and people in need, and all the things...if only—" Dana stopped herself and looked around the table. "I think

I'll skip the political rant." She scooped up a bite of quiche and popped it in her mouth.

Elena sat back in her chair and looked at Al. A dozen emotions flickered across her face. But her eyes were steady, like she was examining Al, sizing her up. Finally, she leaned forward and put her hand on Al's arm. "Chief Jones, I know this is the second time in three days I've had to apologize to you. But I am sorry for taking my frustration out on you. Hazel is right. None of this is your fault. And all you've done is try to be helpful."

Al gulped. She was a pro when it came to approaching and containing a fire. And although Elena's flare-ups took her by surprise, they were fun in a way. They challenged Al's ability to stay calm and keep her sense of humor. It was the unexpected way Elena had of *dousing* a fire, with self-awareness and transparency, that most knocked Al off balance.

Her arm was hot beneath Elena's hand, and the warmth had spread across her chest, up her neck, to her ears.

Dana kicked her again. "Well, what do you say, Al?"

Al blinked, cleared her throat, and shifted again on her chair. "Um...thanks?" She was going to have a bruise on that shin.

Dana's phone started buzzing. "Uh-oh. Duty calls." She pushed her chair away from the table and got up, the phone already halfway to her ear. "Hang on a sec," she said, balancing the phone on her shoulder while pulling money out of her wallet and dropping it on the table. Then she took the phone in hand and muted it the old-fashioned way, by covering it with her other hand.

"It was great to see you all. And, Elena—" She threw a thumb in Al's direction. "Don't let this one give you a hard time. She's a big softie under all that spit and polish."

Al opened her mouth to respond, but Dana put the phone back to her ear and shot out the door before she could say anything.

Hazel gulped down the last bite of quiche, pushed her plate away, and stood up, too. "Gotta get back to work, myself." She gave Elena a quick kiss on the cheek, waved awkwardly at Al, and waddled to the counter to pay up.

Al sat back in her chair. "Is it something I said?"

"Probably," Elena said with a straight face.

"Funny."

Elena cracked a smile. "So are you? A big softie?"

"I am not."

"I'm not sure I believe you."

Elena laughed and poked at her food some more. When she looked up, her eyes glistened, like the pavement after it rains. "You know, Chief. I think maybe we didn't get off to a very good start. Would you like to start over?"

Al took a deep breath, a little startled by her reaction to Elena's question. "Yes, actually. I would."

"You *would*?" Elena sat back, opening her eyes wide.

"I'm willing to start over if you are."

"I would like that." Elena smiled shyly.

Al nodded and smiled back but, without knowing exactly what to say next—and without Dana there to kick her mouth into gear—she dropped her head, picked up her fork, and took some bites of quiche. Elena didn't say anything else, either.

The place was starting to empty out and Knox was busy clearing dishes behind the counter. Al shifted in her chair, trying to get comfortable. But it wasn't the chair making her uncomfortable. She was just starting to think about an exit strategy when her phone buzzed.

"Excuse me," she said as she picked it up, relieved to have something normal to do. "It's probably work."

It wasn't.

It was a text from Dana.

Don't say anything stupid. And ask her out!

Not exactly the relief Al was looking for.

Not even a little.

Chapter Four

Elena studied Al's expression, which was blank. But her body language said something was off. "Is everything okay?"

Al was tapping her fingers on the table, staring at her phone. "Huh? Yeah." She set down the phone and took another bite. "What were we talking about?"

Elena raised an eyebrow. There *was* something going on. Elena was better at reading people than she wanted to be. But Al clearly didn't feel like sharing. And Elena didn't need to go any deeper. She was very young when she learned that knowing more about people than they wanted known never ended well.

"Well, actually. We weren't talking.*"* Elena continued moving food around her plate. She hadn't eaten much since the fire in the hole, despite her mother's best efforts. A sense of impending doom tended to dampen the appetite. "I said I would be open to 'starting over,' after we got off to such a bad start, and you dove into your last bites of quiche like you hadn't eaten all week."

"Oh, right." Al sat back, crossing her arms. "I guess I was just thinking that I'm not sure how to do that."

"Do what?"

Al shrugged. "Start over."

"Hmmm."

Elena took her time responding as Al shifted in her chair, crossing and uncrossing her arms. For someone who walked around like she was wearing a cape, it was remarkably easy to make her squirm.

"I have an idea." Elena smiled. No reason to make this harder than it needed to be. "How about if we ask each other questions? You know, to get to know each other."

"Like truth or dare?" Al lifted an eyebrow. "Because I have to admit, I am very good at dares."

"I don't doubt that, Assistant Fire Chief Jones. I know you make a habit of jumping in front of oncoming cars—"

Al laughed and appeared to settle back into her chair, seeming to recover from whatever it was that had knocked her off-balance a moment before. "First off, I asked you to call me Al. Remember? Second, to be clear, I don't make a *habit* of jumping in front of cars."

"Just *my* car. Okay, got it." Elena waved her hand, playfully brushing away Al's explanations. "Let's start with an easy question. No dare. Just the truth. When did you know you wanted to be a firefighter?"

"That is easy. I mean, who doesn't want to be a firefighter, at some point? Am I right? It's the sickest job in the world. It is literally *fire.*"

"Okay, that's fair. And funny." Elena picked up her glass of water and peered at Al over the top of it. "Your turn."

"Do you want a dare?"

"No. I don't take dares."

"Really? Never?" Al's eyes opened wide, like she was seeing an apparition, something that did not exist in the natural world.

"Never. I mean, I'm not afraid to go after what I want. But I grew up in a funeral home, remember? I've seen what happens when dares go wrong."

Al nodded thoughtfully. "I can see that." Then she sat back and grinned. "I just can't imagine refusing a challenge."

Elena shrugged. Al was a daredevil. Got it. "Well, I hope that turns out well for you."

"It has so far. But whatever. No dare. I got it. A truth then. When did you know you wanted to manage a funeral home?"

Elena almost snorted water out of her nose. "Doesn't *everyone* want to work in a funeral home, at some point? I mean, is there anything *sicker*." It took her a minute to stop cackling before she could talk.

"Actually, it may or may not surprise you to know that I never wanted to work in my family's business. When I was little, I wanted to be a forest ranger. I loved being outdoors. I still do. And I didn't love being around people so much. So that seemed like a good fit. Plus, I thought Smokey the Bear was cute."

"Oh, I like this." Al's face lit up. "We actually have something in common. I wanted to fight fires. And you wanted to prevent them."

Elena chuckled. "I see what you did there."

"So, what happened? What made you break up with Smokey?"

Elena paused, thinking about things she hadn't thought about in years. Al waited patiently, appearing genuinely interested in what Elena was saying.

"The short story is that I fell in love with photography in my freshman year of high school."

"Sounds like a longer story in there somewhere?"

Elena pulled out her phone, and scrolled for a minute. When she found what she was looking for, she held it up so Al could see the picture of a much younger Elena. It was a screenshot of a page in her old yearbook.

"I was fifteen."

Al raised her eyebrows and took a closer look. "That's you, all right. But you look a lot like Wednesday Addams."

Elena laughed. "Yeah, I guess I did."

"Were there a lot of goth kids here back then?"

"Like four. But I was such a loner, I didn't even hang with *them*."

"Sounds lonely."

"It was. But I wasn't lonely just because I dressed like this. My family lived in the apartment above the funeral home—they still do. That would have been enough to make most kids socially outcast.

KELLY & TANA FIRESIDE

And we were, my brothers and me. But I also had a…" Elena took a sip of water, this time without spitting it out of her nose.

"Had a what?"

Elena searched Al's face, trying to decide what and how much to say.

"Let's just say, some things happened when I was a little kid that made people nervous around me."

"Do I need to be worried?" Al shot her a half smile.

"Worried? Nah. Not unless you piss me off." Elena grinned back.

"Noted. Seriously, though. What happened?"

"When I was little, you mean?"

"Yeah."

Elena paused. "I don't like talking about this."

"I'm sorry. I'm not trying to make you uncomfortable. This is your game, though." Al smiled.

She had a point.

"Fine. I'll tell you the version my mother tells." Elena sat back in her seat, crossed her arms, and put one leg over the other. "It took me a long time to learn how to talk. In fact, I didn't say my first word until I was three. And when I finally did, it was notable."

"In what way?"

"Mom had our neighbor, Mrs. McCarthy, over for afternoon tea. I was playing in my little plastic, toy kitchen. Mrs. McCarthy called me over, picked me up, and put me in her lap. She smelled like hair spray and cigarettes and nerves, and she started trying to make me say words. *Who's that, Elena? Can you say mama? Say mama.* Finally, after a few minutes of this harassment, I guess I had enough. So I said my first word."

Al leaned forward. "And…? What was it?"

"Die."

Al's eyebrows hit her hairline. "Your first word was *die*?"

Elena shrugged. "Yep."

"Mrs. McCarthy thought she misunderstood, so she kept saying, *Not 'I,' Elena. Say mama. Not 'I'.* And after a few minutes of that, I said it again, louder and more clearly."

• 70 •

"You said *DIE?*"

"Yep."

"Oh my God. That must have freaked her out."

"That's an understatement. She started sobbing hysterically, was absolutely wrecked. Mom had to call her husband to come get her and take her home."

"No wonder people were nervous around you after that."

"Oh, that wasn't the worst of it. Three months later, Mrs. McCarthy actually did."

"Did what?"

"Die."

Al's jaw practically scraped the tabletop. "Wait. You told her she was going to die, and then she did?"

Elena nodded. "Mom found out later that, just that morning, before she came over to our house for tea, Mrs. McCarthy had gone to the doctor, and gotten bad news. She hadn't told anyone yet and was building up the courage to tell her husband that night. And then—well, apparently whatever treatment they tried on her didn't work."

Al sat back in her chair, hands in her lap, a look of shock on her face. "I don't even know what to say. That might be the strangest story I've ever heard."

Elena shrugged.

"How did you do that? I mean, how could you possibly have known?"

"I have no idea. I didn't really even understand what dying meant at that age."

"You must have just picked up the word somewhere. From hearing your family talk, maybe, and being around a funeral home. It had to just be a coincidence. Right?"

Elena shrugged again.

"Wow, okay." Al crossed her arms. "So, after that happened, you decided to dress like Wednesday Adams. I'm sure that really helped people feel better about having you around."

Elena laughed hollowly, uncrossing her arms and legs. "I can't control how people feel, Al, or what they think. And you know what people are like. They make up whatever stories they want. And they talk. I got sick of it, walking around town knowing that people were whispering behind my back. So, yes, at some point I decided to just...how did you say it the other day? Lean into it. Play the part."

"That makes sense. So, how long were you in your goth phase?"

"I never was actually goth. I mean, I wasn't even into the music or anything. I just played it to annoy my parents. And I wasn't connected to others in the goth community."

"So the outfit was just..."

"A way to keep people away."

Al nodded as if she understood and uncrossed her arms, too. "I bet those were some tough years."

"You could say that. I don't know what I would have done if it hadn't been for my photography teacher. She gave me a key to the darkroom my freshman year, and let me experiment. She built up my confidence behind the camera. My senior year, she encouraged me to apply to the University of Arizona. They still have one of the best programs in the country."

Knox stopped by the table to drop off two pieces of rhubarb pie. "Dana ordered a piece but took off before she could eat it. She sent me a text. This one's on her." He put it down in front of Elena. "And this one's on me, Chief," he said, setting it in front of Al. "I understand rhubarb pie is a British thing."

Al nodded with a smile. "My Gran had a recipe I still dream about."

"Well, I hope you won't be disappointed. Enjoy."

Al picked up a fork and went to work on the pie. Elena followed. She might not have felt much like eating. But nobody turned down Knox's pie.

"Is that when you left town?" Al asked between bites.

Elena nodded. "Four years at the university in Tucson. Then six in LA."

"Did you love it?"

"LA? Yes. No. Sort of. I went because a small gallery included my senior project in a show. It got good reviews and things started to take off. I didn't think I'd ever come back here. Too much history.

But I wasn't in LA for very long before the world shut down. Then it was just lonely. When my dad called and asked me to come home, to help get the business back on track and give him an opportunity to sort of retire, I didn't have to think long."

"Owen Station seems like an odd place for one of the West Coast's up-and-coming photographers to settle down. Even if it is their old hometown."

Elena tilted her head and looked at Al sideways.

"What? I know how to use Google."

"You *Googled* me?"

"Yeah, of course. After I saw your show at the opening last summer."

Elena had been back in town for less than a year when Tessa asked her to show her work at the opening of the new Mujer Fuerte tasting room. And every single piece sold that night. The spooky little kid had come home with a different kind of reputation, an artist on the rise, and the hometown crowd ate it up.

"What did you think of it?"

"The show? I thought it was amazing."

"Amazing?" Elena snorted. "That could mean anything."

"Hmmm. You want more details?" Al shifted in her seat and cleared her throat. "Okay. How about this? Your photos made me look at this town and this landscape in a new way. No, wait. It was like seeing it all for the very first time. You captured the inside of things, somehow, with all their imperfections and blemishes, but their beauty, too. I thought about it for days afterward, and even took my bike out to see some of the places you photographed. My favorite was that shot you took from Boot Hill, overlooking the town at night. It was sad. Foreboding. Like you knew something bad was going to happen. I couldn't look away." Al paused. "It reminded me of a Sally Mann exhibit I saw once."

"Sally Mann?" Elena said softly. "That is high praise. Also, *seriously*? You know who Sally Mann is?"

"Don't look so surprised. I'm a firefighter. Not a Neanderthal."

"Sorry—"

"Again."

Elena smiled. "Yes, again. So…where did you develop an interest in photography?"

Al shook her head. "I don't want to overstate it. I've just been to a lot of museums. My dad moved us around a lot when I was growing up. Air Force. My mom liked to visit the museums in every city we lived, and she dragged me along with her. I was bound to learn *something*."

Elena laughed softly. "Well, I shouldn't be surprised that you have an artistic streak hidden under all the sharp creases and shiny shoes. I've heard you sing."

Al raised an eyebrow. "You have?"

Elena nodded. "Of course. I was at Lace and Tessa's wedding. You sang for their first dance. And your voice…it was *soulful*. It actually made me cry. Of course, I was already crying, just watching the two of them, surrounded by so many friends. The whole town showed up for them, and it made me realize that I hope to have what they have one day."

"What's that?"

"Someplace I feel like I really belong."

"This doesn't?"

Elena sighed. "Not exactly. Not yet. Like I said, for as long as I can remember, I was a loner. So I didn't come back to a bunch of friends. Now that I'm here, I'm having to *make* friends. Just ask Hazel. Or Lace. Or Knox, over there. They were all four years ahead of me in school. They've been super nice to me since I came back and make me feel like I'm part of the gang. But they'll tell you, it wasn't always like that. Actually, you could probably ask any local over the age of twenty-five. The Elena Murphy they remember was a little weirdo who said weird things and talked to dead people."

Elena stopped talking. She definitely had not meant to say that.

"Do you?" Al tilted her head, one eyebrow higher than the other.

"Talk to dead people or say weird things?"

Al laughed. "Yes."

"My brothers are known to say weird, or at least inappropriate, things. Me, not so much. And, no. I don't talk to dead people."

"You don't?"

"No."

"Do they talk to you?"

Well, that was a different question, wasn't it? The answer was more complicated. And this wasn't something she was ready to talk about with Chief Shiny Boots.

"Given how long it's taking to answer my question, I'm guessing the answer is yes." Al's brows furrowed.

Elena shook her head and laughed. "I just think you've gotten more than enough out of me in this little game."

"This game was your idea."

"Fair point. But I think it's my turn to ask a question."

"Okay. Shoot."

"Where is home, for you, Al?"

Al sniffed out a half-laugh. "Home? Nowhere, I guess. Everywhere. The longest I've ever stayed any place is five and a half years. That's when I was living with my grandparents in East London. I liked it there. But then Mum left the military. And moved me here, to the States, so she could be with my dad. I've lived in more than nine different places since then. That's the short story."

"Wow. That must have been hard."

Al grinned. "What part?"

"All of it, I guess. I don't know."

"I like it, actually. I like moving around. Seeing new things. Meeting new people. I like being different. I don't even know what it would feel like to be pigeonholed—or stuck in one place for very long."

"Did you have trouble making friends, growing up?"

Al laughed. "Me? No. I think because of my background, I can pretty much talk to anyone about anything. Music helps, too. The first thing I do, anyplace I live, is join a band, or start one if I need to. Plus, I was always into sports. And I'm funny as hell."

"You are?"

"You haven't noticed?"

"Okay, you're kind of funny."

Elena's phone buzzed and she pulled it out of her purse. It was Dad. She sent him to voice mail and looked up at Al. "Hey, I've got to get back to work. My family is looking for me."

"Understood. I've been gone way too long, too. My boss is probably wondering where I am."

Elena pulled money out of her purse to leave on the table and then paused. Al wasn't moving. She was staring at Elena in a way that made Elena's cheeks get a little warm.

"What?"

Al cleared her throat. "Well, I was just wondering if you might ever be interested in—"

Al paused.

Elena leaned forward. "In what?"

"In, um—"

Before Al could finish, Knox appeared and dropped the *Owen Station Caller* on the table. It was only published on Wednesdays and Sundays. Today was Wednesday. "You two are celebrities."

The headline blared, "Haunted Hole Opens On Old Mine Road." The grainy photo on the front page, which looked like it was shot with someone's phone, was of Al cradling Elena in her arms. The caption read, "Assistant Fire Chief Allison Jones comforts ghost-whisperer Elena Murphy after terrifying encounter with the hole."

"Oh, for God's sake," Al said quietly. She flipped the paper closed and stood up. "This is exactly what I thought might happen."

"It's not like I'm happy about this either," Elena snapped.

Knox stepped back away from the table.

"You need to do something about this, Elena. I can just imagine the way our phone lines are going to light up. Yesterday we got a call from someone who said a ghost chased their cat up into a tree. The day before, a ghost popped out of the refrigerator, almost giving someone a heart attack. What's next? Ghosts pushing people out of bed? Starting kitchen stove fires? Stealing cars and going for a joy ride? My department doesn't have the resources to respond to this kind of nonsense. But *this*—" Al picked up the paper and shook it. "This is fuel for the fire."

Al pulled cash out of her wallet and dropped it, and the paper, on the table. "Knox, thanks for a great lunch, as always."

"Anytime, Chief."

Al turned to Elena, her mouth set in a sharp line. "Elena, it's been a pleasure." Then she turned sharply and marched toward the door.

"Has it, though?" Elena muttered, scowling, watching Al go.

The chief was infuriating. One minute she was charming, funny, attentive, interested, open, comparing her to Sally Freaking Mann.

A minute later, Al was calling her out. And for what? Blaming *her* for things other people said or thought or did.

It was like being on an emotional roller coaster.

Elena shoved the *Caller* into her bag, paid for lunch, said good-bye to Knox, headed back to work, and tried to get Assistant Fire Chief Jones out of her head.

Her brothers helped. Unwittingly, of course.

It turned out, there had been no emergency. Dad was just calling to make sure Elena was planning to have dinner at home that night, which she was. Again. Even though she wasn't sure she could take one more family dinner in a row. As much as she loved them, she really needed to get back into her own house. Working *and* living together was more than she could handle.

Her brothers were arguing when she got to the office.

"I am one hundred percent on this, Conner. It was the Doritos guy. *Jesus*, why don't you ever believe me?"

"Because you're never right, Sean. It wasn't the Doritos guy. No one is going to put their ashes in a Doritos bag, not even the guy who invented them."

"You would if you made a billion dollars off them."

"No." Conner slowed his words, like he was talking to a five-year-old. "In that case, you would be buried with them. Which is what happened to the Doritos guy. He went six feet under with bags of Doritos."

"Well, at least he wouldn't be hungry, if he woke up." Elena swung her bag off her shoulder and dropped it on her desk.

"Very funny, Elena." Sean rolled his eyes.

"Also, a good point." Conner turned back to Sean. "Anyway. It wasn't the Doritos guy. It was the *Pringles* guy. They put his ashes into a can. Which makes way more sense than putting them into a chip bag."

Elena cleared her throat. "Don't you two have a body to move? Prep tables to clean? A family to piss off?"

The boys gave her the exact same blank stare they had been giving her for as long as she could remember. She had no idea how they were all related.

"I had the Truman family in here again this morning." She raised her eyebrows, waiting for a response. Nothing.

"Hello," she said, waving her hand in front of them. "The. Truman. Family. Ring a bell? You picked up Mr. Truman a few nights ago. Made Mrs. Truman cry. Made the daughter furious."

Her brothers delivered a synchronized shrug.

"They were in here today demanding a fifty-percent discount on the funeral, to make up for the pain and suffering you two caused."

A flash of something crossed their faces. Guilt, maybe? Regret? Nope.

Sean punched Conner on the arm. "I'll bet you five bucks it was the Doritos guy." Then they turned and left the office.

Elena's brothers would have done anything to help her if she needed it. They went to LA, loaded a truck with her things, and moved her back to Owen Station. Helped her move into her house and turn the second bedroom into a dark room.

But they had the emotional bandwidth of a pair of slugs. And that might be unfair to the slugs.

They both still lived at home, even though they were a few years older than Elena. They had a macabre sense of humor, a seemingly endless supply of unusual death stories, and a twin brother way of communicating without words that was especially strange because they weren't twins.

But *Elena* was the weirdo in her family?

The *Caller* was peeking out of her bag. She grabbed the paper and snapped it open to the front page. "Fuck."

She hadn't been called ghost whisperer in years. And it did not bring back happy memories. The boys must not have seen the paper yet because they were never going to let her live this down.

Elena looked ludicrous, sprawled out on the ground. Al, on the other hand, looked magnanimous. She had gone down on one knee, with an arm beneath Elena's back, cradling Elena's head against her chest. The other arm encircled Elena's waist protectively. It was impossible to see the expression on her face, because she was looking down at Elena, not at the camera, and she was wearing that ball cap.

Elena studied the image of their bodies together. Al was lean and muscular, strong. But the way her shoulders bent over Elena and her back curved into a full embrace made her look gentle, too. Tender.

Elena looked up, remembering that Al was starting to ask her a question before Knox brought them the paper. The way she was staring at Elena was awkward. It also woke up the lower half of her body.

"Would you ever be interested in—"

Interested in what, exactly?

Was Al Jones about to ask her for a date?

Impossible.

That seemed about as likely as her brothers learning how to read a room.

Al had walked through her house like she was afraid she was going to catch something. After her experience at the hole, she looked at Elena the same way.

That damn hole.

Elena looked back at the photo and shuddered. The hole was in the background. No sign of fire or smoke. In the foreground, some people looked afraid, others curious. But none of them were paying any attention to the hole. They were looking at her.

She had spent her entire adult life trying not to be the weirdo in the room.

And yet, here she was.

Plus, she let herself get cornered into telling Al about Mrs. McCarthy. As if Al needed more of a reason to think she was a freak.

She folded the paper and slammed it into the wastebasket.

Elena didn't care what people thought.

She certainly didn't care what Chief Shiny Boots thought.

The things Elena saw and felt were *real*. She didn't understand it. She didn't want it. But she couldn't stop it, either.

And what she saw at the hole that day really happened. The heat coming off the blaze was so intense she couldn't move. Her lungs had been so full of smoke she couldn't breathe.

She didn't know what it meant. But she knew it was bad.

She tried not to be distracted as she worked the rest of the afternoon. Not by Al. Not by the hole. Not by the photo.

But that's all her family wanted to talk about at dinner that night.

"Hey, look, everyone." Conner half-shouted when she walked through the door. "It's the ghost whisperer."

Elena glared at him.

"Conner, honey, you know your sister doesn't like being called that." Elena's mother sounded almost compassionate. But she knew the real motivation in shutting Conner down was making sure Elena didn't have what her mother called "an emotional response."

After a hundred years in the funeral business, emotions were supposed to have been bred out of the Murphy family.

Instead, Elena got them all.

"Okay, everyone, let's have a nice calm dinner." Mom went into the kitchen to get the food, Dad helped Grandma to the dining room table, and everyone took a seat.

"So what's happening with that hole, Elena?" Her dad asked as he took a large plate of roast beef from Mom and helped himself to a huge serving.

"A whole lot of nothing right now. I ran into Chief Jones at lunch today—"

"You mean your knight in shining armor?" Sean blinked his eyelashes at her, and Conner fanned him like he was going to faint.

Elena ignored them. "The chief said the engineer the city hired thinks an old tunnel collapsed."

"You mean Big Foot didn't do it?"

"Good one, Conner." Sean laughed.

"Hmm." Dad scrunched his forehead. "A tunnel from an old mine? There isn't a mine anywhere near that part of town."

"I know." Elena helped herself to her mother's mashed potatoes. Mom's cooking was one good thing about being home for a few days.

"They *are* going to investigate, aren't they?" Mom asked. "I'm sure we'd all like to know whether there are other tunnels in the neighborhood, just waiting to collapse."

"It doesn't sound like it, Mom."

Dad narrowed his eyes. "Well, they could at least look for the opening. It must be nearby somewhere, maybe up on the hill behind the house?"

Elena shrugged. "I don't know. I've hiked through there more times that I can count and never saw anything."

"It's lucky you didn't find it accidentally and fall in." Conner sounded like he had a mouth full of potatoes, because he actually did.

"Don't talk with your mouth full, dear," Mom said calmly.

"Can we please not talk about this at *all*?"

Everyone turned and stared at Gran. Elena had never heard her raise her voice.

"Gran, are you feeling alright?" Sean asked.

"Yes, of course." She sounded calmer, but her cheeks were pink and, when she took a sip of water, her hand was shaking just a bit more than usual. "I would just like to talk about something else."

"Let's talk about how long I have to share a bedroom with Sean." Conner glanced sideways at Elena. "When are you moving out, anyway?"

"Just as soon as possible, believe me. I'm not sure how much longer I can make it look like I'm wearing a different outfit every day."

"Are you kidding? You wear the same black-and-white clothes every day." Sean scoffed.

"Just because you can't tell the difference in what I wear day-to-day doesn't mean no one does."

"Children. Stop bickering, please."

"We are all in our thirties, Mom. We are not children."

"Well then, why are you whining, Sean?"

Sean crossed his arms over his chest and slouched in his chair.

"Conner, honey, pass the gravy, please."

Conner handed Mom the dish. "You checked in on Gramps at the nursing home today, didn't you, Mom? Ya got any intel? Who should we expect to see in the next month or so?"

"Seriously, Conner?" Elena snapped her head around to look at him. "If that's an attempt at humor, you suck at it."

Sean snickered across the table. "It's called gallows humor, Elena. It's what people do to cope with difficult situations. Like being a mortician, for example. Maybe you've been away for so long you've forgotten."

"You know what I haven't forgotten, Sean? How little you two seem to care about people. I'm not saying you *don't* care. But if you do, you have no idea how to show it. We might work with dead bodies, but the people we actually serve are their family and friends. They need to know that we care about them. They do not need sarcasm or sick jokes or bad behavior. You two have looked at our financials right? We can't keep handing out refunds and discounting our prices because you two have pissed somebody off. Again. Something's gotta change. And maybe that something is you."

"Elena." Mom's voice was sharp. "I know you are feeling stressed, but there's no excuse for having such an emotional response, or for taking it out on your brother."

"I am just stating facts, Mom."

"Okay, enough. Everyone. Can we stop talking about business?" Dad looked exhausted.

But not nearly as exhausted as Elena felt. "What exactly *can* we talk about?"

"Let's talk about what you saw when you fainted the other day?" Conner deadpanned.

Sean booed like a cartoon ghost and waved his fingers in the air. "Did you really see ghosts coming out of that hole, like everyone is saying?"

"Dammit!" Gran threw her napkin on the table and got out of her chair faster than anyone had seen her move in years. "I'm going to my room."

Elena looked at the stunned faces around the table. "It looks like I'm not the only person in this family to have quote-unquote emotional responses."

This should have made her feel better than it did.

But it didn't.

Something was seriously wrong with Gran.

Chapter Five

Al clicked her laptop shut. Her job description included serving as the department's public education officer and that meant managing their social media accounts. She did it. But that didn't mean she had to like it.

Bobby stuck his head in her office. "Everything okay in there, Chief?"

Al tried to smile. "Just dealing with the rumor mill, Garcia."

"Wildfires?"

Al nodded. "And the season is just getting started."

Thankfully, the number of I-saw-a-ghost calls had dropped off. It took six weeks, but the hole was finally closed up and the street repaired. People had mostly moved on.

Then the San Pedro fire kicked off the season a month earlier than usual. It had been quickly contained and was far enough away that it never threatened the town. But the smoke choked the air for a good week. And it seemed like the perfect opportunity to engage people in the county's first ever fire mitigation program. Al had worked with her counterparts across their rural county to win a federal grant that would support home hardening. That meant retrofitting houses with more fire-resistant materials and clearing brush to create defensible space around houses, most of which were a hundred years old.

But first Al had to convince homeowners to apply for the grant and actually get the work done.

"I just don't get it, Bobby. This town is basically a box of matches waiting to be lit, the way these old houses are all built on top of one another. Temperatures are climbing every year and the drought is worsening. You'd think people would be serious about preventing a disaster."

Bobby leaned against the doorframe and crossed his arms. "You'd think. Instead, it's easier to believe leftist radicals are starting the fires on purpose."

Al dropped her head in her hands. "I was just reading about that in the comments section of my post." Al looked up. "Honestly, even if someone was starting the fires on purpose—which, obviously, is not happening—you'd think people would *want* to protect their homes. We've only had about a dozen people apply so far, though. We're going to need to do a lot better than that."

"Anything I can do to help?"

Al shrugged. "You know people in this town better than I do."

"That's true. Lived here my whole life."

"Got any ideas for cutting through the conspiracy noise out there and getting people's attention?"

Bobby was quiet for a minute, thinking, and then a smile stretched across his face. "Actually, I think I do. It'll take me a minute to pull it together, but I think I have just the thing to sexy up your mitigation campaign."

"Sexy it up?"

"That's what I said."

Bobby wasn't kidding, either. He laid out his plan. Al approved it, and got the chief to sign off on it.

That next Saturday, a dozen firefighters showed up outside of an old bungalow on the north edge of town. The homeowner had already signed up for the program and contractors were scheduled for later in the week, to replace the old wood roof with metal and install dual pane windows. But today Bobby had hand-picked a crew of firefighters to clear brush on the property and create defensible space around the home.

And he made sure Elena Murphy was there to capture it all.

She pulled in just after Al arrived.

"She's here!" Bobby, whose face suddenly lit up with a goofy grin, might have had a little crush.

Al couldn't blame him.

Elena was a force. She pulsed with a sense of purpose when she walked. Expected people to listen to her when she talked. And vibrated with so much emotional energy, it was magnetic. Plus, she was cute as hell. Dana said she definitely picked up a vibe between them at the Banter & Brew that day. Al thought she did, too, for a hot minute. Then Knox showed them that stupid photo in the newspaper.

Al hadn't talked to her since.

She had seen Elena a couple of times, including one night out at the Triple D, but Al was hanging with her band mates and Elena was with friends. Some kind of electric charge kept them circling each other, but never let them get close enough to engage. At least, that's how it felt. Magnets have the power to repel, too.

Al was looking forward to seeing Elena, especially here, on Al's turf, where Al was in command. But she would be lying if she said she wasn't a little nervous.

Bobby hurried toward the car, with Al a few steps behind him. As they approached, Elena stepped out of her car wearing gray drop-crotch pants, a white asymmetrical sleeveless tank top, and boots. Al could picture her standing in front of that neat closet, completely surrounded by chaos, with a blinking unicorn behind her.

Everything below Al's waist opened and waves of heat radiated down her legs. Taking a deep breath, she planted herself. Feet spread, she straightened her back, and shoved her hands in her pockets. She reminded herself that she was in charge.

"Thanks for doing this, Elena." Bobby was practically wagging his tail.

"No problem, Bobby. I'm happy to help. My house is in just as much danger as anyone's. If I can take a few pictures to convince more people to sign up for this program, I'm all in."

Elena didn't acknowledge Al or even glance in her direction.

"Sweet. Everyone is excited that you're here. None of us has ever had our picture taken by a famous photographer before."

"I'm not famous, Bobby."

"You are to us." Bobby beamed.

Elena smiled sweetly. "Okay, before we get started. I have a pretty good idea of what you're looking for, and a lot of ideas of my own. But tell me again exactly what you want to use these photos for."

Bobby shot Al a quick look, as if to ask, "Do you want to handle this?"

Al shook her head and crossed her arms over her chest, using an elbow and a head nod to signal that Bobby should keep going.

Bobby looked like a kid whose dad just tossed him keys to the car. "Well, we have a bunch of ideas. We're going to start with a social media campaign. Hashtag #harden-your-home, hashtag #hard-firefighters. We're hoping the pictures will get lots of likes and shares, especially when people find out you took them. That'll help spread the word about the program. If it's as popular as we think it's going to be, we can offer signed prints to people who sign up. And we're talking about creating a calendar that we can sell—Sam said the guys in her last department, somewhere in Michigan, did that. We could use the money to buy things we need in the firehouses." Bobby paused.

"Did I forget anything, Chief?"

Al shook her head.

Again, Elena didn't even sneak a peek in her direction. She was working hard at not looking at Al, but it was so obvious that Elena might as well have been staring at her.

"Sounds like a lot of good ideas, Bobby. I'll do my best."

"I know you will." Bobby's tail was wagging again. "I'm gonna go get everyone ready for you, okay?"

"Sounds good. I'll just grab my gear and be there in a sec."

Elena stood very still, watching Bobby as he moved away. After a long minute, she turned to face Al.

"Hi," she finally said. Her eyes were the color of a cloudless sky.

"Hi."

There was another awkwardly long pause that Al wasn't sure how to fill. She uncrossed her arms and put them in her pockets again.

"How's your house?"

"Fine."

Another long pause.

"And the hole?"

"Gone."

"And the funeral home biz?"

Elena raised an eyebrow and peered up at Al. "Is there something you want to say to me?"

Al swallowed. She wasn't exactly sure. But if Dana had been there, she probably would have given Al a good kick in the shin. And Al realized she actually did know what she needed to say. But that didn't make it any easier.

She took a deep breath, looked Elena and in the eye, and tried to make Dana proud. "I'm sorry."

"Excuse me? I don't think I heard that right."

"I said I'm sorry. I was out of line the last time we saw each other."

"You mean the last time we *talked* to each other, right? Because we have definitely *seen* each other since the last time we talked, including at the Triple D just the other night. You've just been ignoring me."

"I wasn't ignoring you. I just didn't know what to say. And I didn't think you'd necessarily want to talk to me." Al grimaced.

"You mean, because of the way you acted. At Banter & Brew. The day we were on the front page of the paper."

"Yes."

"When you blamed me for things other people are thinking and saying, things that I don't have any control over."

"Yes." Al squeezed her lips shut and squinted.

Elena squinted back. "Okay."

"Okay what?" Al asked hopefully.

"Okay. I forgive you."

"Awesome." Al's shoulders relaxed and she took a breath.

"That doesn't mean I like you."

Al opened her mouth to respond, but nothing came out.

"We're all set, Elena," Bobby called from across the yard.

Elena gave him a thumbs-up, turned toward her car, whipped out a camera and two equipment bags, and was on her way across the yard before Al could think of something to say. Al just stood there, with her mouth hanging open, like the kid who got picked last for kickball.

Which never, ever happened, by the way.

Not once.

Al was picked first. Or she was the team captain. The one doing the picking.

She could walk into the cafeteria of a brand-new school, in a town she had never even visited before, with kids she had never met before, and be sitting at the popular table within fifteen minutes.

It wasn't a party unless Al was there. Usually on center stage with a microphone in her hand.

Ask anyone.

That doesn't mean I like you.

For real?

Elena's words ricocheted around Al's brain.

Al had spent a lifetime learning how to be likable. It didn't matter where she was or who she was with. She could make people want to be on her team. She told jokes. She made music. She could compete on any playing field. Being liked was how Al survived in a world that was constantly being yanked out from underneath her.

She learned all this from the coach she hired after she got the job in Owen Station. Her boss had insisted. Al was lucky to have a chief who was so invested in her success. So, even though she thought it was stupid, she found a coach and went to work. It was the best thing she ever did. The transition, from being part of the crew to being an officer, was tricky. If she was going to be a good one, she had to get over needing to have everyone on the crew like her. Follow her lead, yes. Respect her, yes. Trust her? Absolutely. But like her? No. She was an officer, not their buddy. It felt like she had made a lot of progress.

But Elena's words stung.

"Are you coming, Chief?" Bobby shouted.

Al tipped her chin in Bobby's direction and laughed at herself for letting Elena Freaking Murphy get under her skin. Again.

"Coming."

As Al made her way across the yard, toward the crew, she noticed they were all in various stages of undress. Al knew this was the plan, of course, but it was still a little unnerving.

Sam, her center-stage-stealing bass player and one of the most seasoned young firefighters in the department, was wearing just a sports bra under her overalls. So were the other four women, including Jess, her lead guitarist, who joined the department about six months ago. The four guys, including Bobby, were shirtless.

At least they all had their pants on.

"I'm surprised there are so many women in the department." Elena was talking to Bobby, who was leaning in, hanging on every word. "I mean, I guess I shouldn't be. Right? It's the twenty-first century."

Bobby nodded enthusiastically, but Al stepped in to answer. And reassert her authority.

"To be honest, Elena, most of the department is still men. But they're mostly older guys—"

"Which is why they're not here," Sam yelped. "Bobby just wanted the good-looking ones."

They all hooted and fist-bumped Sam, except Al, who ignored her.

"A lot of rural departments like ours have a hard time recruiting young firefighters. It's getting more competitive and more urgent as the older generation retires. But we've made it clear that we're trying to build a diverse department. That's been compelling enough to attract some really good, young talent."

"It's not the money, that's for sure." Sam cackled, reaching for the high fives coming her way.

Al shot Sam a look that made her back down.

Al was proud of the department she was helping build. Something like seventy percent of career firefighters across the US were white, and just five percent of them were women. Since Al had come on board, they had hired half a dozen new firefighters. The town was growing and lots of the old timers were ready to trade in their fire hose for a fishing pole. Five of their new hires had been people of color and three were women. Al intended to springboard out of Owen Station into a higher profile, higher paying job—but she wasn't just thinking about herself. She had some great mentors, who had encouraged her into leadership and given her opportunities to grow. Her present boss, the chief, included. Now that she was in this position, she was determined to do the same for others.

"Sam's not wrong, Chief." Bobby snapped his suspenders, a big grin on his face. "We're not here for the money. We're here because Elena is about to make us famous."

"That's right. I expect to get a modeling gig out of this." Sam turned and flexed her back, so the scorpion tattoo on her right shoulder looked like it was about to attack.

They all laughed and elbowed each other, but they were getting restless.

"Alright, everyone," Elena said while she assembled equipment. "I know what Bobby wants to get out of this. What about you all? What's the vibe you're looking for?"

"We want to make home hardening sexy as fuck," Sam shouted.

Elena grinned back. "Well, from the look of this group, that shouldn't be too hard to do."

Al's lead guitarist and sometime backup singer, Jess, was flexing very ripped abs. "You're getting in on this, too. Right, Chief?"

Everyone, including Elena, turned toward her.

This hadn't been part of the deal. Bobby asked Al to show up for moral support. Not photos. At thirty-six, Al was at least ten years older than most of the crew. But she never turned down a dare or met a challenge she wasn't willing to take.

She looked around at the crew, looking at her.

"Of course I am." Al peeled off her uniform button down without hesitation.

"A muscle shirt," Sam said. "Nice choice."

Al grinned and was flexing her biceps just as Elena looked up. Al ignored her, but noticed that she didn't look away. Out of the corner of her eye, Al could see Elena watching her. That warmth, which started just below her waist, swept down through her legs again, and Al's heart skipped into a faster rhythm.

Elena might not like her, but she clearly liked what she saw.

"Alright, Elena," Bobby said. "Where do you want us?"

Elena's eyes finally left Al and she turned toward Bobby. "Well, how about if you all just do what you were doing before you took your clothes off. You do you. And leave the rest to me."

Bobby laughed. "That might be a good plan if the job didn't require power tools and sharp objects. I think we might need to do less actual clearing, at this point. And more posing."

"Good point." Elena nodded. "I can get some action shots later." She looked around the yard. "Everyone, pick your favorite tool. We'll get some individual shots, and then I'll put you in twos and threes."

"I volunteer to go first." Sam yelled.

Elena laughed. "I love your enthusiasm." Then Elena turned toward Al. "But I think we should start with you, Chief."

Elena's eyes started up high, on Al's face. They lingered on her lips and then slipped down Al's shoulders before crawling down the full length of Al's body.

It was entirely possible that Elena was just conducting a professional assessment of what she would need in terms of lighting, and whatever else photographers thought about when they studied someone they were getting ready to photograph.

It was probable, even.

For God's sake, Elena was barely talking to Al.

She said she didn't even like her.

So, that's all this once-over was, right? Elena just being a photographer.

And Al was nothing more than the subject of the day.

But that didn't stop it from making Al's ears burn. And when Elena's eyes reached her waist, Al's stomach flipped over. Hard.

Was it a little uncomfortable? Feeling like Elena was examining every inch of her body?

Yes.

But did it feel good?

Fuck, yeah.

Al was in great shape. She worked out hard, every day. She did it so that she would be ready for whatever situation she found herself in. She didn't expect her crew to do anything out in the field that she wasn't willing and able to do.

But right at the moment, all that work was paying off in a different way.

Elena's eyes finally made their way back up to Al's face, and met Al's eyes. Her face was expressionless, except for the eyebrow she raised. "Well, Chief. Are you ready to kick things off?"

Al grinned. Kicking things off is what she was best at. "Let's go."

"Okay, then. Let's see what you've got."

Al scanned the yard and quickly spotted her tool of choice. A chainsaw.

"Go big or go home, Chief," Sam shouted as Al picked up the heavy piece of equipment.

"You know it, Sammy."

Elena might have rolled her eyes. Al couldn't be sure, but she just laughed. She was going to take this moment and make the most of it.

"What's the matter, Elena?" Al grabbed the rear handle of the chainsaw with one hand and the front handle with the other, holding it at her waist like a zombie-killing machine. "Is this too much?"

Elena just shook her head and laughed, but the crew was loving it.

For the next fifteen minutes, Elena's camera clicked maniacally, capturing what felt like every move, every flex, every second. Then she switched cameras and shot for another ten.

Al played to the camera, putting on the performance of a lifetime. She hoisted the machine up onto her shoulder, held it over her head, stood with it dangling just below her waist. She looked at the camera, away from the camera, off in the distance. She flexed and twisted and turned, summoning a full range of expressions, from sultry to fierce to vulnerable, as the crew whistled and hooted, encouraging her.

It didn't take long before Elena was totally there for it, too. She kept snapping, even as she shouted directions. "Look up, Al. No, *up*. To the right. No, wait. Turn around. All the way. Now, put your foot up on the stump. Yes. Like that. Let me see the muscles in your arms. Harder. I want them to bulge. Okay, now hold that chainsaw like you mean it."

Al was sweating and out of breath by the time they finished. She had dived into the whole thing hard, completely losing herself in the experience of being on the other side of Elena's lens. Forgetting everything that had come between them, before that moment. Instinctively trusting Elena to co-direct her body, sometimes ceding control of her own movements, at other times taking charge and demanding that Elena follow her lead. It was like they were listening to a beat only the two of them could hear.

It wasn't clear who decided the shoot was over. Both. Neither. Their session just came to what felt like a natural end.

When they finished, the whole crew was staring at them. No one was fiddling with their phone. No one was laughing or joking or horsing around.

Sam whistled softly. "That was *sick.*"

"Chief for the win," Bobby said proudly, coming in for a fist bump. "Way to get this party started."

Al took an exaggerated bow.

They all clamored to be next. Elena didn't take as long with anyone else as she had with Al. But everyone got into it. She took solo and group shots with all the tools. Axes, machetes, handsaws, shovels, even a weed whacker. Everything a homeowner would need to clear brush and create a barrier between their house and a potential fire. These pictures weren't just going to get people's attention and inspire them to harden their homes against fire, these photos were going to teach them how to do it.

Al found a stump and sat down to watch Elena work. She was constant motion. And completely focused. Her directions were clear enough that no one ever felt like they were playing Twister. She was enthusiastic, and she was encouraging.

"Yes!"

"Just like that."

"Hold it right there."

"I see a modeling contract in your future."

Unlike her shoot with Al, Elena would stop in the middle of each one to show her subject what she was seeing on her screen. Jess decided, after she saw the first photos Elena took of her, to pull her hair tie out and let her hair down. One of the guys decided he wanted to take some shots smiling.

"I look like a serial killer." He laughed at himself, totally at ease.

They all were.

Elena knew what to say to each of them to help them overcome whatever insecurities they were carrying around. She didn't tell stupid jokes or use one-liners, like Al had seen other photographers do. She was just herself with them. Open. Confident. Caring.

They ate it up.

After the individual and small group shots, everyone put their clothes back on and went to work—Al, too—so Elena could get them in action. They just did their job, and they were in a good mood doing it.

"I feel like a freaking supermodel." Sam shouted.

"Supermodel Sam. Is that your new handle?"

"It oughta be."

It felt great to be working alongside the crew like that. Al missed it. And after a few minutes, she almost forgot Elena was there. Almost.

Al told stories from her days at the fire academy, impressed them with the number of accents she could do, and got them all singing Alicia's "Girl On Fire." This was what she loved about the fire service. The teamwork, the camaraderie. The feeling of doing something physical, something that matters, side-by-side. No hierarchy. Just hard work and a good time, getting shit done.

Al hadn't been a hundred percent about Bobby's idea. And when she went to get her boss's approval, she was totally prepared for him to nix it. She wouldn't even have been upset. But he loved it.

"That's why I brought you in here, Al. Fresh perspective. New ideas."

"Actually, it was Garcia, Chief. This was his idea."

"Whatever. You let him think it, didn't you? You listened to him."

Al nodded. "And you really think we outta do it?"

"The sooner the better."

Bobby was thrilled when he got the okay to contact Elena and recruit the team. Al was happy for him but was ready to prop him up if things didn't go the way he hoped.

The last thing Al was prepared for was to actually have fun.

Ninety minutes after they started working, the yard was clear and Elena said she had what she needed.

Al was sorry it was over.

"Hey! Wait. We need one more picture." Bobby shouted.

Elena looked surprised. She had been shooting for going on three hours at that point.

"We need a group photo with you in it, Elena."

Everyone started yelling.

"Come on, Elena."

"Let's go."

"Okay, okay." Elena's eyes were bright. "Give me a minute."

She quickly set up a tripod and attached her camera. Then she told everyone where to stand, while she looked through the lens. She put Al in the back row, dead center. "Alright, everyone, squeeze together like you like each other."

Then she set a timer and hurried to get into the frame.

After they heard the click, they all gave a cheer, and started high-fiving Elena.

"What a fun day, Elena."

"Thanks for everything, Elena."

"Make me a star, Elena."

The team started packing up their equipment, and Elena crouched down to gather hers. Bobby moved toward her at the same time Al did, to help. But Al waved him off.

"I got this, Garcia. Great job today."

Bobby grinned, gave Al a thumbs-up, and went back to helping the team pack up.

Al reached out to take Elena's bags. "Can I give you a hand with that? You must be tired."

"You're kidding, right? I just watched you clearing brush for ninety minutes straight. All I did was point and shoot."

Al snorted. "That's funny." She held her hand out until Elena let her take the bags. "It was really inspiring. Watching you work today."

Elena tilted her head quizzically. "Really? In what way?"

"In *every* way. The way you put everyone at ease. Helped a bunch of goons hyped on energy drinks actually relax enough to spend hours getting their pictures taken. How encouraging you were. It's like you could see through all their joking around. Like you knew how nervous everyone really was. And you knew just what to say and do to make them feel okay about it and actually have fun. Where did you learn to do that?"

Elena's smile faded just a little, and tiny lines appeared between her brows. "It doesn't feel like something I learned. It's just something that happens. I've always been able to sort of sense what's going on with people, I guess. Feel their energy."

"Like with Mrs. McCarthy."

"Like that."

"Well, after watching it in action today, I think it's a real gift."

Elena took a deep breath. "It's taken me a long time to think of it that way. Most of the time, I try to block it out. Knowing what people are feeling and sometimes even what they're thinking doesn't always end well. But sometimes, like today, it's super helpful."

"I can't even imagine how great those photos are going to be. They're going to be *bomb*, as Sam would say."

"Sam would say that." Elena laughed.

"Seriously. I can't thank you enough. I know these photos are going to support our campaign, and that's important. But just as important, you gave us a huge morale boost today." Al looked off in the distance. "Sometimes this work is really hard."

"I can't even imagine. I mean, the physical demands alone—"

"That's not what I mean." Al looked back at Elena. "Most of us actually live for the physical stuff. Fighting fires is what we're trained for. And this might sound weird to say, but when we actually get to fight one, it's a huge rush. When I say the job can be hard, I'm talking about the rest of it. Like the bureaucracy, and the paperwork, and dealing with the rumors people spread. It makes our work so much harder."

Elena raised an eyebrow. "You mean rumors like there are ghosts in the hole."

"Yes, like that. Please don't get mad. I know it sounds petty. But those stories that get started end up costing the department resources. And we don't have many to begin with. Besides, spreading rumors about ghosts is nothing compared to some of the other things people say and do. Like when people won't take care of their property because they don't think wildfires are real."

Elena's eyes widened. "You mean there are people who believe wildfires are fake news? We can actually see the smoke. And *smell* it when the fires get close enough."

"Not exactly. But they believe all kinds of fake stories about what starts them and how to stop them. So they don't do the things that would really make a difference."

"Like clearing their property and replacing their roofs?"

Al nodded.

"Well, hopefully these pictures will help."

"I hope so, too. But I want you to know that, even aside from the pictures, what you did today was really great. I haven't had this much fun with the crew since I got to Owen Station two years ago. It was good for me. I think it was good for all of us. So thank you."

"You're welcome." Elena's blue eyes were smiling, and her hair shimmered in the midday sun. "It was really fun watching you work today, too."

"Yeah. I'm pretty good at spreading mulch."

Elena laughed. "Yes, you are. But that's not what I was talking about."

"No?"

"No. I mean the way you are with the team. Letting Bobby run with his ideas. Encouraging him to lead. You do an amazing job of keeping everybody focused, too, without being a—"

"Dick?"

Elena grinned. "Exactly. There's never a question that you're in charge, but you make everyone feel like they matter. You never ask them to do something you're not willing to do. You make space for them to be themselves. And—those stories you told. The way you got them all laughing. And singing."

She held Al's eyes for a few seconds. "They know you care, Al."

Al took a deep breath. Sometimes it all felt like an act, the things she did to make people like her. A suit of armor to protect her from whatever might happen if they didn't. Elena saw the truth.

"I do care, Elena." Al released her breath, and the tension she was holding in her stomach and across her shoulders melted away. "I care a lot."

Elena took Al's hand and squeezed it. "Thanks for letting me see that."

Al squeezed back. "I'm not sure I had a choice, did I?"

"You always have a choice," Elena laughed. "I can't see what you don't want me to see."

Bobby came up from behind Al, clearing his throat, and Al quickly dropped Elena's hand.

"We're all packed up and ready to go, Chief. Are you all set, Elena?"

"I am. Thanks again for today, Bobby. It was really fun to be with you all."

She gave Bobby a quick hug, and then did the same to Al. Before she left, she promised to have photos on Al's desk within a week.

They were ready in less than forty-eight hours.

Bobby picked them up from Elena's house and dropped them in a folder on Al's desk, along with a thumb drive.

"They're good, Chief." Bobby grinned.

He wasn't wrong.

Al flipped through the pile of black-and-white portraits, and a stack of candids. Elena had captured the essence of the young firefighters on her crew. Their passion. Their bravado. The purity of their dedication to doing good.

Also, they looked all kinds of hot.

"I think these might break the internet." Al smiled. "And I think, yes, we should do that calendar."

Bobby left and Al took another, closer look at the photos. Elena really did have a gift. It was like she was able to pull out whatever was *inside* of her subjects, making each photo seem almost multi-dimensional.

Al examined her own portrait, the one where she was shouldering the chainsaw. She was staring at the camera with such intensity it made Al catch her breath.

Viewers would have their own interpretation of what Al was looking at, and why she was wearing such a fiery expression.

But Al knew. She remembered the exact moment Elena snapped that photo.

Al was looking at the person behind the camera.

A heat missile shot straight up through Al's body, and then down again, finding its target right between Al's legs.

Al quickly shoved the photo back inside the folder.

And that's when she saw the group shot Elena took, at Bobby's request. They all had their arms around each other, broad smiles on their faces. Elena was sandwiched between two young firefighters in the front row. And everyone, including Elena, was grinning straight ahead right into the camera.

Al looked closer.

There was one exception.

There in the back row, Al had one arm around Bobby and the other around Sam.

But Al wasn't focused in the same direction as everyone else.

Her eyes were on Elena.

CHAPTER SIX

Elena gave the counter one last swipe and then stood back to appreciate her work. Dishes washed, dried, and put away. Stovetop scrubbed. Unrecognizable leftovers cleared out of the fridge. Floor mopped.

Even Chief Shiny Boots would have to approve.

She had thought about Al every day, but it had been a few weeks since Elena had seen her. Not since the photo shoot. The funeral business had been very lively. That's how her brothers described it, anyway. Lively. And Elena had been busy. They all had.

The flu had gone through the assisted living complex into which Grandpa had been court-ordered, after his dementia nearly caused a tragic accident. It was very late in the season for the flu, almost the beginning of May, and it took everyone by surprise. Grandpa was fine, but several other residents didn't make it.

The boys tried to pitch Elena on a new tagline in the middle of it all.

Murphy Funeral Home and Mortuary: We come to life when you can't.

Elena rolled her eyes just thinking about them.

Apparently needing her attention, Casper chose that moment to jump on the counter, meowing.

"Hey. You know you don't belong here. I just cleaned that. Get down."

Casper glared at her and hopped down with one last meow. But then he rubbed his head against her and circled between her legs.

She crouched down to scratch his ears. "See, this is better, little guy. You catch more flies with honey than vinegar, as Grandma always says. Although I have no idea why anyone would want to catch flies. Especially in their honey."

Casper pushed his head up harder against Elena's hand.

"Are you hungry? Is that what you're trying to tell me?"

She gave him one last scratch, and then filled his dish with kibble.

Then she flipped her tablet open to the recipe she wanted and propped it on the counter. Following the directions, she set the oven to three fifty and started pulling supplies out of the cupboards. A large mixing bowl, a baking sheet, the cast iron skillet, measuring cups, and all the ingredients for homemade biscuits and sausage gravy.

Gran was coming for brunch.

Elena was worried about her after that outburst a few months ago and was making a point of spending more time with her. Plus, Gran was turning ninety in November. And even though she was in great shape for her age—she was driving herself over to brunch—Elena wasn't taking anything for granted.

The timer for the biscuits dinged just as Gran's car rolled into the driveway. Elena pulled them out and went to help Gran up the front porch stairs.

"Give your grandmother a kiss, Elena. Here, I brought you something." Gran turned a cheek toward Elena as she shoved a bouquet of daffodils and purple irises into Elena's hand.

"I told you not to bring anything, Gran. But these are beautiful. Thank you." Elena kissed her and then reached for her arm.

Her grandmother swatted her away.

"I don't need help, young lady."

Elena laughed. "I'm sorry."

Elena kept pace beside her as she made her way up the sidewalk to the front stairs, where she paused to look up at the house. "I admit, I wasn't happy when your parents told me I needed to move in with them, even though I didn't like being here alone after your grandfather moved out. But now that you're here, it just feels right."

"I love this house, Gran."

Gran nodded and climbed the stairs, taking it slow but doing it on her own. At the top, she paused to catch her breath and turned to look at the street.

"You wouldn't know there was a big hole there just a few months ago." She looked at Elena. "Would you?"

Elena shook her head. But she was lying.

She knew that hole had been there.

She could still feel it.

Al had been right, of course. The city hired an engineering firm to reinforce and fill in the hole and repair the street. There was no investigation. There wouldn't be one.

The mayor gave a quote to the *Caller* for their story on the lack of funding to find and close up old mines across the state. "If you live in an old mining town, in a state that was built on the mining industry, you've just got to expect that, every once in a while, someone's going to fall in a hole."

Not very helpful.

But it wasn't just the potential danger of future holes that haunted Elena. It was what she had heard and seen and smelled the day *her* hole opened up.

That is what woke her up in the middle of the night, in a panic.

Something happened inside that hole. She didn't know what or when or to whom. But she knew one thing. It had been terrible. And someone, somewhere, seemed to want her to know about it.

"I still can't believe the city just fixed that hole and walked away." Elena followed her grandma into the house and down the hallway toward the kitchen. "We have a right to know where that tunnel led and what happened inside of it, and whether or not the shaft opening has been properly closed up. It has to be around here somewhere. It's probably nearby. And who knows how many others are around, just waiting to swallow the next car. Or person."

Grandma slowly turned around at the kitchen door, blocking Elena's way. Her face was white granite, her eyes dark. "Elena

Marie Murphy. Why can't you just let this go? No one cares. If there was an open shaft up on our hill somewhere, don't you think someone would have found it by now? You sound crazy the way you keep talking about it. You need to stop letting your emotions carry you away."

Elena's heart skipped but she kept her mouth shut. Mom had been handing these lectures out since before Elena went to kindergarten. But she wasn't used to hearing it from Gran.

She took a deep breath. "I'm sorry if I got you worked up—"

"I'm not the one who is worked up, dear."

"Of course." Elena tried to smile. "Come on. I made your favorite. Let's go eat."

All she wanted was a nice brunch with her grandmother. She should have known better than to bring up a topic that was going to cause upset. Even if it made absolutely no sense for Gran to *be* that upset about some random hole in the street.

Then again, she was ninety. That gave her permission to be whatever she wanted to be.

Gran perked up the moment Elena put a plate of biscuits and gravy in front of her. "Oh, my goodness, Elena. This looks delicious."

Elena grinned. "I hope it tastes good, too."

Gran took a bite and moaned.

"Is that a smirtle on your face, Gran?"

The mischievous smile deepened. "Your mother never cooks like this for me. She has me on a heart-healthy diet. Or at least that's what she calls it. More like a cardboard diet. I'm ninety years old, for God's sake. Is a little butter or salt going to kill me? It hasn't so far. And if it did, I would go out with a smile on my face."

"Don't tell Mom, but I'm on your side."

"I know, dear. That's why you're my favorite granddaughter."

"I'm your only granddaughter."

Gran winked, and dug back into her plate of food like it was her last meal.

After they finished, Elena cleared the table and put a kettle on for tea.

"So, tell me everything, Elena. What are you working on these days? And I don't mean the business. When is your next show?"

Elena leaned against the counter. "It really makes me happy that you're so interested in my work, Gran. No one else in the family seems to be."

"Don't be too tough on them, Elena."

Elena raised an eyebrow and gave her grandmother side-eye.

Gran wagged a finger at her. "Now, don't be like that. I know they can be difficult."

Elena snorted. "Difficult? Yes. If by that you mean emotionally shut off from everyone and everything. Unwilling to deal with anything even remotely unpleasant. Utterly lacking in empathy."

Grandma sat back in her chair without responding. And the longer she was silent, the guiltier Elena felt.

"I guess I have some things to work through, don't I." Elena chuckled.

Gran nodded. "It does seem that way. You are not wrong about them, though." She dropped her head. "I blame myself."

"What do you mean?"

Gran's eyes slowly met Elena's. "Don't be so shocked to hear me say that. All that unhealthy behavior had to come from somewhere, didn't it?"

Elena wasn't sure what to think. Almost nothing about Gran had seemed normal since that night at dinner, when she stormed off to her room.

"Are you feeling alright, Gran?" She put her hand on Grandma's shoulder.

"Yes, of course." She squeezed Elena's hand and then let go. "I want you to listen to me, though. It doesn't matter what your family thinks. It doesn't matter. Everyone should be allowed to follow their passion. Don't get me wrong. The family needs you right now, and I'm thankful you came home to help. But don't ever give up on your art, Elena. Never, ever give up on what you love. Or *who* you love, for that matter, when the time comes. No matter what anyone says. Or doesn't say. Never let go of your dreams. You deserve to be happy. Everyone does."

"Yes, ma'am." Elena smiled.

"I mean it."

"I know." Elena grabbed the whistling kettle and poured water into a small ceramic tea pot.

"So, when are you going to open your own gallery?"

"Ah, you haven't forgotten."

"No, of course not."

Elena pulled two teacups from a cupboard, grabbed some honey and lemon, put it all on the table near the tea pot, and sat back down.

"I'm not sure, to be honest. I expected to be further along by now. But between the business, getting settled into this house, and all the drama with that, um…with the mess in my front yard…I haven't even had time to look at property."

"Do you plan to open your gallery on Main Street?"

"Maybe. Or maybe in the old downtown."

"Where all the renovations are planned."

Elena nodded. Hazel's fiancée, Sena Abrigo, was a developer who had come to Owen Station almost two years ago with a vision for renewing their old downtown, and the means to make it happen. The work was progressing more slowly than she had planned because she was collaborating closely with local people to ensure any new building honored the town's past, and to make sure people weren't being displaced by the new development. But many of the buildings, which had been vacant for decades, since the mines closed down and thousands of residents streamed out of town in search of work elsewhere, were already being restored.

Sena would have loved Elena to open her gallery right in the middle of it all.

"So you haven't changed your mind?" Gran smiled. "You *are* going to open a gallery. Here in Owen Station. Which means you plan to stay."

Elena thought about that for a long minute. "Yes. I'm…going to stay." She paused, pulling on the strings that were dangling over the edge of the tea pot, and then she looked up at Grandma. "That's the first time I've said that out loud to anyone."

"It's a very big decision."

Elena laughed. "Yes, I guess it is."

She had expected it to feel strange, coming back to Owen Station. And it was. But it also felt right to be there. It didn't feel like home, exactly. Not yet. But it would.

Elena poured the tea and Gran added a heaping spoonful of honey.

"Well, I'm glad you're staying, Elena. I'm very thankful that you feel comfortable here. And safe."

Elena blinked. "Why wouldn't I feel safe?"

Suddenly, a picture of Al's face, looking confused and disapproving when she realized Elena didn't lock her doors, flashed through her mind. But Al didn't know Owen Station the way Elena did. She had never felt unsafe there.

"Why *wouldn't* I feel safe?" she asked again.

Gran tapped her spoon on the cup and placed it gently on the saucer. She didn't look at Elena. "I don't mean that you *shouldn't* feel safe. I just mean…"

In the silence of her kitchen, Elena waited. A car backfired somewhere down the street, and a gust of wind rattled the window. They hadn't had much rain that spring. Everything was dry. Hopefully, the wind was bringing in some wetter weather.

Finally, Grandma looked up at her. "I don't know what I mean. I just know that this town hasn't always been a very nice place for people like you."

"People like me?" Elena frowned. "Do you mean ghost whisperers?"

"No." Grandma tilted her head and looked sideways at Elena, squinting as if to see her better. "Well, maybe it hasn't always been a good place for those, either. But what I meant was…*women* like you."

"Do you mean women who like women?"

Gran nodded.

"Ah." Elena poured herself some tea and squeezed in a little lemon. "I suppose not."

"Your generation takes it for granted. It wasn't that long ago that women like you had to hide in this town. Most of them spent their lives alone. Or they stayed hidden inside of a marriage. The suffering they went through was…"

Gran looked away, as if seeing something Elena couldn't see.

"When I was your age, I never could have imagined going to a wedding like the one we all went to a few months ago. The whole town turned out for Tessa and Lace. Two women! It boggles the mind."

Elena let that settle while she sipped her tea. Casper came in, jumped up onto a kitchen chair, and let Elena scratch her ear.

"I hear you, Gran. Owen Station is a special place, especially for being such a small town."

"I think it happened when the mines closed. Your parents were still in high school at the time. Overnight, it seemed like ninety percent of the town just up and left. The people who stayed were different. We believed in this place, even though it broke our hearts. We wanted it to be a place where everyone who stuck it out with us felt like they belonged. We didn't want to lose anyone else." Grandma paused. "But it wasn't like that before. When I was younger. We did lose people. People like you. It just wasn't safe for them to be open about who they were."

Elena nodded. "I get that. But I know people who are still having to hide. For all kinds of reasons and in all kinds of places. Not everyone has people in their lives who accept them for who they are."

"I know. It makes me want to spit."

So, this was new. Talking to Grandma about being queer.

"Seriously, Gran. What is going on? I've never heard you talk about any of these things before."

Grandma sighed and sat back in her chair. "Nothing's going on, Elena. I don't know what's wrong with me. I'm just being an old lady, I guess. Thinking about the past. About what might have been."

"Well, when I'm ninety, I want to be able to think about and say and do whatever I want. So, you're allowed."

Elena's tablet dinged on the counter, and she got up to check her messages. It was a text from Bobby Garcia.

Thought you'd like to see these.

He followed that with links to all of the department's official social media pages.

The photos were up.

Elena clicked one of the sites open and watched as the likes and comments multiplied right in front of her eyes. Bobby was a genius.

"Check this out, Gran. This is one of the projects I've been working on." Elena sat down right next to Grandma, and opened the tablet so she could see. "I took these for the fire department, to help them get word out about a new program they've started. They're helping homeowners make their houses more resistant to fire. Apparently, not many people were paying attention before."

"Well, it looks like they are now. Look at all those likes."

Elena snapped her eyes toward Grandma. "All those what? Are you telling me you know what *likes* are? Do you even know what social media is?"

"Of course I do. I'm ninety. Not dead. I have my own page. Sean helped me set it up."

It was like learning that Pluto wasn't actually a planet.

"I really like this one." Grandma pointed at the photo of Al, where she was shouldering the chainsaw. Then she used her thumb and forefinger to zoom in. Which made Elena's head spin.

Grandma knew how to use a touch screen.

"That's our new fire chief, isn't it?"

"Assistant fire chief."

Grandma grinned. "She looks tough." Then she zoomed in even closer, so that Al's face filled the screen. "But look. There is something else there, too. Loneliness, maybe? There is an ache of some kind. Can you see it?"

"Hmmm." Elena stared at Al, who was staring at her. Grandma wasn't wrong. "I imagine she has a very hard job."

"She's handsome." Grandma sat up straight. "You should go on a date with her."

"Grandma!"

"What? Are you dating anyone else?"

Elena shook her head. "When exactly am I supposed to have time to date, Gran? Between the business, my photography, everything happening with the hole, this house, the family—"

"In other words, I'm hearing you say that you are not dating anyone else."

"No. I just said—"

"So what's the problem?"

"Grandma." Elena tried to summon her best schoolteacher voice. "You don't even know whether or not she's gay."

Gran dropped her chin and looked at her over her glasses. "Seriously?"

Elena laughed. "Alright, fine. But you don't *know* her. She and I could not be more different."

"Pardon me, but are you kidding me? You're both smart. You're both strong. You both care about other people—"

"You're getting this from a picture on social media?"

"She is a *fire chief*, Elena. Of course she is all those things." Grandma had a point there. "Plus, she's a girl. You're a girl. You both like girls. And I saw the way she was looking at you in that picture that was in the *Caller*. The one where you fainted and she was—"

"I got it, Gran." Elena's cheeks were hot, but she managed to roll her eyes. "She might be all those things. But she's also bossy. She's so rigid, her pants squeak when she walks. She has no roots. In fact, she's never lived anywhere for more than a few years, and I'm sure she's only here until she gets a better job somewhere else. She has an unnatural need to be the center of attention, and she's always taking dares, like she's a teenager or something. Do you know she jumped in front of my car one day and I almost ran her over? Yes, she has her moments when she doesn't seem like a total pain in the rear. And she is really good and kind to her team. They clearly love and respect her. And she is doing a really good job for the fire department and for the town. I mean, just look at this social media campaign. She didn't come up with the idea, but she had the good sense to listen to her crew and helped make it happen. But she blames me for things that are not my fault, and she is constantly judging me. Also, she thinks she is funny and she is not. I could not be less interested in dating her."

"You certainly seem to be very passionate about this person you say you're not interested in. Also, my dear, you are blushing."

Elena scowled. "I am not blushing."

"Don't use that tone with me, young lady. All I'm saying is that I'm glad you're going to settle down here. But you shouldn't be alone. You need to find someone to share your life with. Think about all the women who were never able to do that. Women right here. In this town. Who had to spend their lives hiding who they really are. Who had no choice but to be alone. Or worse, who were trapped in loveless marriages. With no escape. No hope. You have so many options available to you now. But it's up to you to make it happen. I mean, listen. What's the point of being *out* if you're not actually *out* there—"

"I got it, Grandma. I got it."

Gran shrugged and pushed the tablet away. "She seems nice, is all I'm saying."

Elena shook her head and forced a smile. There was no point in talking about this anymore.

"I'm going to do up the dishes. How about if you go out into the backyard and look at the little garden I put in last week. It's not much. Just some tomatoes and a few herbs. But it's fun. I also spent a few hours cleaning up out there and clearing brush away from the house. I even pulled down all the old, dried vines that were on the retaining wall back there. It's a fire safety thing. I learned it at the photo shoot—"

"The one with your new girlfriend?"

"Grandma."

"I'm kidding, Elena. Have a sense of humor." Laughing to herself, Gran got up and started toward the door. "Don't be long."

"I won't. Be careful going down those stairs. Hold onto the rail."

"Oh, for God's sake, Elena. I'm not a child. Also, clearly Chief Jones isn't the only bossy one."

Elena stuck out her tongue, and then turned to open the curtain over the kitchen sink. She wanted to be able to keep an eye on things out there while she cleaned up.

Gran was being careful, and Elena was happy to see it. She had aged so much over the past few years, especially over the last two or three months. But she was also feistier. It was like something was opening up in her, after a lifetime of being buttoned down. She was talking about things Elena had never heard before. She was even critiquing family dynamics. Interjecting herself into Elena's love life. And she was having emotions. Big ones.

Gran bent over, rubbed a basil leaf, and smelled her fingers. Elena loved seeing how much Gran was enjoying the improvements to the yard. It really did look good. It had become too much for Grandma and Grandpa to care for during those last years they were in the house. It was satisfying to be able to bring the place back to life. There was a lot more work to do. But Elena was staying. This was going to be her home. She had made that decision. So, she had time.

Casper started scratching at the back door.

"What's wrong, little guy?"

He was not an outdoor cat.

When he didn't stop, Elena turned the water off and went over to pick him up. But when she pulled him into her arms he meowed loudly and struggled to get free. She let him go and he leaped onto the floor, where he immediately began scratching at the door again.

"What in the world is wrong—"

"Elena!" The fear in Grandma's voice made the breath catch in Elena's throat.

"Coming." Elena scooted Casper out of the way and threw open the door.

Gran had one hand on her heart and, with the other, she was pointing at the hill behind the house. Elena didn't need to see what she was pointing at, though. She could smell it.

"Fire!" Grandma yelled, right before falling to her knees.

"Gran." Elena ran to her. "Gran, what's wrong?"

Her grandmother didn't answer, but her eyes screamed that something awful was happening. She was holding her chest.

"Oh my God. Gran." Elena helped her grandmother sit down. "Don't go anywhere. Don't do anything. Don't you dare do anything. I will be right back."

Grandma nodded and waved at Elena to go. She raced back into the house to get her phone. Her hands were trembling badly, but she was able to pick it up and dial 911.

"Nine-one-one. What's your emerg—"

Elena jumped in. "My hill is on fire. My grandma is hurt. I think she might be having a heart attack."

"Okay, we're going to get help to you right away. What is your address?"

Elena's mind went blank.

"Ma'am, please. What is the address where your grandmother is located right now?"

Thank God for muscle memory. She had known that address since she was a child. "One eighty-five Old Mine Road."

"Is that where the fire is?"

"Yes, it's in back of the house. On the southwest side of Murphy Hill."

"What is your name."

"Elena. Elena Murphy."

"You mean the same name as the hill?"

Elena raised her voice, on the edge of hysteria. "Yes. It is our hill. I mean, it was named after my—oh my God. Can you please hurry? My grandmother is—"

"Elena, help is already on the way. What is your phone number, just in case we get cut off?"

Elena gave her the number, but her patience was gone. "My grandma is in the backyard. She is sitting down on the ground. She has her hands over her heart. The fire is on Murphy Hill, right behind my house. There is an old shack up there but mostly just some small trees and a lot of brush. I can't tell how bad it is. There is a lot of smoke. I can see flames, but it looks like they're closer to the old road, up on top of the hill. Like I think the fire is between my house and that road."

"Elena, this is all very good information. You're doing great. Is your grandma safe where she is?"

"From the fire? Yes, I think so."

"Can you move her, if you need to?"

"I don't know." Gran was bigger than she was. Heavy. "I don't know if she can walk. She's too big for me to carry."

"Okay, listen. Help is on the way. I can hear sirens through the phone. Can you hear them?"

Elena realized that she could, in fact. They were far away. But they were coming. "Yes."

"Good. I want you to go back to your grandma and see if she can walk. If she can, then take her into the front yard. If she is able, go across the street. The street is a natural fire barrier. The important thing is to get as far away from that hill and the house and the fire as you can. And wait for help to come."

"What if she can't walk?" Elena was having trouble breathing. It wasn't the smoke, though. It was the panic.

"Just try, Elena. Try."

Elena shoved the phone in her pocket and ran back out the door. Gran was still sitting there, with her hands over her chest. Casper was in her lap. Smoke was starting to fill the yard and Elena could hear the crackling of a fire.

"Gran, we have to get out of here. We have to get across the street. Can you walk?"

Grandma nodded and started to get up. This time, she let Elena help. Leaning heavily on Elena, she took two steps forward and then stopped.

"Get Casper," Gran whispered.

Elena scooped him up with one arm, still holding onto Grandma. Then the three of them made their way around the house, through the front yard, and across the street. Mr. Martinez saw them coming and brought a folding camp chair out to them. He and Elena got Gran settled into the chair just as the first fire truck barreled up the street.

Elena was clutching Casper with one arm and had her other hand on Gran's back. She tried to slow her breathing and tell herself everything was going to be okay.

But now that Gran was in a safe location and all she could do was wait for help, Elena felt the panic rise. Her heart was racing and she was having trouble taking a deep breath.

She closed her eyes and tried to picture something, anything, that would help her calm down.

The first image that came into her mind was Al.

Al would know just what to do.

Al would show up in her creased pants and shiny boots and her badge, and she would make sure everything was okay.

Elena never doubted that Al was on her way.

She took a deep breath while counting to four, held it for four, and then slowly let it out. She did that three more times.

Then she opened her eyes and stared down the street, willing Al's truck to appear.

CHAPTER SEVEN

The fire alert on Al's watch went off in Banter & Brew as she was listening to the mayor brag about his efforts to keep a US post office in town. She was at the monthly chamber of commerce luncheon, filling in for her boss, who was on a Disney vacation with his wife and grandkids. One of the hardest things for Al to get used to, now that she was an assistant chief, was how much time she spent behind her desk, online, and making public appearances. She missed the adrenaline rush of regularly being on the front lines. But she was thankful that Owen Station had very few emergencies that actually required her presence.

Based on what she was seeing on her watch, this was not one of them.

To be clear, any fire in that town was a BFD. A *big fucking deal*. The houses were mostly hundred-year-old bungalows. Wooden structures. Built by miners who immigrated there from all over the world, way before modern fire codes. Many of the houses had never been updated. They were, as the guys kidded, kindling. Except it was no joke. Many houses were stacked on top of one another. In some cases, literally. Built one right above another, all the way up the side of a mountain. Plus, they were in a high desert ecosystem where extreme temperatures were becoming more and more common. And they had been in a drought for more than six years.

The potential for disaster hung over them like thick, black smoke.

KELLY & TANA FIRESIDE

But based on information from dispatch, this was just a one-alarm fire with a medical emergency, which meant two engines, a rescue unit, and a ladder truck responding. This was a fire that should be relatively easy to contain and extinguish. A brush fire, most likely. The lowest threat level. Bobby could handle it. He wouldn't even expect Al to show up, especially while the chief was out of town. Also, as a new captain, Bobby *needed* to be free to handle it, without having Al looking over his shoulder.

Al should have just sucked it up and looked interested in whatever it was the mayor was saying. She had strict orders from the chief to pitch the mayor on the need for an increased budget next year, in order to replace their aging air packs and hire more firefighters to meet the needs of a growing town. And she had Knox's pie to look forward to.

There was absolutely no good reason for her to skip out on the luncheon, ditch the mayor, and go racing across town to a fire that Garcia and the dedicated men and women of the Owen Station Fire Department could easily handle.

But Al recognized the address on the call right away.

Elena.

And there was an undefined medical emergency.

Someone at the scene was hurt.

Elena?

Images of Elena flashed through Al's mind. That day at Banter & Brew, when she demanded answers, seemingly unintimidated by the uniforms at the table, looking a foot taller than she really was.

And the morning they met. Right after a giant hole opened up in the middle of her street. When Elena almost ran her down. Leaping out of her car, waving her arms around, shaking her finger at Al. Like a lone, terrified hiker confronting a black bear, making herself look twice as big as she really was. Fierce. But fragile.

Elena at the photo shoot, contorting her body, crouching on the ground, climbing walls, all just to get just the right shot. The way she tamed those firefighters, assuring them that it was safe to be vulnerable on the other side of her lens, getting them to move and pose in exactly the way she wanted.

The moment Elena saw her.

Really saw her.

After she had spent the afternoon working beside the crew.

They know you care, Al.

Even Al didn't realize how true that was until Elena said it.

It took her about five seconds to decide. She quickly mumbled an apology to the mayor, waved at Knox, and flew out of Banter & Brew. Her turnout gear was always ready in the SUV. She jumped in and flipped on the lights and siren.

Within seven minutes, she was at the scene and parked. She knew from her car radio that the truck, engines, and an ambulance were already at the scene. Bobby was doing an initial size-up, as the crew assembled.

Al hopped out of her truck, yanked on her turnout coat, grabbed her helmet, and went looking for Elena.

A crowd had gathered in the street and on the sidewalk, across from the smoking hill, and police were directing them to retreat. Al assumed they were going to close off the whole street. But at the moment, it looked like a whole lot of people were in the wrong place at the wrong time.

And no sign of Elena.

Al pushed forward through the crowd, which was moving in the opposite direction, her heart racing, scanning faces. She had the benefit of height, but Elena was short, which would make it hard to find her. Al saw a glimpse of someone wearing black and white, but it was just a teenager in a hoodie. Then she saw the ER nurse. The one who didn't end up in a hole.

"Have you seen Elena?" Al asked breathlessly, grabbing the nurse by the elbow.

The woman looked confused and a little frightened. "Who?"

"Elena. The girl who talks to ghosts. Works at the funeral home. Lives in *that* house," Al said too gruffly.

"Oh. I think she's over there." The nurse took her arm back, pointed down the street, in the direction of the fire, and kept moving.

Al elbowed her way as quickly and carefully as she could through the crowd, trying to find exactly where "over there" was, doing her best not to look as panicked as she felt. It wasn't easy.

Finally, she spotted her. Elena was on her knees, which is why it had been so hard to find her. She was in the front yard of the house directly across from her own—pajama man's house—and an elderly woman, holding Casper, was sitting in a camp chair beside her. Two paramedics were with them.

"Elena!"

At the sound of Al's voice, Elena spun toward her, her face contorted by fear and confusion. She tried to stand quickly, and stumbled forward. Al grabbed her, holding her arms to steady her.

"Elena," Al said softly, looking into eyes that had turned a cloudy gray. Al pulled her close and wrapped her arms tightly around her. Then she bent her neck and pressed her cheek against the top of Elena's head. She would have held her like that all day if Elena needed it.

After a long few moments, Elena's grip on Al softened, her shoulders stopped shaking, and her breathing finally slowed.

Holding her by the shoulders, Al stepped back to take a good look at her from head to toe. Elena appeared to be unharmed, but Al searched her face for signs of distress. "Are you hurt? Dispatch said there was a medical emergency."

Elena was pale, her face crumpled in worry, her eyes moist. "It's not me. It's my grandmother."

Al looked over Elena's shoulder and did a quick assessment. One of the paramedics was kneeling beside the folding chair. He was holding a blood pressure cuff and talking calmly to the grandmother, who looked tired and scared but didn't appear to be in pain. The other paramedic was standing nearby, scrolling through her phone.

The situation did not look critical, but it would be frightening to be in the middle of it all. Dozens of first responders scurried around them, performing an urgent but familiar choreography, as emergency lights flashed and white smoke rose from the hillside across the street. Al knew that everything was going to be okay, but Elena couldn't necessarily have known that.

She looked down at Elena. "I was scared. When I heard the call. And realized it was coming from your house. From you."

"I was too—until you got here."

Elena laid her head on Al's chest again, and Al let her.

"What's going to happen, Al?"

Al gave her a gentle squeeze. "Everything is going to be okay. Bobby is managing the fire response. Everyone knows what to do, and they're doing it."

"But my grandma." Elena pushed away. "She was holding her chest. She fell. I didn't know what to do. I didn't know if she could walk, or if I could get her away from the house. She was having a hard time catching her breath. Oh my God, Al. She's *ninety*."

Elena's eyes looked wet and Al was expecting her to cry, but she was working hard to hold it together, like one of Al's crew managing a hose under pressure.

"It's okay, Elena. I know it was scary. But you did great. You made the call and got us all out here right away. Now, you're safe. And your grandmother is safe."

"Is she, though?" Elena's voice rose an octave. "She is still so weak. And pale. And I don't know what's going to happen to her."

Al squeezed her shoulders. "Come on. Let's go find out what's going on."

Elena nodded and Al released her. Then she guided Elena over to the paramedic who was standing nearby. "So, what have we got, Becca?"

The paramedic slipped her phone back into her pocket. "Hey, Chief. We've got a woman, ninety years old, reporting shortness of breath and dizziness. Never lost consciousness. Said she can walk but feels a little shaky. We're giving her a minute. Her granddaughter here said she was holding her chest and thought it was a heart attack—"

Becca paused and looked sympathetically at Elena. "Which was understandable."

Then she looked back at Al. "But Grandma is reporting no prior pain, and no pain now, in the chest, neck, back, or jaw. Blood pressure and pulse rate are elevated, but within normal range. We're thinking it was a panic attack, but we're going to take her to the bus to do an ECG just to be sure."

Al nodded and turned back to Elena. "Did you get all that?"

Elena's wide eyes met Al's. "So...no heart attack?"

"We can't say that for sure just yet. But she is in good hands. The best. They are going to take her to the ambulance to do a test. But that's what it looks like. No heart attack. Just a very understandable reaction to a very scary situation."

Elena grabbed Al's hand, closed her eyes, and took a deep breath.

Al faced her and waited for her to open her eyes. She really did have the longest lashes. She was clenching and unclenching her jaw, and her right eye was twitching. The last twenty minutes must have been terrifying. Al knew what a one-alarm meant. She knew what her crews were capable of, and what the likely outcome of this situation was going to be. All Elena knew was that the hillside behind her house was on fire and her elderly grandmother couldn't breathe.

When Elena opened her eyes again, Al pulled her gently by the hand and led her to a spot not far from her grandmother, but far enough that they would not be overheard. "Listen. It looks like your grandmother is going to be fine. Okay? These are two of the best paramedics I've ever worked with. They're going to take her to the ambulance, and you can go with them. Stay with your grandmother the whole time while they do the test."

Al bent closer to make sure Elena's eyes were fixed on her own and took both her hands. "Elena, listen to me. I need to go check on my crew. But I need to know if you're going to be okay on your own. I'll stay with you if you need me to."

Elena's eyes did not waver. They stayed glued to Al's as she swallowed hard. But finally, she shook her head. "You don't need to stay. You need to go. Do your superhero stuff. I will be fine. I promise."

Al nodded. "Do you have your phone?"

Elena reached down, pulled it out of her pocket, and gave it to Al.

"I'm going to put my personal cell number in here, okay? So you can call me if you need to."

Al added her number, then called herself from Elena's phone to get Elena in her contact list. She wanted to know it was Elena, if and when she called.

Elena's hands were trembling when she reached to take back the phone.

Al took them and held them steady. "Are you sure you're okay?"

"Yes." She squeezed Al's hands. "Thank you."

"Stay with your grandmother. Stay safe. Don't leave the ambulance. If and when they decide they need to take her to the hospital—and she'll let them—let me know right away, and I'll come with you. Otherwise, I'll be back to check on you as soon as I can."

"Okay." Elena's voice was shaky.

"O-*kay*?" Al shook Elena's hands, gently, smiling. She wanted to know Elena was actually going to be alright if she left her.

Finally, Elena's shoulders relaxed, and she smiled and nodded. "Yes, Al. For real. I am o-*kay.*" Elena's jaw was set. She was tough.

"Alright, good." Al grinned. "Also, I think we really have to stop meeting this way."

"What way?"

"In the middle of your street, at the center of a crisis. Now that you have my number, just *call* me if you want to see me. No drama required."

Elena opened her mouth to respond, but Al put a finger over her lips, and then quickly stepped around her, toward Elena's grandmother.

"Elena is going to go with you to the ambulance, Mrs. Murphy. You're in good hands."

The grandmother gave Al a wobbly thumbs-up.

"Take care of these two," Al told the paramedics.

"You got it, Chief."

"Good. Okay, Mrs. Murphy. Don't give my crew too much trouble, you hear?"

Elena's grandmother grinned. "I'll do my best. Be careful out there, Chief."

Al saluted and shot one last grin at Elena, who was still standing there with her mouth slightly open, looking bemused. Then she turned and jogged across the street toward where Bobby was managing the fire response.

"I'm surprised to see you, Chief. Thought you had a luncheon with the bigwigs today. Are you taking command?" Bobby asked as Al walked up beside him.

Al shook her head, smiling. "Not at all. You've got this, Captain. But you know how much I hate those events—I'll take any excuse to scoot out a little early. I'm just here for moral support, and to check on a friend."

Bobby swiveled his head around to see where Al had come from. "The ghost whisperer?"

"*Elena.* Yes. She's been through a lot already, with the hole and everything. I knew paramedics were responding. Didn't know the nature of the emergency. Just wanted to make sure she was okay."

Bobby grinned. "Got it."

It was suddenly a little warm inside her turnout coat. Al looked around at the small army of first responders swarming the area. There were still a few civilians in the vicinity, too, who hadn't been moved to safety yet. Most of them had phones out, taking pictures. Then she looked across the street at Elena, who was back kneeling beside her grandmother. At this point, there was a clear line of sight to them from almost every direction. Al's interactions would have been visible for anyone with eyes to see. Or a camera on their phone. And the crew would most certainly have noticed that when Al arrived, she shot over to Elena before checking in with them.

Al pictured what it must all look like through their eyes, took a deep breath, loosened her tie, and undid the top button of her uniform shirt. Then she turned around, toward the only situation she should have eyes on right in that moment, and tried to focus. "Alright. Captain. What have we got?"

Bobby snapped to attention. "We have a fire on sloped terrain. It is approximately half an acre in diameter. We're seeing light, white smoke. Our main fuel will be brush, some lowland oaks and pines, and dried grasses. Flames are less than three feet tall. The point of origin appears to be a quarter of a mile from here, near a small wooden shed that appears abandoned. It is the only structure under immediate threat. We have a northeast wind at six miles an hour, blowing away from our location. A mountain road just north of the fire is creating a natural barrier, but there are a half dozen homes on the other side. Residents there, and on this block, all along this side of the street, are being evacuated."

"What's your attack?"

"Offensive. We're approaching from the black. The anchor point is at the end of this driveway. Engine One has secured a water source. We are stretching hand lines now. Ladder One is in position. It's giving us eyes on the fire, and it's going to help us get our personnel and hand tools up over that retaining wall, onto the hill. We should be mopping this up within a few hours."

Al was proud of the kid. He knew what he was doing. And based on what she was seeing, the dozen women and men in turnout gear, who were all doing their jobs with purpose and confidence, knew he did, too.

"Looks like you've got things under control, Garcia. Good work."

"Well, it's not under control yet, Chief." He meant the fire, of course. "But it will be."

Al hung out next to Bobby for a while, watching and listening, giving advice when asked, and sometimes when she wasn't. A pillar of gray smoke went up, signaling that old shack was giving more fuel to the fire, but the team was all over it. Even from where she was standing, Al could see that they were making progress.

Al glanced over at the ambulance for about the tenth time, trying to figure out what was happening with Elena and her grandmother. The bus hadn't moved, and no one was in sight. What was happening? And what was taking so long?

"Hey, Chief?"

"Yeah?"

"If there's something else you need to be doing—you know, like another meet and greet luncheon with the big shots—by all means, go do it. I've got things covered here."

Bobby's grin said he knew exactly what else Al wanted to be doing, and it wasn't some bullshit luncheon. But the kid was smooth. And decent. Just like his mom.

"I know you've got this, Bobby. I've just been enjoying watching a future fire chief in action."

Bobby glowed under the praise. "Alright then, Chief. Get after it."

Al was more eager than she wanted him to know to get back to Elena. "Obviously, call me if you need me. And let me know when you move into the mopping up phase."

Bobby nodded and tipped his chin in the direction of the bus, sending Al on her way. Al didn't need to be told twice. She spun around and jogged toward the ambulance.

But Elena wasn't there.

Her grandmother was sitting on a bench inside the bus, holding Casper, with the two paramedics beside her, and they were mid-guffaw when Al arrived.

"Hi, Chief." Mrs. Murphy said brightly.

"Mrs. Murphy." Al nodded. "It looks like you are feeling a little better."

"I feel better than ever. I mean, look at the company I'm keeping. Becca and Pablo are taking such good care of me."

Becca smiled and shrugged at Al. "Her ECG looks great. Vitals are all good. Dizziness is gone. Breathing is normal. We suggested that it would be good to take a little trip to the hospital, for additional tests, just to be sure, but—"

"I told them that is *entirely* unnecessary."

Al didn't have to wonder where Elena got her self-assertiveness from.

"It might seem unnecessary, Mrs. Murphy," Becca scolded her. "But you can't be too safe. Especially at your age—"

"At *my* age, the last place I want to be wasting time is in the emergency room of some hospital. I would much rather be here, with you young people. Why does everyone think *old* people should be more careful, take more naps, and stop eating all the things that make life delicious? We don't have that much time left! We should be living every second like it's the very last one, and enjoying ourselves. Honey, I'm not going to some hospital to get poked and prodded. This is the most excitement I've had in years. Decades, maybe."

"She's waiting for her son to come pick her up," Pablo said.

"And in the meantime, they are being kind enough to listen to my whole life's story. Can you believe I was born in 1934? I have a LOT of stories."

Al couldn't help but grin. "I'm sure you do, ma'am."

"Don't call me ma'am, young lady." Mrs. Murphy shot her a sly smile. "It makes me sound old. My name is Mary Ellen."

"You got it, Mrs. Murphy." Al liked this woman. Elena had the same feisty energy. "I'm glad you're feeling better. And I'm glad you're enjoying yourself."

"I just wish my granddaughter was here right now. I'm sure she would like to see you. You two have a lot in common, you know."

"We do?"

"The important things." Mrs. Murphy spoke with such authority, it was clear there would be no follow-up questions.

"Speaking of Elena. Where is she?"

"She said she had to make a phone call." Becca shrugged, and then turned back to her grandma with a big grin on her face. "So. Mrs. Murphy. You were telling us about the time there were two bodies that looked alike, and you and your husband accidentally put them in the wrong caskets…"

Al backed away from the bus and pulled out her phone. No missed calls. So, the phone call Elena was off making wasn't a call to Al. Maybe she was calling her father, to see what the holdup was and when Grandma was going to get picked up.

Al scanned the area. The police had been effective at clearing the street of everyone who didn't have a job to do. Elena would have been obviously out of place if she was just wandering around, the only person out of uniform.

So where was she?

"Hey, Sam." Al saw her bass player working Engine 2.

"'Sup, Chief?"

"Have you seen Elena?"

"Picture-taker? Yeah, sure."

"Where is she?"

"Said she was going to get her camera. She's taking pictures of us in action." Sam grinned. "I can't wait to see them."

"She went to get her camera?" Al enunciated every word. "In the *house*? A house on a street that we have evacuated?"

"Yeah. She said she was here to shoot the fire."

Al scowled. "She did, huh?"

"Uh-oh. Is she not supposed to be here?"

"Did you not notice that she doesn't have a coat on?" Al was doing her best not to take Sam's head off. "Since when do we allow civilians to wander around the scene of a fire? Especially without protection?"

Sam's eyes widened and her mouth scrunched into an apologetic frown. "Sorry, Chief."

But Al barely registered the apology. She sprinted across the street and through the front yard, took the porch stairs in one giant step, and burst through the front door of Elena's house. Which was unlocked, of course.

No sign of Elena.

Al called her name and swept through the house, opening each door, checking each room, looking for her.

She wasn't there.

She was *shooting the fire.*

What the absolute fuck was she thinking?

Al flew into the kitchen, through the back door, and out into the backyard. Where Elena was, in fact, shooting.

Huge billows of smoke hung on the hillside right above them. The flames were in the distance, but clearly visible. The fire didn't sound nearly as angry as a lot of them Al had fought, but it was making its presence known. The truck was dousing it with water while teams of firefighters on the hillside used hand tools to clear brush along the edges, depriving it of the fuel it needed to survive.

Elena was crouched down and she had her camera trained on the handline team that was making sure the truck had water. She had no coat. No helmet. No protection of any kind. And she seemed completely oblivious to the danger.

"Elena!" Al called as she ran to her.

Elena stood up and turned around just as Al reached her.

"Elena, I told you to stay with your grandmother. In the ambulance. I told you not to go wandering around. I told you to stay *safe*. What in the world do you think you're doing out here?" Al grabbed her by the elbow.

Elena looked confused. "I'm…taking pictures."

"I can see that. I'm saying *why* are you out here?"

Elena furrowed her eyebrows, yanked her elbow free, and set her jaw. "Because I am a photographer. It's what I do."

Elena's back was straight and her feet were slightly apart, like a tiny, immovable statue, daring Al to make her move or try to stop her from doing her job.

Al shook her head. "Elena, listen to me. We have evacuated this area for a reason. It might look like everything is under control, but you can never count on a fire to do what you want it to. Fires have a mind of their own. And they like to *bite*."

As if wanting to be proven right, the fire issued a whooshing sound as a gust of wind blew down the hillside, scattering leaves in Elena's backyard.

"Bump back! Bump back!" The ladder crew yelled to the teams on the hillside. The wind had shifted direction, which meant the fire would, too.

Al put her arm around Elena. "I need to get you out of here. I mean *now*."

But Elena twisted away from Al's reach and pointed her camera at the action on the hill, clicking maniacally as men and women in yellow turnout coats scrambled to move back, away from the fire. Then she shifted toward the activity on the ground, running back toward the street, stopping to shoot the engine crew along the way. She circled the crew twice, shooting them from every angle. When she got to Bobby, she did a similar dance, oblivious to everything and anything that wasn't directly in her frame.

At least she was moving in the right direction, *away* from the fire.

Al was livid. She ran up behind Elena and took her firmly by the arm. They moved quickly to cross the street, away from the action, and once on the sidewalk, Al spun her around so that they were face to face. Keeping a tight grip on her, Al leaned in, words ready. Elena was impudent. Irresponsible.

She could have gotten hurt.

Elena looked up defiantly, lips set in a hard line she dared Al to cross. But her eyes betrayed her. She glanced around wide-eyed at the scene behind Al, where firefighters were shouting and smoke poured off the hill, and then looked back at Al. The lines around her mouth softened and her eyes could have swallowed Al whole. Al gave her arm a light yank, bringing Elena a step closer. Close enough for Elena to hear her, if she whispered. Al looked deeper into those eyes, splashing around in a sea of emotions she didn't exactly know what to do with. And Elena's lips parted, not so much for something to come out, as for something to come in.

She could have gotten *hurt*. The words rang in Al's ears, filled her brain. What was she *thinking*?

Al straightened up, hardened her jaw and her heart, and snapped around. Then she led Elena by the arm, back toward the bus, without saying a word.

Inside the ambulance, Al found Mrs. Murphy regaling Pablo and Becca with a story about a pastor who cussed like a sailor all through a funeral sermon. Understandably, it turned out to be his last, and the end of his career in ministry, even though the family thought it was hysterical.

They stopped laughing when they saw Al's face.

She sat Elena down in the back of the ambulance. "*You.* Stay here."

She glared at Becca and Pablo. "*You.* Keep an eye on her. Do. Not. Lose. Her. Again."

Then she spun back around and headed back to Bobby, to see what help she could offer. The crew was moving less frantically by the time Al reached him. Bobby was on the radio. When he clicked off, Al stepped up and stood beside him, without making eye contact. This was fucking embarrassing.

"Chief," Bobby said somberly, staring straight ahead.

Al nodded. "Captain. You got this?"

"I do. We had a pretty strong gust and thought the wind was shifting, but it's moving northeast again. We're back on the offensive."

Bobby turned with a raised eyebrow to look at Al, and tipped his chin toward the bus where Elena was on house arrest. "Do *you* got this, Chief?"

Al sighed heavily. "Bobby, I have no idea."

Chapter Eight

Elena's life at home had been chaos for months, since the hole opened up. The fire a week ago had only added to it. But work was a constant.

"Can we please move on?" Her head hurt.

Her brothers had been arguing for twenty minutes about the new ambient scent machine Elena had ordered.

Conner scowled. "I don't even understand what this is. *Non-nebulizing.* Is that even a word?"

"Yes, it is a word, Conner." Elena had explained the way it works at least four times. "It means that the vapor mist it produces isn't wet. The machine uses a fine particle dry vapor mist to diffuse the scent through the HVAC system."

"This is *dank*." Sean was reading the box. "Look, Conner. You control it with an app on your phone."

"I'm not sure this context is the best use of the word, *dank*, Sean." Elena rolled her eyes. "But, yes, it's a smart machine."

"What do we need this for, anyway?" Conner's scowl deepened. "What's wrong with the little plug-in air fresheners we always use? They're cheap and you can, you know, put extras around whenever a room needs a little boost."

"That's a good point, Conner." Sean looked up from his phone, where he was no doubt searching for the app. "Plus, what about all the flowers that are in here all the time?"

Conner slapped the desk in front of him. "Exactly. And the candles. Between the plug-ins, the flowers, and the candles, what more do we need?"

Elena sighed. "Okay, look. This is an old building. It's got a hundred years of all kinds of odors trapped in these walls. And we all know there are a lot of unpleasant smells that waft through here from the prep room. It's just part of the job. But trying to cover them up with fifteen different powerful scents, all competing for attention, isn't helping."

Sean and Conner both opened their mouths to argue, but Elena cut them off. "Let me finish. We're starting to get complaints. Remember when Mrs. Truman fainted in the middle of her husband's service? She said it felt like she was assaulted by a cacophony of odors."

"Not the Trumans again." Conner rolled his eyes.

"It's not just the Trumans. Even I get a headache if I'm in this building too long." The competing odors were not even the main reason that was true, but Elena didn't need to say that. "This scent machine is just part of the solution. The new air filtration system being installed is the most important part of the plan. This machine will just help us control what people *do* smell. We can make it soothing and consistent throughout the building. If we do it right, it will become part of our brand."

"I vote for pine. I love that smell. It's like being around a campfire."

"Don't be stupid, Sean. Pine, as in a pine box? Get it? No one wants to be buried in an old pine box."

"Okay, fine. Let's do vanilla, then. That always makes me think of Gran's cookies."

"Like anyone wants to eat cookies during a funeral." Conner scoffed.

"*Everyone* wants to eat cookies, especially during a funeral."

Elena sighed again and sat back in her chair. Maybe weekly meetings with her brothers wasn't such a good idea.

An air filtration system, though? That definitely was.

She needed one for her house, too.

The smell of smoke was the first thing that hit her when she got home later that afternoon. Even after a week, it clung to her furniture, her rugs, her clothes.

It was spring and the weather was idyllic, low humidity, lots of sun, temperatures in the low eighties during the day, in the sixties at night. Her favorite time of year. So, she had her windows open day and night.

But still the smell lingered.

The only good thing to come out of that hillside fire was it gave meaning to the experience Elena had at the hole, when she had seen fire and smelled smoke so thick she couldn't breathe. She had been terrified. But it finally all made sense.

That day the hole opened, Elena had a premonition of the fire to come, and the danger her grandmother would be in. If she had been paying attention, she might have been more prepared. But she had only ever had a few premonitions before. The first was Mrs. McCarthy, the one that freaked out her family and the whole town.

They were not her favorite things.

Casper met her at the front door. Elena dropped her bag on the living room couch and kicked off her shoes, then headed to the kitchen. Casper followed her, meowing.

"Oh no you don't. I could not deal with those boys for one more minute. So, since it's Friday afternoon, I decided to come home early. But it isn't even close to dinner time, Bucko."

Casper would eat all day long if she let him. He sat next to his empty dish and stared at her.

"I said, not yet. I'm going for a hike. And, yes. I do think I'll take my camera with me, thank you very much."

She had been spending a lot of time on a series of black-and-whites that she had begun shooting in LA before everything shut down. Queer women at work. She had some great new pieces to add from her last year and a half in Owen Station, too. It would be the show that opened her gallery.

If she ever had time to find a space, do the buildout, and actually get it off the ground.

Pieces of that show were in various stages of readiness, all over her living room.

But right now, she was dying to get up onto the hillside behind her house, to see the effects of the fire. She planned to add photos of the fire's aftermath to the ones she took at the scene of the fire, and those from the home hardening campaign shoot. A second exhibit, maybe? She didn't know exactly. But she was pretty sure they were good.

She grabbed a water bottle from the cabinet and filled it. Then she headed to her bedroom to change into hiking clothes. Casper followed and jumped onto the bed to watch.

"You're not going to make me feel guilty, Casper. You know I can't take you with me."

The cat just kept staring.

"Whatever." Elena frowned at him but scratched behind his ears. He could be cranky, but she couldn't imagine life without him. Plus, he had been through a lot over the past few months. He spent six weeks mostly hiding under the bed during the hole drama. Not only were workers and heavy equipment out in front of the house every single day, crowds of curious locals were out there, too, watching it all happen. Then there was the whole fire fiasco, and an hours-long confinement on Grandma's lap in the ambulance. It was a lot. He deserved a break.

It took less than a minute for Elena to pull on a white T-shirt, gray hiking shorts, and her favorite boots. Then she grabbed her camera and backpack, shoved the water bottle in a side pocket, and headed out the door.

An eight-foot retaining wall in the backyard kept Murphy Hill from sliding down into her house. So getting up there meant walking a couple of blocks through town to a trailhead.

The trail was in decent shape. It wasn't too steep of an incline, but it was a bit of a rugged climb up the back side of the hill, and Elena was thankful for a solid pair of boots. A lizard scurried across the path, reminding her to watch her step, and a flash of something white caught her eye, off in the distance. A white-tailed deer, most likely.

Elena had been hiking through the Mule Mountains since she was a kid. And she spent many afternoons up on Murphy Hill, behind her grandparents' house, alone. It was quiet up there. No people gawking at her, asking her if a dead relative was still hanging around.

No dead relatives showing up to bug her, either.

Just the peace and quiet that only nature could provide.

The fire hadn't touched this side of the mountain, and spring was in full bloom. The ground on either side of the rocky path was alive with deep purple and vibrant yellow wildflowers, and hummingbirds darted in and out of the brush.

The trail climbed about five hundred feet, until it reached an old paved road, which took her around to the front side of the hill. From there Elena could see her house, in the distance, below. And between her house and where she was standing, the devastation.

At least two acres of her beautiful hillside had been scorched. The fire had stripped the earth of anything organic, leaving nothing but bare soil and patches of charred vegetation in its wake.

Elena closed her eyes and tears formed beneath them, but she steadied herself, clenched her jaw, took deep breaths, and forced the tears not to fall. She was a professional. Taking photos was what she did. Even if what she was seeing through the lens broke her heart.

Nothing could ever be more difficult than the photo series she took her senior year, documenting the resiliency of desperate and exhausted families who had been detained along the border, and then dumped off at the bus station in Tucson, all trying to figure out how to make their way through a land and a system that could not have been more foreign or more unforgiving.

That project was what took her to LA and launched her career.

Their faces haunted her dreams.

Elena opened her eyes, pulled her camera out of its case, and began her descent across the blackened hillside. The late afternoon sun cast shadows off the charred remains and craggy limestone. This could have been so much worse if not for the quick response and decisive action of the firefighters that day.

Al had pissed her off. Badly. Treating her like a child, instead of a pro. Chasing her down, interrupting her work.

But seeing the extent of the damage, Elena had to admit Al wasn't wrong to be cautious.

From below, the fire had seemed so far away from the house, and the retaining wall felt like a shield. Especially after the work Elena had done to clear her property and clean that wall. But from up here, she could see just how little space actually lay between where the fire was burning and the roof of her house.

She couldn't blame Al for being so tough on her.

"Well, what is that?" She squinted, using a hand to block the sun, trying to get a better view.

A single yellow wildflower clung to the earth. A lone bit of color visible on a wide expanse of blackened ground. A tenacious splash of life.

It reminded her of the firefighters, in yellow coats, scrambling up the hillside. How often did they fight against what must sometimes seem like insurmountable odds?

Elena had seen enough death and despair in her lifetime—on the border, in the funeral home, in the encounters she occasionally had with souls on the other side—to fill Ramsey Canyon. So, no matter how challenging or haunting her photos might be, Elena strove to inject her work with hopefulness.

She dropped to her belly and began shooting. Then she jumped into a squat position and circled the flower, trying to catch every angle, determined to find the best way to tell this story of hope against hope.

The phone in her pocket buzzed just as she was finishing. She got up and shook out her legs, feeling the blood rush back to her feet.

It was a text from Al.

Do you have a minute to talk?

It took a moment to decide how to respond. A breeze had kicked up, and Elena closed her eyes, picking up the scent of star jasmine in full bloom. Her feelings for Al were complicated. But she couldn't deny that she had them.

Yes.

Her phone rang immediately.

"Hello?"

"Hi, thanks for taking my call."

Elena didn't respond. Now that she was hearing Al's voice, she wasn't sure this had been a good idea. When everything went sideways, and she was finally able to get Gran across the street, and she knew help was on its way, and she was shaking so badly she could hardly stand...all she wanted was Al. Al made her crazy. But she was confident and strong. She would know what to do, and she would protect them. Then Al showed up, and she was all of those things and more. She was compassionate and funny and kind. She made Gran smile and made Elena feel safe. Her arms were strong and her heart beat steady as Elena leaned against her chest.

But Elena hadn't seen Al since she had been marched over to that ambulance last Friday, like a child in time-out.

"Are you there?" Al said, like anyone would if it sounded like the call suddenly dropped.

"Yes."

"Okay, good. It just got quiet for a sec."

"I'm here."

"I wanted to call because we've discovered how the fire started. It will probably be in the *Caller* on Sunday. But I thought you might like to hear it right away."

"Oh. I actually thought you might be calling to apologize."

Al was silent for a moment, and Elena prepared herself for a lecture. She was a *civilian*. She didn't belong there. She put herself and others in danger. She didn't follow orders. Blah. Blah. Double blah.

"I'm sorry."

Elena let her mouth drop open. "You're *what*?"

"I'm sorry. For being so tough on you the other day."

"You mean when you interrupted my work. And humiliated me by putting me in lockdown and giving your team orders to watch me and then storming away?"

Al was quiet again. Elena could hear a tapping sound through the phone. Like a pen or fingers tapping nervously on a hard surface. Voices in the background were muffled, as if far away. Elena wondered where Al was, what her office looked like, whose picture sat on her desk.

"Yes. That. I was just doing my job, Elena. But I know you were just doing yours, too. I admire that, even if I didn't like it."

Now it was Elena's turn to be silent. She looked down at the ground. The sun was glistening off the petals of that yellow wildflower.

"Thank you for saying that, Al."

"You're welcome."

Elena paused. Al did owe her an apology. But she didn't need to offer one.

She also wasn't the only one who had been in the wrong.

Elena took a breath.

"As much as I hate to admit it, I know you were just trying to keep me safe. And that's *your* job. So, thank you."

"Thanks for saying that, Elena."

"You're welcome. Also…thanks for being so great with my grandma, and everything else you did that day. I was really thankful you were there. Until you locked me in that ambulance, I mean." Elena half-smiled.

"I didn't *lock* you in the ambulance, Elena."

Did she hear a smile through the phone? It seemed like she did.

"You know what I mean. What I'm saying is, I really appreciated the way you showed up. For my grandma. And for me."

"Your grandmother is something else. I see where you get it."

"Where I get *what?*"

Al chuckled. "Never mind. I don't want to get myself in trouble again. I'm just saying I really like your grandmother."

"Well, I have to say, the feeling is mutual."

"It is? That's good information. What does she like? My charming personality? My sense of humor? My strikingly good looks?"

"Oh my God. Here we go, again. Can you ever be serious for more than a minute? Sometimes, talking to you is like talking to my brothers."

"You mean the pasty pair?"

Elena was stunned. "That is not funny, Al."

This was not going well. But wasn't that how it always was with Al Jones? Just when it seemed like there was something beneath the jokey, bruh exterior, she said or did something like this. Showing a complete lack of empathy. Maybe she didn't know any better, or maybe she knew and just didn't care.

"*What?*" Al sounded incredulous. "Isn't that what everyone calls them?"

"Yes, but that doesn't make it okay."

"I'm pretty sure they call *themselves* that, Elena. Remember last Copper King Festival, when they entered the Annual Donkey Race under the team name the *Pasty Pair*? One of them was the front end and one was the back. They even won. The name is a joke that they're in on."

Elena sighed. Maybe next year Al and her brothers could enter a four-legged race together.

They were three of a kind.

"Look. I just called to tell you how the fire started. Are you interested?"

Elena sighed and started walking back up, across the scorched earth toward the road. There was something irresistible about Al. She was dynamic and charming. Strong. Reliable. It was easy to be held by her. But just when it felt like she had Al in focus and could see her clearly, the picture blurred and she wasn't sure what she was seeing.

Maybe it was best if she and Al just kept things professional.

"Yes, of course I'm interested. Tell me. How did the fire start?"

"A man from Phoenix was down here getting ready for a big reveal party he was planning to surprise his wife."

"A reveal party? You mean where pregnant parents announce whether it's a boy or a girl?" Elena grimaced and started walking slowly along the road.

"Exactly."

"Even though it contributes to the gender binary, reinforces societal stereotypes, and puts children into starkly defined boxes even before they're born."

"Well said. Yep. One of those."

"Not a party I want to attend."

"Me, neither. Anyway, the dad-to-be was with his brother last Friday. His brother is from Phoenix, too, but owns a second home down here. They were testing the pyrotechnics before the big event the next day."

"You have to be kidding me." Elena stopped mid-stride.

"No."

"I heard it, Al. The explosion. I was in my kitchen, having brunch with my grandmother. I thought a car backfired. Oh my God."

Al sighed. "Yes, that was probably it."

"What in the world were they thinking? Playing with fire in the middle of a drought."

"I wish I could say it was unusual, Elena. But when you believe the conspiracy theories, you know, climate change isn't real, there is no drought, wildfires are being intentionally set—"

"If you believe that, then you don't exactly give two shits about fire safety."

"Exactly."

"How did you find out?" Elena stopped and took a swig from her water bottle.

"The brother is back down this weekend. Got into town last night and was talking about it down at the Miner's Hole. Came in drunk, tried to get drunker. Said he had recently escaped a fiery death." Al snorted. "He was being very dramatic about it all. Anyway, Ricki was behind the bar. She overheard him and called Chief Dana."

"What an idiot."

Elena started walking again and, because the road had begun descending, she took it a little more slowly.

"What's going to happen to them?"

"They're being charged with arson. The burning of wild lands is a serious offense, even if it's accidental. They were reckless, and they didn't report it. Property could have been damaged. People could have been killed. They could be looking at fines, probation, even jail time."

"What a stupid waste," Elena said. "And his wife is pregnant."

"Apparently, they also have a two-year old."

"And for *what*?" Elena looked at the ugly scar below her. "The earth looks angry, Al. It's like someone peeled its skin off. It's painful to see."

"Where are you, Elena? Are you there now? Aren't you at work?"

"I am not at the funeral home, if that's what you mean. But I am at work. I'm on the old mountain road, above where the fire started, right behind my house. I hiked up to—"

"Take more pictures."

"That *is* what I do."

"I know, I know. Just…Elena. Be careful."

Elena shuddered as she hung up the phone.

Al probably didn't mean anything by those last words. It was just the kind of thing Al would say. Like *don't set off fireworks in the middle of dry brush.* Or *always keep your fire extinguisher charged and fresh batteries in your smoke detectors.*

Be careful.

Or, who knows? Maybe Al had really wanted to say something else but didn't know how.

Whatever Al meant, her words sent a shiver through Elena.

She had been gazing down at the burn as she took each careful step on the descent, but something made her stop when she got to the spot directly behind her house. She slowly turned around to look at the brush that lined the far side of the road, and that's when she realized her fingers were tingling again. They had been since she got back up onto road. And the farther west she walked, the worse it had gotten. She just hadn't been paying attention.

Elena gave both hands a hard shake, trying to get blood flowing to her fingers, to make it stop. But it didn't.

She should have known better.

That had never worked.

Neither had holding her hands up in the air, over her head, to drain her fingers of blood. Or sticking them in ice. Or folding them into a hot pad. Or wrapping them in bandages, to hold them still.

She had tried everything.

The only way to stop her fingers from feeling like they were going to vibrate off her hands was to listen to whatever it was someone was trying to tell her.

To pay attention.

At the moment, however, Elena didn't hear anything. Because there was no sound.

The hummingbirds had disappeared.

In fact, nothing at all was moving. Not a bird, not a lizard. Even the air was still.

The road had dropped about four hundred feet from the highest point, where the fire had finally been stopped.

Her house was directly behind her.

She heard something rustle in the brush, maybe twenty feet off the road. She couldn't see it, but it was definitely there.

She took a step off the road, into the grass, careful to avoid stepping on wildflowers. And then she stood very still, squinting into the brush, listening for the thing she could not see.

It was clear firefighters had been through there. She remembered seeing them, on either side of the black, coming up behind the fire, using hand tools to cut grasses and clear as much brush as they could on the side of road. She knew from the photo shoot that what they were doing was creating a stronger barrier, to make it harder for the fire to spread.

Her fingers were beyond tingling. They were twitching now, so she balled her hands into fists and held them against her chest.

She took three more steps off the road, deeper into the rocky terrain. Then two more. Still no sign of anything, and she hadn't heard that sound again.

"This is ridiculous." She spun back around toward the road.

That's when something enormous came crashing through the brush, under a low-hanging tree, right at her. Elena screamed and leaped backward out of the way.

Javelina.

A mama and three babies.

Like anyone who lived in the southwest, Elena knew them by their smell, even before she saw them. They looked like large wild boars, smelled like dirty socks, didn't eat meat, and were so short-sighted, they would never see you coming.

Elena probably scared the crap out of them.

But she wasn't worried about them. They had hurried away down the road.

Elena, on the other hand, had landed on her butt.

She kind of wanted to cry.

Instead, she started laughing.

It had been a hell of a few months.

First, the giant hole. The fire inside it.

Then, the mess in front of her house. The fire behind it.

Gran falling. Casper hiding. Her gallery on hold. Her brothers irritating half their clients. Being home but not feeling settled. The resurrection of the ghost whisperer.

And then there was Al.

Assistant Fire Chief Allison Freaking Jones.

Chief Shiny Boots.

Charismatic, handsome, irritating Al.

Her fingers were twitching, but she didn't even care. It had all just been too much. Elena held her head in her hands and laughed until her sides hurt.

Finally, she was exhausted. She wiped her face and took a few deep breaths. Then, she put one hand on the ground to brace herself as she stood up.

But the ground beneath her gave way and swallowed her arm up to her elbow.

She screamed, yanked her arm up out of the ground, and jumped up, holding her arm tight against her body, as if the earth might come for it again.

"What the *fuck.*"

Her fingers weren't just twitching now, it felt like they were on fire. Whatever it was she was supposed to be listening to was here.

It was right here.

She looked around on the ground and found a long stick, which she used to examine the ground that swallowed her arm. Except, it wasn't ground at all. She had inadvertently pushed her hand between two rotting pieces of wood.

Which were covering a hole of some kind.

Elena shrugged off her backpack and camera and put them on the ground. Then she pulled a pair of hiking gloves out of her pack, slipped them on, and went to work.

After about fifteen minutes, she had removed the brush that had hidden the hole and discovered that it wasn't a hole at all.

She stood back and stared at it.

Elena never would have seen it if she hadn't been knocked on her butt. But without its camouflage, it was obvious. She was looking at an opening about three feet in diameter, blasted right into the side of Murphy Hill.

She didn't know how she knew, but she knew it to be true— this was the opening to the mine that led to the tunnel, the one that collapsed, leaving a gaping hole in front of her house.

She pulled a flashlight out of her pack and made a decision. She was going in.

She ducked through the opening and found herself in an underground portal, which was large enough for her to be able to stand upright. The walls and ceiling were reinforced by thick wooden planks the size of large trees.

Using her flashlight, she could see immediately that the entire structure was blackened and charred. Like the earth on Murphy Hill. But this damage wasn't from a recent fire.

Elena's fingers were twitching so violently, she dropped her flashlight. When she bent over to pick it up, a blast of smoke came up from the tunnel, filling the portal and her lungs, and the shaft glowed an angry red.

Elena dropped into a squat and covered her head with her hands.

After what felt like an hour, the glow faded and the smoke cleared. Except, of course, there was no sign of an active fire.

Just the remnants of a very old one.

Trembling, Elena reached into her pocket for her phone. Surprisingly, she had a signal, so she opened it up, looking for Al's number. Al would know what to make of this.

That's when she realized her fingers had stopped twitching.

Apparently, whoever was trying to send her a message felt pretty confident that it had been received.

Now she just had to figure out what it meant.

Chapter Nine

Al flipped through a short stack of résumés. A very short one.

Applications to join the service were down by an average of fifty percent across the country since Al graduated from the academy, and it was even worse for small and rural communities like hers. But their department was going to lose about half its force to retirement within the next six years, and part of Al's job was to make sure they had seasoned firefighters to take their place. That was going to mean training them, so the race for new, young recruits was on.

The applications she had on her desk were for the handful of people who had applied *and* passed the written exam. It was a good crop of candidates, but it wouldn't be enough.

Al picked up the résumés, shoved them in her top drawer, and pushed away from her desk. She needed ideas for how to get more applications coming in. So she headed to the one place she knew had more ideas than they knew what to do with.

The kitchen table.

Al's office was in the Owen Station Fire Department's administration building, and it was attached to Station One. She often visited the other houses to check in on the men and women who were on twenty-four-hour shifts. They worked, ate, slept, played cards, and lived together there.

And they talked. Endlessly. About all kinds of things.

Al missed that life. It was one reason she made a point of hanging out at the kitchen table with the crew. Plus, it was the best way for her to stay in touch with how they were actually doing and find out what they needed to do their jobs better. They loved it, too, and she knew it boosted morale.

Because Station One was right next door, though, it kind of felt like Al's house. Usually, when she pushed the station door open, the crew would greet her pretty enthusiastically.

"Hey, Chief.

"How's it going, Chief?"

"Hey, Bruce! Pour the chief a cup of that sludge you made."

This time when Al walked in, though, no one said anything. Everyone snapped their heads around to look at her, like she caught them in the act.

Or like they had to suddenly shut up…because they were talking about her.

Al stopped short and looked around, confused.

"Lose something, Chief?" Sam asked.

And then they all busted up laughing.

Al rolled her head back, looked at the ceiling, and sighed.

She wasn't surprised the firehouse was full of gossip about her since the fire. There was no doubt they all noticed that the first thing Al did when she got to the scene was look for Elena instead of checking in on them. Never mind that Al knew without a doubt that Bobby had a handle on things. Never mind that, ordinarily, she wouldn't even have left her desk for a one-alarm brush fire. As much as she craved the adrenaline rush of being on a 911 schedule, that wasn't her job anymore. That was a big reason she had gotten herself a coach, to help her make the mental switch to being on a forty-hour schedule, to appreciate the importance of her new role, and to help her calm the fuck down, so she didn't drive herself—or the crew—crazy.

If it hadn't been a call from Elena's house, she wouldn't have been at the scene of that fire at all.

But she was there.

And the crew would have made a quick note of that.

Elena going rogue—so Al had to chase her down and stick her back in the bus—just made it worse.

Al looked back down and gave Sam a big dose of side-eye. "No, Sam. I have not lost anything."

"Not even a brunette?"

They all cracked up again, slapping each other on the back.

"Alright, everybody, back to work, or whatever the hell you were doing," Bobby said. But even he was grinning. Then he looked at Al. "What's up, Chief?"

"Well, I was coming over here for some advice. But I'm not sure these goons are going to be very helpful today."

"Oh, come on, Chief. We're just kidding around." Sam headed over to the table, waving her hand. "Come on, guys. The chief needs our brains."

Within moments, Al had her focus group.

"I'm not getting enough applications in the door, and I think we need to do a better job of getting the word out there. You got any brilliant ideas for how we can attract some new recruits?"

"Actually, yeah. We were just talking about this last night." Bruce put a pot of coffee in the middle of the table and dropped off some mugs.

Sam filled one and shoved it in front of Al. "We should do some videos, is what we should do. Fun ones, you know? For social media."

"Sam wants to be an influencer." Bobby rolled his eyes.

Sam laughed. "Like the chief, you mean?"

That photo Elena had taken for the home hardening campaign, the one of Al where she was shouldering the chainsaw, had blown up on social media. More than a thousand likes, and hundreds of shares, most from people who didn't even live in Owen Station. There were more than a dozen marriage proposals in the comments, and a few menacing comments that didn't make it through the filter—not everyone was a fan of female firefighters. Much less officers. But Al didn't share those with anyone except her boss.

Al scowled. "That campaign was supposed to convince *Owenites* to do fire preparedness."

"Well, it did do that, Chief. Grant applications from local homeowners quadrupled almost overnight." Bobby grinned. "You becoming a social media meme, on the other hand, is just—"

Al shot Bobby a look that shut him up.

It was one thing to know that her photo might inspire people to reconsider what leadership looked like. She was still a rarity in the fire service, and if that brought some notoriety, it was all for a good cause. But there was another version of her photo out there, too. Someone had edited it, adding #smoldering underneath her image. There was no way to know how much action the meme was getting online, but her mother saw it somewhere and sent it to Al in a text with a long string of question marks.

"Can we get back to the topic of how we get more applications in the door, please?"

"Roger that, Chief." Bobby looked around the table, and switched his captain voice back on. "Alright, everybody. What have ya got?"

"How about doing an online open house?" Bruce asked.

Every head at the table snapped up to look at him. Bruce was one of the older guys, and a halfway decent cook, but nobody would have called him creative. And he had never expressed an interest in the future of the department. He was already thinking about how much fishing he was going to do when he retired in a few years.

"Okay, Bruce," Al said. "You have our attention. What would an online open house look like?"

"I don't know exactly. But I actually went to a few online tours of nursing homes when I was trying to help my sister—the one who lives up in Scottsdale—when she was looking for a place for my mom a few years ago."

"I freaking love this idea." Sam said. "I think we should do it live. We bring people on a tour inside the department, virtually, you know? That way they don't have to be local or drive all the way out here. We could reach people all over the country."

Bobby nodded. "There have to be a lot of people out there, sick of the rat race in big towns, who would jump at the chance to live somewhere like Owen Station. We could show them around one of the houses and the equipment and let them meet members of the crew."

"Let them meet the *hot* members of the crew, you mean?" Sam flexed her biceps. "These babies were born to be on live TV."

"I do think it would be good to let people see how diverse our crew is, Chief," Bobby said, ignoring Sam. "If people see firefighters who look like them, they can imagine themselves doing the job."

"After the tour, we gotta take them to meet the chief, though. Am I right?" Sam asked. "Everybody's gonna want to see her, now that she's hashtag #smoldering famous."

Everyone started laughing. Only Bobby kept a straight face, even though he was clearly amused. Al shook her head scowling, but she didn't interrupt. Unfortunately, Sam wasn't wrong. If the likes and comments filling the department's social media pages were any indicator, people were going to want to hear from her.

"You could give a little pep talk, Chief." Bobby was doing his best to keep the conversation on track. "Explain all the reasons being a firefighter is so great."

"You get to be part of a team," Bruce suggested. "And you're always solving problems."

"I love that it's so physical," Sam added.

"For me, it's knowing that I get to show up for people on the worst day of their lives and actually do something that makes a difference."

Everybody turned and looked at Jess, surprised that she had spoken up. She was a damn good guitarist, the one member of the band Al and Dana had struggled most to find. But she was a rookie firefighter, the newest member of the crew, and she didn't tend to talk much.

"Exactly." Bobby said. "Like that, Chief. You'll inspire them. Then we open it up for questions. And close with easy-to-follow instructions for how to apply."

Al sat back in her chair. "Not bad, everybody. Not bad at all. I like this idea. How would you feel about putting together a plan for me?"

"You got it, Chief." Bobby said.

"Great. Just tell me what you need to get this done."

Bobby jumped up when Al got up and walked her to the door.

"Hey, Bobby," Al said, just before she headed out. "You are doing a really great job here."

The kid just about melted right there on the floor.

Al's phone had buzzed a couple of times while she was at the kitchen table, and she opened it up to see what she had missed as she walked back to her office. Dana had called but didn't leave a message. Hopefully, she had an update on the Murphy Hill fire starters. Somebody from a women's health magazine based in Philly wanted an interview—they had seen Al's picture online. A recruiting agency wanted her to call them back about an opportunity with a large fire department somewhere.

And Elena had texted her three times.

I need you to meet me on Murphy Hill right now.

Are you there?

Please answer.

The last text was five minutes ago.

Al didn't even stop at her office. She was out of the building and in her truck within thirty seconds. She dialed Elena while en route but got no response.

"What have you gotten yourself into now, Elena?"

Al gripped the steering wheel hard and moved as quickly as she could through town without breaking any traffic laws. Everybody knew her SUV, so driving it was like always being under a spotlight. When a school bus pulled out in front of her, she almost lost her mind. It was that time of day, though, on a Friday afternoon, so it wasn't unexpected. The bus rolled to a slow stop every block. The stop sign popped out on the driver's side, and everything on the road came to a halt as kids with backpacks clambered down the stairs and spilled out onto the sidewalk.

Al propped her elbow on the window and held her head in her hand as she waited while she tapped the steering wheel nervously with the other hand.

She told her phone to call Elena again. Still no response.

Finally, Al turned onto Old Mine Road and rolled slowly past Elena's house. There was no sign that she was home, so she must have still been up on the hillside.

Al had two choices. Go to the trail head and hike up to the old mountain road or drive three miles outside of town to the nearest entry point by car. She was still learning her way around the Mule Mountains and had never hiked that trail. Given that, the time of day, and the urgency of Elena's text, Al opted to take the road.

It used to be one of the main roads in and out of town, but it was rarely used anymore. Al didn't pass a car all the way up.

She noted where the trail popped out onto the road, on her left, and kept climbing another few hundred feet, at which point she saw the expanse of blackened, charred earth stretch out below her. As long as she had been doing this job, she never got used to the ravages of fire.

Elena's house was visible in the distance, and Al sped up. Elena said she was right off the mountain road, directly behind her house.

Al did her best to line up with those directions, parked her truck, hopped out, and called Elena's name.

Nothing.

"Elena!"

It was still a couple of hours until sunset, but the light was already changing, throwing shadows across the hillside. Al squinted into the brush, scanning the ground for any sign that Elena might have been there. Then she left the road, stepping carefully into the brush, minding the rocky terrain.

"Elena, can you hear me?" She yelled loudly enough that Elena should have been able to hear her, even if she was in her own kitchen, six hundred feet below.

"Al!"

She heard Elena's voice, but couldn't see her right away. Then, about twenty feet into the thick brush and off to her left, she saw Elena's head sticking out of what looked like a hole in the side of the mountain.

"Over here, Al."

Al inhaled sharply and realized that she had been holding her breath since she went running out of her office. Now that she had eyes on Elena, though, the adrenaline coursing through her body flipped the anger switch.

"What in the hell, Elena?" She took several long strides toward Elena's disembodied head. "Why haven't you been answering my calls? And *what are you doing* in there?"

"I found it, Al. I found the mine that connects to the tunnel that collapsed in front of my house."

"That is a *mine shaft*? Are you insane?"

"No, of course not." Elena waved one hand in a circle, around the opening. "This is an *adit*, a passage into the mine."

"This sounds like semantics, Elena. You're literally inside an old mine right now. I don't care what it's called."

"I've been wandering around in here for, I don't know how long. Since the first text message I sent you. I'm being careful. But there's something in here I want you to see."

"Elena, come out of there now."

"No, Al. I will not come out. I want you to come in."

"I'm not doing that."

"Are you afraid?" Elena's voice rose, matching her eyebrow. "Aren't you the daredevil, who loves running into burning buildings?"

"No one loves running into burning buildings, Elena." Al rolled her eyes. "But, no. I am not afraid. I'm just *smart*. You need to get out of there right now."

"Al, I'm serious. You need to come in here and see what I've found. Do you have a flashlight in your truck? Go get it."

Then Elena pulled her head back inside the shaft. Correction, the *adit*.

Al growled. How did she get herself into this situation?

She was already the subject of kitchen table gossip. The butt of jokes. That wasn't all she was, but dammit. Al had worked too hard to earn their respect—especially after getting a job that some of the guys thought should have gone to someone inside the department. It didn't matter that, after the chief changed the requirements to include a degree, there weren't enough internal candidates who qualified. It had taken a good two years for Al to prove herself to them.

And overnight, Elena had made her look like a fool.

On second thought, she couldn't blame Elena. Al had done it to herself.

She wasn't going to make that mistake again.

Elena needed to come out of that mine, like now. If Elena was right, that mine was connected to a tunnel that had just *collapsed.* Could there be a more dangerous situation? But Al wasn't about to call a crew to come save Elena's butt. Al would never live it down.

She needed to clean up this mess herself.

She wheeled around and headed to her truck. If she was going in after Elena, she was going to be prepared for anything.

Fortunately, there was everything she could possibly need, for almost any imaginable situation, in that SUV. She opened the tailgate and pulled out anything that seemed like it might come in handy when diving into a hundred-year-old abandoned mine. The last thing she grabbed was her helmet, to which she attached a head lamp. Then she headed back toward Elena.

The opening was about three or four feet in diameter. Al folded herself over, tucked her head, and stepped through the portal. Then, to her surprise, she stood up.

"Mines were built so workers could stand up in them." Elena was shining her flashlight on the ground in front of Al. She was smiling.

"Here," Al said, thrusting her helmet at Elena. "Put this on."

"I'm not going to put your helmet on. *You* put it on."

"Elena, I am in here against my better judgment. I should throw you over my shoulder and carry you out of here. But you are insisting that we be in here, for some crazy reason. The least you can do for me is put this helmet on. If I had two in my truck, I would wear one, too. But I don't. So, please, put the damn thing on."

Al shoved the helmet toward her, again.

With a huff and an eye roll, Elena snatched it from Al and shoved it onto her head. "This is heavy."

"It'll keep you from having your skull crushed when this shaft falls in."

"This is not a shaft, Al. A shaft is a tunnel that goes straight down. This is a *drift*, a horizontal tunnel. I'm sure there is a shaft in here, though, maybe several, so watch where you're walking."

Al quickly looked down at her feet to make sure she wasn't standing on the edge of one. She was more jittery about being inside that mine than she was going to admit. "How do you know so much about mines?"

Elena shrugged. "I know next to nothing. But having grown up here, it would be impossible to actually know *nothing*. Even though active mining stopped decades ago, the mines themselves are all still here. We didn't know there were any on *this* end of town, until that hole opened up in front of my house. But there is a boarded-up entrance to the biggest mine in town located right at the end of Main Street, just a few blocks from Banter & Brew. And from there, if you know what you're looking for, you can see half a dozen openings to half a dozen mines up in the mountains."

Al used her flashlight to sweep the area looking for potential hazards. There were so many. "I'm assuming, then, that you know how dangerous it is in here?"

Elena turned to look at Al, which meant the headlamp on Elena's helmet shone right on Al's face, which made Al shield her eyes with her hand.

"Oh, sorry," Elena said, tilting her head down and away to get the light out of Al's eyes. "Yes, of course I know the dangers. They're drilled into us from the time we can walk. Falling. Toxic air. Abandoned explosives. Wildlife."

"Snakes."

"*Where?*" Elena jumped and Al caught the helmet, which came flying off Elena's head, with one hand.

"Nowhere. I just meant snakes are a potential hazard."

"Oh my God, Al. Don't do that. I thought you actually *saw* a snake."

"I did not see a snake." Al put the helmet back on Elena's head, trying not to laugh. "And I'm sorry I scared you."

"There is nothing funny about this."

"I'm not laughing."

"You are, too."

"Okay, maybe a little."

"Because I'm afraid of snakes?"

"Because this is a ridiculous situation, Elena. And, yes, because of all the things that could go wrong down here, you're afraid of snakes."

Elena looked up at Al.

"Again?" Al used a hand to block the light from blinding her.

"I told you I didn't want to wear this."

Elena started to take the helmet off again, but Al reached out for her hand to stop her. "Leave it on," Al said gently, squeezing her hand. "It's safer."

"But I keep blasting you—"

"It's okay." Al did not let go of her hand, because she absolutely was not going to let Elena take that helmet off.

Also, Elena's hand was soft. And warm. And it felt tiny. If there had been music, Al might have lifted it above Elena's head and given her a spin. It was just a hunch, but Elena seemed like she might enjoy dancing, and she was probably good at it.

"Just try looking at me with your eyes rather than your whole face."

Elena dropped Al's hand, took three steps backward, and gave it a try. She pointed her head slightly away from Al's face, and used just her eyes to look up and sort of sideways at her. "Like this?"

Al nodded and Elena did it several more times, practicing.

Al started to laugh again.

"What? What's so funny?"

"Nothing. You're doing great...you just look a little like a cartoon."

"I look like a cartoon?"

"A little. I mean, the helmet is so big it's a little wobbly. We're in the middle of this dark cave and your face looks a little like it's disembodied, floating around the cave. And now the way you're looking up at me like that, with those Smurfette eyes. Well, yeah. A cartoon."

"Nice. That's really nice, Al." She sounded snarky, but she was smiling.

"So alright. What is so important that you had us both climb in here?"

Elena grabbed both of Al's hands, keeping her eyes on Al's face, but pointing the lamp away from her. "Al, *this is the mine*. The one that leads to the tunnel that collapsed in front of my house."

"I heard you say that before, Elena. But how do you know? How could you possibly know that this hole we're in leads to your house?"

"Well, first off, I just know, okay. You can believe me or not. But I *know*. Second, it's directly up the hill from where the tunnel collapsed, so it makes sense."

"But Hazel said the area is probably covered with abandoned mines."

Elena nodded, and the helmet bobbled up and down. "I know. Although I have hiked all over this mountain since I was a kid, and I've never seen one. Until today. And I'm telling you, Al, this is the one. Look."

Elena swiveled her head toward the wall and pointed her flashlight at the old wooden structure. It was blackened and charred. There had been a fire in that shaft. Or drift. Or whatever it was called.

Then Elena swiveled back toward Al and looked at her with an expression that could only mean, "See, I told you."

"I don't get it, Elena. It looks like there was a fire in here at some point. From the looks of it, probably decades ago. How does that translate into this is the mine that leads to the tunnel that opened up in front of your house?"

"Because there was a *fire* in the hole, Al."

Elena practically shouted it. But that didn't make it make any more sense than if she had whispered it.

"There was a fire in *what* hole?"

"The one in front of my house."

Al couldn't understand why *Elena* sounded exasperated. "Elena, the only fire at your house, at least as far as I know, was the one on this hill last week. There was no fire in that hole."

Elena closed her eyes and sighed heavily. When she opened them again, there were wrinkles across her forehead.

"Okay, listen. Remember when I couldn't breathe?" Elena sounded a little like a kindergarten teacher, trying to be patient with a struggling student.

Al nodded.

"It was because of the smoke."

"The smoke?"

"Yes. I had a bad feeling about that hole right away, as soon as I saw it. But when we came out of the house, I saw *fire* coming out of it, Al. A huge fire. And the smoke was overwhelming. And I was trying to get everyone to move away from it, but I couldn't breathe. And that's when I passed out."

"Are you telling me you had some kind of vision?"

"You make it sound stupid."

"I'm just trying to understand."

"You don't believe me."

Al sighed. "I believe that you think you saw something, Elena."

"I don't *think* I saw something, Al. I saw it. I didn't know what it meant at the time. Last week, when the hillside was on fire and I thought my grandma could die, I thought I understood. I thought the fire I saw in the hole in front of my house was some kind of premonition. But it wasn't. The fire I saw wasn't going to happen in the future. It happened in the past. It happened right *here*."

"Okay, fine. Let's say you're right. And you saw a vision of a fire that happened in the past. So what? I mean, not to be disrespectful or anything. But what difference does that make that there was a fire here? Why does it matter—"

"Shh," Elena hissed sharply.

"What—"

"Shh!" She hissed louder and held her hand up to stop Al from saying another word. She was looking past Al, deep into the tunnel.

Al snapped around, toward whatever it was Elena was seeing, and used her flashlight to scan the area. But she saw nothing.

"I saw something move, Al," Elena whispered. "Over there."

"What? Where? What was it?" Al's heart was racing.

"I don't know. But whatever it was went that way, deeper into the mine."

Elena adjusted the helmet on her head, so the headlamp was pointed straight in front of her and aimed her flashlight in the direction of whatever it was she thought she saw. Then she started following it.

"Elena, what are you doing?"

"I need to see what it was, Al."

And before Al could even yell at her for doing such a stupid thing, much less grab her to pull her back, Elena was off.

Al was close behind.

About thirty feet deeper inside the mine, Elena stopped so suddenly Al almost ran her down.

She was shining a light on the ground.

"Are those…human?" Elena whispered.

Al used her own flashlight and crouched down for a better look. Then she turned her head and looked back at Elena, whose mouth was open and eyes were wide with shock. "Yes, I'm pretty sure these are human bones."

Elena started trembling so bad the helmet on her head wobbled. Al jumped up and grabbed her. "Let's get out of here."

Elena didn't resist. She let Al guide her back the way they came. Looking over her shoulder to make sure whatever it was Elena had seen wasn't following them, Al snatched Elena's bags and camera and her own gear off the ground, and then led Elena out through the entrance.

"Come on. I have my truck."

When they got to the SUV, Al opened the tailgate and helped Elena sit down. After she called Dana to report what they had found inside the mine, Al turned to Elena.

"I think you can take this off now." Al smiled softly and took the helmet off Elena's head.

Elena looked up at her, dazed. "I knew something bad was on the other side of that hole, Al. I told you. I didn't know exactly what it was. But I could feel it. Do you believe me now?"

That was a good question. Al wasn't a big believer in the supernatural. If there weren't facts and hard evidence, she wasn't interested. She assumed the Owen Station ghost tours, that were so popular with tourists were just a corny type of community theater. And she thought the rumors about Station Two being haunted were just stories the old-timers told the new recruits to keep them up at night. But Dana reminded her that many cultures and lots of very smart, wise people believed that, just because you can't see something, doesn't mean it's not there.

Al wasn't exactly convinced. But this much was true—*Elena* believed. She was seeing things that led her into one dangerous situation after another, and she was willing to put herself at risk to discover the truth. And that willingness had led to a disturbing discovery.

"Let's put it this way." Al thought carefully before speaking. "I think you are foolish for taking so many risks. But I also think you are very brave. And I don't *not* believe you."

Elena let out a deep breath and her shoulders relaxed. Then she grabbed Al's hands and looked up into her eyes. "You don't know how much that means to me, Al. I swear to God, I could kiss you right now."

A wind swept across the mountain and the sky was pinking up as the sun got ready to set. A siren, growing louder by the second, told Al that Dana wasn't far away.

And Elena's lashes, framing those deep blue eyes, were so long.

It was just a throwaway comment, right? Elena wasn't really going to kiss her. Was she?

"What did you say?" Al said quietly, letting the warmth from Elena's hands radiate up her arms and down through her body.

There was no fear in Elena's eyes. And nothing hidden.

Her eyes dropped to Al's mouth.

"I said, I could kiss you."

Then Elena pulled Al toward her.

Their lips touched, and Al tasted citrus and smelled rosemary, and Al's body melted, like steel inside an inferno.

Finally, Elena gave her hands a hard squeeze, let go, and pulled away.

Al tried to catch her breath as she searched Elena's face, for the first time unable to read what she was feeling.

Then she turned around to watch Dana's truck coming toward them, as questions floated in the air like burning embers ahead of a fire front.

CHAPTER TEN

It had been a long time since Elena had such a poor night's sleep.

But it wasn't the mystery up on Murphy Hill that kept her awake, tossing and turning. She had led the authorities to the bones, but there wasn't anything more she could do. Solving the puzzle of who those bones belonged to and what happened inside that mine was up to the experts now, and she knew that. So, when Al offered to give her a lift, shortly after the county coroner arrived, she was ready to go home. But Elena chose to hike down the hill, instead. She needed to clear her head. All the way down, all she could think about was—what was with that kiss? And what happened now?

Finally, around midnight, Casper jumped off the bed with a thud, meowing his disapproval about having to endure such a restless night. He spent the remainder of the night chasing something around the house.

By the time the sun came up, Elena was almost grateful to have an excuse to get out of bed and quit pretending sleep was going to come.

Casper jumped up next to her, meowing.

"Good morning to you, too. I'm sorry I kept you up all night."

Casper meowed louder.

"Oh. Are you starving, you poor thing?"

The sarcasm was lost on him.

"Okay, I'll answer for you. You most definitely are not starving. I bet you still have kibble in your bowl, you little chow hound."

As if knowing she was on to him, Casper plopped down and rolled over for his morning belly scratches. He would have stayed there all day, but Elena had a family coming in to make arrangements that morning. She did her best not to make appointments on Saturday, but sometimes it just couldn't be avoided. Today was one of those days.

Casper kneaded the bedspread as Elena loved on him.

"So, you got any advice for me, Casper?"

He rolled over and stared at her.

"No, huh? What use are you?"

He stretched his front legs dramatically, got up, and jumped off the bed.

"I'm sorry. I didn't mean to offend you."

With his tail twitching in the air, he marched out of the bedroom.

"You're such a diva," she called after him. But he didn't have an answer to that.

Her phone buzzed on the nightstand just as she was about to get out of bed herself. She rolled over to grab it, hoping her brothers hadn't already annoyed someone. It was way too early.

It wasn't her brothers, though. It was a text from Al. Elena's stomach did a double backflip. How did she even have the number?

It took a minute to remember they exchanged contact info at the fire.

Good morning. How'd you sleep?

How did she sleep? She didn't, that's how. Every time she closed her eyes, all five foot, ten inches of Al Jones was there. Making some sarcastic observation. Swooping in to save the day.

Kissing her.

Elena dropped her head back into her pillow and groaned. What had she done?

She hadn't planned to kiss Al, that's for sure. Not that she hadn't thought about it. Al was the kind of beautiful that made you look twice, like a rugged mountain range. Powerful. Real. Naturally beautiful in a way that didn't require embellishment.

She was nothing like any woman Elena had ever been with.

Her last girlfriend had been a finance lawyer, well known in the art world for collecting work by artists she thought would be valuable one day. She not only knew what to wear to a five-star restaurant, she didn't think twice about picking up the tab. She spent endless hours name-dropping, debating the pros and cons of art in the digital age, and perseverating over the latest fads in skincare. Heidi didn't care that Elena had special abilities, she didn't even know it. Because the only thing she really cared about was herself. In the end, Elena discovered that Heidi didn't just collect art—she collected artists. Elena learned about the affairs a year into the pandemic and, honestly, the worst part was thinking about how many germs she had been exposed to.

It had all been so exciting. Until it wasn't.

Maybe it was time for a new type.

Elena picked up her phone to respond to Al's text.

Didn't sleep well at all, actually. Yesterday was—

Elena paused to think about what adjective would best sum up the experience. The scorched earth. The yellow wildflower. Almost being run down by javelina. Discovering the mine. The deep darkness. The remains of a fire. Whatever she saw skirting through the tunnel. The bones.

The kiss.

Finally, she typed the only two words that could capture it all.

—a lot.

Yesterday was a lot.

Al responded immediately.

Are you doing okay?

Elena wasn't sure how to respond to that, either. Okay about what? The dead body that was hidden in a hole behind her family's house for who knew how long? The scar on the hillside she had loved for as long as she could remember? The way her stomach flipped every time she thought about kissing Al? The way it sunk when she thought about the possibility of never kissing Al again?

Elena responded with the only answer she could think of that would be simple enough to put in a text, even if it wasn't entirely true.

Yes.

All things considered, she was doing okay.

Will you be at the tasting room tonight? The Fireballs are playing.

Elena took a deep breath and read Al's text twice. She had, in fact, been planning to go. It was a Mujer Fuerte new release event, members only. Elena had joined the wine club at the opening of the new tasting room almost a year ago. She already had arrangements to meet Hazel there.

But now, she wasn't so sure. The *Fireballs* were playing. Al would be there. And right in the moment, Elena wasn't sure how she felt about that.

It did seem as though Al knew how she felt, though.

Al wanted to see her.

She wouldn't be asking, otherwise. Right?

Every inch of Elena's body was painfully awake.

Was she going to be at the tasting room tonight?

Maybe. I'm not sure. I think so.

Al responded quickly.

Good. We should talk about that kiss.

Elena threw her phone down on the bed, slunk down, and pulled the sheet up over her head.

It wasn't fair. She had initiated the kiss. All Al wanted to do was talk about it.

But Elena wasn't sure what there was to say.

Or why she had done it.

Because she was emotionally exhausted?

Physically drained?

Grateful that Al had shown up when she called?

Relieved that Al believed her—or at least didn't *not* believe her?

Curious?

All of that was true.

But it wasn't as true as the truest thing, the thing she had been trying to ignore for months.

She had a serious crush on Owen Station's assistant fire chief.

A woman who rode motorcycles and ran toward danger, who lived in a uniform and played in cargo pants, who needed to be the boss of everything and sometimes seemed to hide her real feelings so deeply, under jokes and sarcasm, that she didn't even seem to know they were there.

She had a crush on Al.

She closed her eyes and let herself picture Al that day at the photo shoot. In a muscle shirt and those creased uniform pants. The sun on her face and glistening off her shoulders. Lithe, muscular arms. A blindingly bright smile. Abs with such definition Elena could see them through her fitted shirt. But what really got Elena's attention were Al's eyes, where light and shadow swirled deep, in endless shades of blue, a study in contrast, boasting resilience, hinting at vulnerability. Elena could have gotten lost in them. But she couldn't help wondering.

What was it like to look at the world through those eyes?

A world that had been pulled out from under her more times than she could count, as her family moved from place to place. A world without stability, where every year, every day was a new challenge. A world that, even now, was full of expectations and biases and dangers that Elena couldn't even imagine. A world that demanded that you be larger than life just to be seen and accepted and safe.

She had a crush on Al.

But what in the world—in *Al's* world—would make her think Al might have a crush on her? A woman so privileged, in so many ways, that her family had part of a mountain range named after them, who couldn't take orders and was constantly getting herself in trouble, who thought snakes were scary and fainted in front of a crowd.

What in the world was she thinking when she pulled Al in for that kiss?

Al most likely wanted to talk about it because it had been such a huge mistake. Inappropriate. Uncomfortable.

Elena shrunk deeper under the sheets, willing herself to disappear.

She might have stayed like that forever, but Casper jumped up and started pawing at her. Finally, Elena sat up. She didn't have time for this. She had a job to get to. A cat to feed. And other important things she just couldn't think of right then. But she knew there was a list.

She threw on a gray pair of leggings and a white linen sleeveless tunic and made her way to the kitchen. Casper circled in and out of her legs while she put her espresso pot on the stove, reloaded Casper's dish with kibble, and refilled his water fountain. When the coffee was ready, she frothed some milk, filled her thermos, and headed to work.

Her office door was open when she got there. Sean was hiding behind it, with a sheet over his head. Like a ghost. Waiting to jump out, screaming boo, to scare her.

It worked.

"For Christ's sake, Sean," she yelped.

"I heard you found my bones, Elena," he moaned dramatically. "Do you know who I am?"

She grabbed the sheet and yanked it off him. "Are you ever going to grow up?"

The speaker phone on her desk crackled next. "Hello? Elena?" A spooky voice cried. "I am calling from the great beyond…"

"Hang up the phone, Conner. I swear to God. Do you two not have anything better to do?"

The boys were laughing so hard they couldn't talk.

"Get out of my office," she said, pushing Sean out and closing the door behind him. "Both of you." At her desk, she ended the call and silenced the phone.

Of course her brothers would have heard about the find at the mine the night before. They would know that she had been there. And of course she would never hear the end of it.

It would probably be in tomorrow's *Caller*.

Ten minutes later, there was a knock on her door. "Can I come in?"

That was a voice she wasn't used to hearing at work.

"Gran? Of course."

Elena hopped out of her chair and greeted her grandmother with a hug. Gran was wearing her hair in a classic chin-skimming, silver-gray bob. Elena remembered going with her at least once a year to the makeup counter in a Tucson department store. Even now, at ninety, her makeup was understated and perfect—no garish orange lipstick bleeding through the wrinkles in her lips. She was a class act, never trendy, always current. She had influenced Elena's own style, in a way.

Elena helped Grandma get seated and then sat back down in her own chair. "You look fabulous as always, Gran. You know, I want to be you when I grow up."

"Don't be ridiculous, Elena. You are far more already than I would ever hope to be. Look at you. An accomplished photographer. The family business is getting back on track because of you. You look fantastic."

Elena waved her hand to brush away the compliments, but it felt good to hear them. "So, what's up? What are you doing down here?"

"Isn't it okay for me to pop in on my favorite granddaughter?"

"Of course. You can pop in on me anytime. I just wasn't expecting you. You never come to see me here." Elena smiled, thankful for the unexpected visit.

"Well, I just want to tell you I am very happy that, from the sounds of it, you're taking my advice about that fire chief."

Elena tilted her head. "What do you mean?"

"I heard you were at the mine with Chief Jones yesterday."

Elena sighed and rubbed her temples. "News does travel fast in this town, doesn't it?"

Grandma nodded. "It does."

Then Grandma sat up bone straight, folded her hands in her lap, and cleared her throat. "Speaking of the mine. Would you mind telling me exactly what you saw in there yesterday?"

"In the mine? Um…sure. Why?"

"Because I'm curious."

"Okay. Why?"

"Stop asking questions, Elena. Just tell me what you saw."

Elena leaned back in her chair. "Well, it was dark."

Grandma rolled her eyes. "No duh."

Elena laughed. Where did she get this stuff?

"It was very dark. But we could tell that there had been some kind of fire inside. The beams were charred."

"I heard you found something in there."

"About twenty or thirty feet inside the tunnel we found bones."

"Human bones."

Elena nodded. "We couldn't be sure, but the police confirmed it, and they called the coroner."

"Anything else?"

Elena shook her head but then stopped. She remembered looking further down the tunnel, after she saw something move. "A flash of red. Maybe part of a shirt or a blanket or something. It was on the ground. I didn't get a good look at it. We moved pretty quickly to get out of there as soon as we realized what we had found." Elena thought for a few seconds more and shrugged. "And that's it."

Grandma pursed her lips, frowning, but didn't say anything more.

"Why are you so curious about this, Gran?"

"No reason." Then she got up as quickly as a ninety-year-old could move. "Thank you, Elena. I'm tired and I'm going back upstairs for a nap."

"Okay." Elena came around the desk and gave her a hug. "Take care of yourself."

Her grandmother left the office, but a minute later she circled back and stood in the doorway. "You go get that fire chief of yours, Elena. She's one of the good ones."

And then she was gone.

Elena sat back down. Had everyone lost their minds?

Her brothers impersonating ghosts. Grandma wandering around, quizzing her, giving her dating advice. Al—well, Al hadn't lost her mind, as far as Elena knew. But Elena felt like she might, thinking about having to see Al that night, and having to come up with some kind of explanation for that kiss.

It was going to be a long day. And she was going to need something to look forward to. She picked up her phone and dialed Hazel's number. Hazel answered on the first ring.

"Elena? What's up? Everyone's talking about you and Mystery Mine. Which I think is what it's going to end up being called, by the way. I can't find a record of it anywhere."

Elena laughed. "Hello to you, too."

"Oops. Sorry. Hi. I've just spent the last couple of hours searching all the old records I have here in the library. And... nothing. But that's probably not why you called."

"Well, it's sort of related."

"Tell me. What do you need?"

"I need a drink," Elena laughed. "And a friend."

"It's a little early for a drink, don't you think? But I got the friend part covered."

"I don't mean I need a drink right this minute. But I am wondering if you want to meet me a little earlier than we had planned tonight."

"I can do that. Like, for dinner? You want to meet at Banter & Brew before we head over to the tasting room?"

"If the morning I'm having is any indication, by this afternoon I'm going to need something stronger than Knox's coffee and rhubarb pie, as good as that is. How about just heading to the tasting room early?"

"That sounds good. I'm excited to try the new non-alcoholic options Tessa is offering."

"And her cheeseboard will make a perfect dinner."

"Sounds great. Meet you there around four thirty?"

"Perfect."

According to the invitation Elena had received to the members-only event, music was scheduled to start at six. That would give her an hour and a half to pull herself together before she had to see Al.

The rest of the day actually went much more smoothly than the first few hours had gone. The family she met with had worked out a lot of the details on their own before they even came in. Sean and Conner had retrieved their loved one directly from the hospital, so the family never even had to deal with them. And they seemed genuinely thankful for Elena's kindness and efficiency.

They did have questions, though.

About what Elena had seen inside of Mystery Mine.

So did the flower delivery person.

And the plumber who came in to deal with the drainage system problem in the prep room.

And her father, who also wandered downstairs just to "check in." Which he very rarely ever did now that Elena was in charge, allowing him to fully and finally retire.

Everyone wanted to know the same thing.

"What did you see, Elena?"

"Who do those bones belong to?"

"What happened in that mine?"

She had stopped trying to explain herself to people a long time ago. She wasn't psychic. She couldn't read minds. She didn't talk to ghosts. She rarely even saw what you'd call a ghost, not any more often than most Owenites, anyway. She mostly just had a feeling about things. And sometimes those things were related to people and situations that existed in the past. It was like being on the other end of the bat phone. When someone called, she answered. Even if she didn't want to. Most of the time the call was subtle. Sometimes it erupted out of a hole and knocked her out. She didn't know how it worked and she couldn't control it. Sometimes she didn't even know what it meant. So people could come at her with questions all day long. She didn't have answers. But that didn't stop them from asking. It never had.

At three o'clock, she was ready to call it. She packed up her bag and headed home to get ready to meet Hazel.

Casper was sitting by his empty food dish waiting for her.

"You are the piggiest little kitty I've ever known." She bent down and gave him a good ear scratch. "But I love you."

Casper followed Elena into the darkroom, where fifteen black-and-white test prints hung. She had been working on this series for years and finished the last one a few nights ago. Most of the work she did was digital, but she loved being in the darkroom. It wasn't just nostalgia, although there was some of that, to be sure. This had been her safe place since high school. But even more, the darkroom was the place where she did magic. In the darkroom she could use toning techniques to add contrast, emphasizing shadows, giving her photos depth, imbuing them with a kind of transcendent timelessness. That's the look she wanted for this show. And this was the show she wanted to open her gallery with. She was eager to share them with someone, and tonight that someone was going to be Hazel. She put them in her portfolio to take with her and got ready to head out.

An hour later, she was walking into Mujer Fuerte. Tessa immediately came around the counter to greet her with a hug.

"Tessa, you cannot open a bottle fast enough."

"A bottle kind of day, huh?"

"It's been a bottle kind of week. Actually, if I'm honest, it's been a few months."

Tessa nodded. "I hear you. Do you want to sit here at the bar, over on a couch, or at a table?"

"I'll grab a table. Hazel is joining me."

"Okay. How would you like to try our new release? The party doesn't start for an hour or so. But I'll make an exception for you." Tessa winked. "We labeled the new bubbly this week. It's a rosé, refreshingly crisp. Just the right amount of acidity and fruitiness. I think you will love it. I'll bring it over."

"That sounds perfect."

Elena was putting her bags down at the table when Hazel walked in.

"Girl, you are looking very pregnant." Elena smiled as she hugged her.

Hazel beamed. "I am so ready."

"Can I get in on this?" Tessa asked, coming up behind them. She put her tray on the table and gave Hazel a warm hug. "You are radiant."

"I am huge. But thank you." Hazel grinned.

After they sat down, Tessa served them. She put a bottle of her new ginger beer in front of Hazel and set a bottle of bubbly in the center of the table with three glasses.

Elena was puzzled. "I was just kidding about having a bottle."

"And I'm not drinking—" Hazel added.

"I know." Tessa smiled. "The second glass is for Lace. My beautiful wife has someone closing up Frisky Business tonight, so she can come early. She should be popping over in a minute or two, and I know she'll want to sit with you. If that's okay?"

"Of course it is," Hazel and Elena both said at the same time.

"And one of the glasses is for me, just in case I get the chance to come hang out. This is on the house tonight."

Elena started to argue, but Tessa held up her hand. "It is the least I can do for your help with Mrs. Owen." Lace and Tessa lived in the old Owen Mansion, and the original Mrs. Owen had been hanging around for a hundred years. Elena actually didn't have much to do with Mrs. Owen deciding it was time to go, but she had been able to confirm that she was gone.

"I was happy to do it."

"How about if I bring over a cheese board, too?"

"You were reading my mind."

"Awesome. We just got in a beautifully aged, super creamy, bloomy rind goat cheese. It takes so much time to make, the cheese maker doesn't have it very often, so I scoop up as much as I can when she does. It'll blow your mind. We're pairing it with the lavash crackers I've been getting from the farmers market. A local baker is using Sonoran white wheat with a little mesquite flour to make them. Add some prickly pear jam, and…wow. Paired with this rosé, it's pretty spectacular. What grows together, goes together, you know."

"Sounds amazing."

Tessa opened the bottle, poured a few ounces into Elena's glass, and headed off to get the board ready. "I'll bring a bucket back, too, to keep this chilled."

"Honestly, Hazel, I'm looking forward to having my mind blown by something delicious for a change." She held her glass up for a toast and Hazel clicked it with her bottle.

"You've had your hands full, haven't you?"

"It has been a wild few months, that's for sure."

"Did someone say wild?" Lace slid into a chair next to Hazel, brushing her pompadour back with a silly grin. "Here I am."

Hazel kissed her on the cheek. "You are ridiculous."

These two had been part of the same gang since they were in grade school. Elena remembered watching them out of the corner of her eye as she sat alone in the cafeteria. They were four years ahead of her, and never in a million years did she imagine that one day they would all be friends. Of course, in those days, Elena couldn't imagine having even one.

Tessa brought the cheeseboard and a bucket for the bubbles, and then headed back to help her daughter, Madison, finish getting ready for the crowd they were expecting.

"So, Elena. Tell us everything." Lace poured herself a taste and refilled Elena's glass. "You have pretty much been the main attraction in this town for the past six months."

"Main distraction, you mean." Elena frowned. "It's starting to feel a little too familiar—like I'm the weird little kid everyone talks *about* but no one wants to actually be with, all over again."

Lace and Hazel exchanged a quick look.

"I wasn't just talking about all the drama," Lace said apologetically. "I mean, there *has* been a lot of drama. But, also, people are still talking about your first show, here in the tasting room. We're all waiting to find out when you're going to open your gallery. And I've heard so many people talking about the way you're wrangling those brothers of yours. My family has been using Murphy's for generations, like a lot of families. Things had really gone downhill. Until you got back."

Hazel reached across the table to squeeze one of Elena's hands. "I know we were all hard on you, Elena. Before. It must have been so lonely. I am truly sorry about that."

Lace nodded vigorously. "It really is great to have you back in town. And not just because you helped us solve the mystery of Mrs. Owen."

Elena sighed. "Thanks for trying to make me feel better, you two. And thanks for the apology. But I was as much at fault as anyone in cultivating a reputation as the ghost whisperer. I don't think I could have tried harder to scare people off. Unfortunately, I was very good at it. And as much as you're trying to convince me, I know that people aren't just talking about my photography and my family's business."

Hazel gave her a crooked smile. "There has been a lot of other excitement, hasn't there?"

"Excitement? I guess you could call it that. First, the tunnel collapsed, opening up that hole in front of my house. Then, the Murphy Hill fire and a near miss with my grandma. Now, I've got a dead body in the side of the mountain behind my house."

Hazel's eyebrows jumped. "They did move the body, didn't they?"

"Yes. I didn't mean it was still there. But it was there for who knows how long."

Lace held up a hand, using her fingers to count. "First, the hole. Second, the fire. Third, the bones. They say things come in threes, right? I think you're golden."

"It would be great to think I was done for a while." Elena took a breath and sat back in her chair. Then she remembered her portfolio. "Oh! I brought something I want to show you."

"New photos?" Hazel exclaimed, watching Elena reach into her portfolio as Tessa took a seat at the table.

"It's a show I'm working on. I think I want this to open my new gallery, if I ever get it opened, that is."

"I keep telling you, you need to talk to Sena, to help you find a space," Hazel scolded her.

"I know, I know. I just haven't had time."

"Once Sena is involved, you'll have that gallery open in no time," Tessa said encouragingly. "She made this tasting room happen in less than six months."

"Okay already." Elena smiled. "I'll talk to her."

She opened the folder and spread fifteen photos on the table. "No one has seen these yet. The draft title for the show is *Queer Work*."

"Oh my God." Tessa was looking at a photograph of herself, between the vines as the sun set behind her. She looked up at Elena, wide-eyed. "This is beautiful, Elena."

"Look at this one." Lace held up a photo of herself, at a table during a town festival, giving a dental dam demo to a trio of young women. "I look so—"

"Soft," Tessa said quietly, making Lace blush. "You look soft, Lace, and warm. Most people just see the fun, goofy you. But Elena has captured the you I see, the you who cares so deeply about helping people find love and joy."

"Look how officious I am in this one." Hazel said, holding up a photo of herself in the library, in the special collections room, with her gloves on, showing the mayor some historic photos. "And look at Sena," Hazel said dreamily. Elena had taken the shot of Sena downtown, with Knox at a ribbon cutting after they purchased the Banter & Brew building together, to turn it into an incubator for locally owned small businesses.

The three women were an appreciative audience. They spent time with each photo. It had taken years to shoot them. There was a two-spirit person on horseback at the Tucson rodeo. Another wore heart-shaped glasses and a head scarf, handing out love is love swag on a street corner in LA. A dock worker operated a forklift, moving cargo off a large ship in San Diego.

But it was the photo of Al that got the most attention. Her shadowed face peaked out from beneath her helmet. Elena had caught her the day of the fire, looking up at the hillside, before she knew Elena was out shooting. She looked concerned, but also determined, confident.

"These are amazing." Tessa's eyes looked a little watery. "I don't know how you do it, Elena. I don't even have words. You have captured the unique beauty of each one of us."

Hazel nodded. "We all look so strong. Resilient. Like we're just doing life on our terms."

Elena breathed deep. This is exactly what she hoped they would see.

"Yeah, yeah. She's brilliant." Lace laughed. "But I want to talk about this picture of Al. It certainly does not look like it was taken by someone who was terrified their grandma was dying and their house might get engulfed in flames."

Hazel took a second look while Lace poured a splash of bubbly into Tessa's glass and topped off Elena's.

"She's right." Hazel shifted her eyes to Elena and held them steady, as if looking for something.

Elena laughed nervously. "It was a terrifying day. My grandmother scared me half to death. But once Al got there, and the paramedics did some tests in the ambulance, and we found out it definitely was not a heart attack, Gran leaned over and told me to go get my camera. Then she distracted the paramedics with all her stories—you know how she is—and I was able to slip away. I caught this picture of Al right before she chased me around the property and pulled me by my ear back into the ambulance."

"Oh my God, I would have loved to have seen that," Hazel cackled.

"What's the story with you two, anyway?" Lace leaned in.

"What do you mean?" Elena did her best to sound innocent, taking a big gulp of bubbles, followed by a tiny hiccup.

"What do you mean, what do I mean?" Lace's eyebrows narrowed. "We're hearing the rumors. You two seem to be popping up together all over the place."

"Including the front page of the paper," Hazel added. "There's another one of the two of you, from the scene at Mystery Mine yesterday, in tomorrow's *Caller*."

"Oh, no." Elena took another sip. "Al is going to hate that."

"So? What's the story?"

"There is no story."

Tessa folded her hands on the table, with one eyebrow practically in the air. Hazel and Lace followed. And then they all just sat there, waiting. Clearly, they weren't going to let this go.

"Okay, fine. I kissed her," Elena squealed.

The table erupted.

"Go, Elena. Go, Elena," Lace started chanting in a sing-song voice and the other two joined in.

"Shush." Elena looked around the room to see who might have prying eyes and ears, and then tried to talk quietly. "It was nothing. Just one kiss. In Al's truck, right after we found the bones. But Dana was just pulling up, and it kind of killed the mood." She paused and cracked a grin. "No pun intended."

"I knew it," Lace yelped.

"Oh my gosh, Elena. I'm so happy for you." Hazel beamed.

"Hold on, everyone. I said it was nothing." Elena poured herself a full glass.

"Did she kiss you back?" Tessa asked quietly. They were all aware of the people around them now.

Elena felt her cheeks get warm.

"Oh my God," Lace said in a loud whisper. "She did!"

"I need more wine." Elena reached for the bottle. But she was grinning.

"Al is so handsome, Elena," Hazel said sweetly.

"Look at you, fan-girling." Lace laughed. "In your condition, you shouldn't be thinking about anyone except Sena."

Hazel flipped the bangs of her bright red hair back off her forehead. "I'm pregnant, Lace. I'm not dead."

"So, what's next?" Tessa asked.

Elena shook her head. "I have no idea. Al wants to talk about it. Tonight. But I don't even know what to say."

"I recommend using as few words as possible," Lace said authoritatively. "Actions say more than words."

"Says the toy queen." Tessa grinned.

"What I mean is, I don't even know what to *think* about it." Elena put her glass down. "Al isn't exactly my type."

"You mean tall, handsome, and charming? What is there not to like?" Hazel looked confused.

"I mean…" Elena paused. "She's so—"

"Dynamic, smart, and funny?" Tessa interrupted this time.

Elena laughed. They were right. Al was all of those things. She was also—

"Annoying. Bossy. And she always blames me for things I have no control over. Like what people are going to say when they see the front page of the *Caller* tomorrow."

The three just nodded at her, like bobbleheads lined up on a dashboard, each with one eyebrow raised.

Elena took another gulp of wine and looked at her watch.

The Fireballs were scheduled to arrive at any moment.

CHAPTER ELEVEN

This was not how Al had planned to spend her Saturday morning.

She sat at her kitchen table for twenty minutes, just staring at her phone, reading and rereading the text she had just sent.

We should talk about that kiss.

Little dots appeared a couple of times and waved at her from the screen, teasing her. But Elena did not respond.

Al laughed and shook her head.

She loved a challenge.

And Elena Murphy qualified.

One minute, she was pulling Al in for a kiss. The next, she was pushing Al away.

At least she wasn't trying to run Al over anymore.

She thought about heading over to Elena's house. Calling her bluff. Seeing where things went.

They had been doing this little dance together for months. Dana noticed it first. Then, everyone did.

"Lose something, Chief?" Leave it to Sam to needle her about it publicly. The firehouse was no doubt still laughing.

And Al couldn't blame them. She probably did look like an idiot, chasing Elena around the house the day of the fire. It was impossible not to see the connection she and Elena had, even for a bunch of firefighters amped up on Bruce's coffee and adrenaline.

She should totally have gotten up right then and there, left the breakfast dishes in the middle of her kitchen counter, and gone over to Elena's house to have a chat about what was going on between them. And to see if Elena was brave enough to go any further than a kiss.

Not that it wasn't a good kiss.

It was better than good.

Elena had started it, so Al let her lead.

When Elena's tongue slipped between Al's lips, just for a second, it sent a rush of electricity coursing through Al's body.

At the sound of Dana's truck coming down the road, Elena pulled away and let go of Al's hands.

What would have happened if there hadn't been that interruption?

Al wanted to know.

And the only way to find out was to *talk about that kiss.*

Which she couldn't do unless Elena actually answered her text, or Al went and knocked on her door.

After all, it was Saturday morning. And she had nothing else to do.

Also, *she had nothing else to do.*

Al scowled, shoved her chair back, got up, and put her breakfast dishes in the sink.

Then she turned around and looked at her apartment. It wasn't small. It took up the entire second floor of a large house. It was nice, too. The house had all the character of a home built in the first few decades of the 1900s. Built-in cabinets. Original pine flooring. An old claw foot tub.

But it wasn't hers.

She hoped and planned that Owen Station would just be a small data point on her career trajectory to a big job in a big city. Buying a house in such a small market, in an uncertain economy, one that she didn't intend to own for long, didn't make sense.

Most of the stuff in it wasn't hers, either. Her apartment in Tempe had been filled with rented everything, and this place came furnished. What was the point of collecting a lot of furniture when she knew she wasn't going to stay anyplace longer than a few years?

Al traveled light.

And moved often.

And that's just the way she liked it.

But she had never been at a loss for things to do on a day off.

There was always a group of firefighters to hang with. They'd go see a game or play pool or go for a ride or whatever.

It was different now.

She was an officer, and that meant she was no longer just one of the guys.

The blank walls in her apartment stared back at her.

Dana would have been happy to have her join them for whatever family activities they had planned for the day, if Al asked. But did she really want to go hang with someone else's family? Sit on the edge with her feet dangling in the pool of someone else's life?

Al looked at her phone, sitting on the table.

For the first time in a couple of years, she thought about calling Maria. But Maria was up to her eyeballs prepping for Saturday, the busiest day in a restaurant's week.

She picked up her phone.

Still no response from Elena.

And then, before she could overthink it, she punched in her mother's number.

"Al?" Mum picked up on the first ring, sounding breathless. "Is everything okay?"

Al sighed. "Yes, Mum. Everything is fine."

"Well, why are you calling?"

"Does something have to be wrong in order for me to call you?"

"I don't know, dear. You tell me."

Al sighed again. Maybe this call was a mistake.

"I'm sorry I've been MIA. It's just been a little busy in the firefighting universe. I'm calling now, though."

"Well, that's nice, honey. How are you doing?"

Actually, that was a very good question. Al was Al, so of course she was doing well. Great, even. Living her best life.

Just feeling a tiny bit lonely.

Okay, maybe more than a tiny bit.

"I'm good, Mum. How are you and Dad?"

"Oh, you know. Same as always."

Which probably meant Dad was doing whatever the hell he felt like, wherever and with whomever he wanted.

"I do have a bit of news, though. You'll never guess who I ran into at the mall last week."

"I don't know, Mum. Who did you run into?"

"Maria." Mum sounded more excited than she should have.

"Maria, my ex-girlfriend, Maria?"

"Yes, of course. And you'll never guess what else?"

Al rolled her eyes. "What else, Mum?"

"She's pregnant."

"She's...*what*?"

"Pregnant! She got married a year and a half ago, and she and her wife started trying to have a baby right away. She said she's always wanted to have children, and the clock was tick, tick, ticking." Al's mother sighed. "I always liked her, Al."

Al closed her eyes and shook her head, trying to remember if she and Maria had ever, even once, had a conversation about getting married. Or having children.

Nope. Never.

"Al? Are you still there?

"I'm here, Mum."

"Oh, good. I thought I lost you. So, honey...why *did* you call?"

There was a long pause, as Al tried to imagine what in the world she was thinking when she decided to dial her mother's number.

"Well, actually, I was wondering if you wanted to meet me for an early lunch."

"Today?" Mum made it sound like she had just been asked to captain a flight to Mars.

"Yeah, today. I was thinking about going out for a ride, and thought maybe you'd want to meet me halfway. Like, in Tucson somewhere."

"Tucson? Oh, I don't know, Al. You know I don't like driving so far on my own."

"Mum, sometimes you sound like you're ninety, not sixty-something."

"It's not that. You know I'll just never get used to driving on the wrong side of the road. Besides, your dad is taking me out to lunch and a movie this afternoon."

Al's mouth dropped open. "*Dad*. Is taking you. To a movie?"

"Uh-huh. And lunch." Like it was no big deal at all.

"Since when?"

"Since when *what*, dear?"

"Since when do you two go on...*dates*?"

"Oh, Al." Her mother laughed. "I wish I could meet you today. I would love to see you. How about if we try planning something. In advance, next time?"

Dad said something in the background, which made Mum giggle, and she said she had to go.

Al hung up feeling like the earth just shifted.

And more alone than ever.

She spent the next three hours numbing that feeling with the vibration of a Harley beneath her. One of the things Al loved most about riding was that it took such concentration and focus, she couldn't really think about anything else. She was totally in the moment. She wasn't thinking about Maria, or her parents, or her blank walls, or whatever the crew was gossiping about around the kitchen table, or how the fire prevention social media campaign was going, or the women's health magazine that was putting her picture on the cover, or whatever opportunity she might have in some other city somewhere, or finding bones inside a mountain.

She wasn't even thinking about Elena.

Mostly.

All that mattered was the road, the wind, and the machine. Plus, it was a glorious day to be riding through the mountains. The desert was in full bloom. Bright orange ocotillo, green palo verde trees, and wildflowers in every color flashed like a kaleidoscope as she flew by under a clear, blue sky.

By the time she got home, she would be totally recentered.

But there was one stop she needed to make before she headed back to her apartment.

She turned up the old mountain road and rode to the spot where her truck had been parked yesterday, when Elena kissed her.

Two police cars and a dark gray sedan were parked there instead. Al could see Elena's house below but quickly noted that no one appeared to be home. No car in the drive. No lights on. No doors or windows open.

But she wasn't there to suss out Elena's whereabouts.

She pulled a flashlight out of her saddle bag, left her bike parked on the side of the road, and stepped into the brush. The perimeter around the old mine was still taped off. Two uniforms were standing around shooting the breeze.

"Hey, Chief," one of them said as she approached.

"Officer..." She looked at his name badge. "Lopez. What's happening here today?"

The other one, Hatch, nodded in the direction of the mine. "A couple of detectives are inside, just making sure nothing got missed yesterday."

"You were here, weren't you, Chief?" Lopez asked.

"She found the remains," Hatch said with an implied *duh*.

Al had stuck around last night until Dana's team arrived and preserved the scene. As soon as they confirmed the remains were human, the county coroner was called. They were going to be collecting evidence until late into the evening, so Al sent Elena home, promising to let her know as soon as they had information to share. Al took off not long after that.

There was nothing either of them could do to be helpful.

"Mind if I check in with the detectives?" Al asked.

"Go right ahead, Chief."

Al folded herself over and stepped through the entrance to the mine. Portable lights had been set up inside, which were casting odd shadows on the walls. A shiver went up Al's spine, thinking about whatever it was Elena saw moving in there yesterday.

Two detectives were glaring at her.

"Chief Jones?" The crisp tone conveyed the real message— *what the hell are you doing inside our crime scene?*

"Good afternoon, Detectives." Al tried to sound more professional than she looked at the moment. It wasn't like she had been out riding in uniform, on her day off.

Al flashed her light up at the charred beams above. "I know you two are the pros here. I just wanted to double-check to make sure you're collecting samples from the remains of the fire."

"The fire isn't relevant to the case."

"It was probably set by a homeless guy."

"Or it happened a hundred years ago, when the mine was still operating."

Al tried to be patient as she was cop-splained. She cleared her throat. "Exactly. You can't tell how long ago a fire happened just by looking at the remains. So, we don't know for sure that the fire *didn't* have something to do with this case."

"The coroner said it didn't look like the bones had been burned."

"And I'm sure the doc is going to do testing to confirm that," Al said calmly. "So, just in case, how about if we collect some samples?" She spread her hands out, then folded them into a fist, and rested them on her belly. She could wait all day. And if they weren't going to do it, she would do it herself.

The two men looked at each other and shrugged.

"Okay, Chief. Whatever you say."

"We'll take some samples of the burnt wood."

Al nodded. "That's great, guys. Thank you. Be sure to grab some samples of the soil in this area, too. Depending on what the doc finds, we may end up wanting to know if there was an accelerant used in here, or evidence of some kind of incendiary device."

"Like a bomb?" One of the detectives snickered.

"There are all kinds of things that can be used to start and accelerate a fire. Chemicals. Ignitable liquids. Arson candles." Al paused and smiled. "But you're forensic experts, right? So you know all about this stuff."

They smiled back stiffly and shrugged.

Al thanked the detectives for their service, said good-bye to Lopez and Hatch, and hopped back on her bike.

Who knew whether or not there was a connection between that fire and whoever those bones belonged to? She didn't. The detectives didn't.

But Al knew one person who believed that fire was important to this case.

And for the moment, Al was ready to give Elena the benefit of the doubt.

If she had been home, Al might have stopped in. To give her an update on what she had learned at the mine.

And to ask about that kiss.

It was just as well that Elena wasn't home, though. Because Al had a gig to get ready for.

The last time the Fireballs played at the new Mujer Fuerte tasting room was about six months ago, for Lace and Tessa's wedding, and Al was looking forward to it. The whole band was. It was a members-only release party. The theme, Love Wins, was kicking off Pride month at the winery. The band spent endless hours pulling together a list of love songs to perform, spanning genres and also reflecting their diverse backgrounds. Al planned to sing her first song, an old favorite of Dana's, in Spanish.

She took a quick shower and opened her closet. Uniform shirts and pants hung neatly on one side, play clothes on the other. Shoes and boots lined up neatly along the floor. Al laughed, remembering Elena's closet.

"That should have been my first clue," Al said out loud.

In the middle of all that chaos, Elena's closet was as neat and organized as Al's.

The woman was a puzzle.

Al could never be sure whether calm, rational Elena was going to show up. Or the Elena whose emotions sprayed everywhere, like a cat in heat. She was as likely to fall into Al's arms, as she was to throw hands.

It excited Al in ways no woman had before.

When Al got dressed for the gig, she did it with Elena in mind. She didn't know for sure that Elena was going to be there. "Maybe," she had texted. But given her friendship with Tessa and Hazel and that gang, it seemed likely. Al was going to be ready just in case.

She pulled out a pair of oversized cargo pants and took a crisp, white, cropped T-shirt off a hanger. Like all of Al's clothes, it had been pressed before it was even put away. Then she slipped into her camel-colored Timbs.

She stopped in front of the full-length mirror hanging on her bedroom door before she headed out to the kitchen. Her mother's blue eyes and freckled nose looked back at her. But she definitely had her father's build. Tall, lean, muscular.

And damn if she didn't look good.

She strutted out to the kitchen and made herself a Sarnie—crisp bacon between two slices of buttered bread. She liked hers with brown sauce, just like Granddad made them. He usually ate them for breakfast. But Al ate them anytime, especially when she needed a taste of home. Then she poured herself a tall glass of milk. Before she could sit down, her phone buzzed. It was a text from Dana.

You on your way?

Al fired off a quick response. *Not yet. Soon.*

Al watched the dots dance while Dana typed.

Don't be late. Just because your instrument is your voice, doesn't mean you don't have to help us carry ours.

Al snorted, thankful she had already swallowed that last gulp of milk, and typed. *Roger that, Mum.*

Dana responded with a laughing emoji.

She could be so bossy.

But Al ate her sandwich standing up, and twenty minutes later, she was carrying a bass drum from Dana's truck into the tasting room.

Tessa shot over to greet them with big hugs. "We're so glad you're here."

We?

Al looked over Tessa's shoulder. Elena was at a table across the room, with Hazel and Lace, who both waved wildly with big smiles on their faces. Elena stuck her hand up like she was swearing an oath in court and shot a shy wave in Al's direction.

Al's hands were full at the moment, so she returned their greeting with a tip of her chin.

Dana cleared her throat. "We got this, Al, if there's something else you need to do, or somewhere you need to be."

"Huh?" Al looked over at her.

Dana had her cymbals bag over one shoulder, a gig bag over the other, and a drum case in each hand.

"Don't be like that," Al laughed. "If I let you carry all this stuff in by yourself, I'll never hear the end of it."

"I'm just saying." Dana raised a knowing eyebrow and tipped her chin in Elena's direction. "You might have something else you'd rather be doing."

"I can help carry stuff," Tessa volunteered, her eyes shifting between Al and Elena's table.

"Seriously? You too, Tess?"

Tessa grinned. "I'm just feeling the vibe here. Love wins, remember?"

Al laughed. "Well, there's no love happening for me tonight except up on that stage. I expect a full house and an adoring audience."

Dana rolled her eyes. "When do you ever *not* have an adoring audience, my handsome friend?"

"I'll do my best to deliver for you, Al." Tessa grinned. "I think we're going to have a very full house tonight. Stop by the table and say hello to everyone after you get set up."

Al carried the bass drum to the stage and set it down, then went out to Dana's truck for another couple of loads, while Dana started setting up. Out of the corner of her eye, Al could see Elena watching her as she went in and out to the truck. It was impossible to tell what she was thinking.

Yesterday, Elena had kissed her.

But today?

Elena never did respond to her text.

Those moments inside that dark mine, especially when Elena thought she saw something move, and then right after, when they spotted those remains, had been tense. For Elena, they might have been terrifying. The whole experience had been a little overwhelming, even for Al. All she could think about was getting Elena out of there and getting her to safety.

Maybe, once she was safely inside of Al's truck, knowing that help was on the way, Elena had been thankful. Relieved. Or maybe she was just confused.

Maybe that kiss was an accident.

Maybe Elena thought it was a mistake.

Why else would Elena have refused to answer her text?

Al didn't think it was a mistake, though.

And she wanted more.

Fifteen minutes later, everything was unloaded, and Al was ready for a glass of wine.

"Let me know when you're ready for a sound check." Al could help the band carry in their equipment, but she couldn't do much when it came to setting it all up. "I'm going to grab a glass and say hello to Tessa and her crew."

"Uh-huh," Dana said, grinning. "You do that."

"Sounds good, Chief." Sam pulled her bass guitar out of its case without looking up, a shit-eating grin on her face. "Try not to lose anything tonight, okay?"

Jess snickered.

Al ignored both of them.

"Let's just work on getting a balanced sound tonight, okay?"

"You got it, Chief," Sam said happily.

Al rolled her eyes and started to say something, but Dana waved her off, mouthing *I got this.* Dana told Al that she had talked to Sam about backing off. But Al would believe it when she heard it.

Tessa's daughter, Madison, was behind the bar, getting things set for the event. She had just turned twenty-one but was already a full partner in the winery. "What can I get you, Chief?"

"What do you recommend?"

Madison smiled broadly. "Well, love is in the air, isn't it? What goes better than a glass of pink bubbles? We're releasing a new vintage tonight. Want to give it a try?"

Love? Al must have looked as confused as she felt. Until she realized Madison was talking about the event's theme, not whatever was going on inside Al's head.

"Why not?" Al smiled weakly.

Madison pulled out a glass, and popped open a bottle. "This is the Lily. Mom named it after Lily Bollinger, one of the grand dames of champagne."

After Madison finished pouring, she gave Al the bottle. "We put Lily's favorite quote on the label."

Al read it out loud. "I drink champagne when I'm happy and when I'm sad. Sometimes I drink it when I'm alone. When I have company I consider it obligatory. I trifle with it if I'm not hungry and drink it when I am. Otherwise, I never touch it—unless I'm thirsty."

Al laughed as she set down the bottle and picked up her glass. "Sounds good to me."

"Me, too." Elena had silently appeared, and was standing beside Al at the bar, a half full glass in her hand. "Cheers."

Al turned toward Elena, clinked her glass, and took a sip. Madison winked at Al, excused herself, and headed down the bar to set out glasses.

"What are we toasting to?"

Elena smiled. "Love, of course. Happy Pride."

Al tilted her head and studied Elena's face. "Happy Pride."

"You look good tonight, Chief." Elena's eyes sparkled.

"I'm glad you approve. I dressed for you."

Elena's mouth opened and her eyebrows jumped an inch.

Al chuckled. "Just kidding. I always look this good when I go out."

Elena closed her mouth and laughed. "Oh my God. You are something else."

"Some kind of awesome, you mean."

"Umm—"

"Psht. Don't answer that, Elena." Smiling, Al put her finger across Elena's lips. "You can tell me later how amazing you think I am. But it looks like the band is ready for a sound check."

As if on cue, Dana clicked her sticks together four times and the band drove into the opening measures of their first song.

"Gotta go." Al left Elena standing at the bar with a crooked smile on her face.

Tessa wasn't lying about the size of the crowd. She opened the doors right as the band finished their sound check, and the tasting room was packed by the time they all came back from their last pre-show pit stop in the bathroom.

Al pulled Dana aside before they went on stage. "Nice job setting the levels. I might not have to kill Sam tonight."

Dana chuckled. "Good. I'd hate to have to book you into the town jail tonight. Especially because, from the looks of it, you're going to have other plans."

Al's cheeks got warm, and a tingle shot up her back and across her shoulders. "I don't know exactly where things are headed with Elena, Dana. But I do know we've got a show to do."

Dana slapped Al on the back. "Then let's do this."

By the middle of the second song, at the start of their first set, people had moved tables off to the side to create a small dance floor. Al led them through one genre after another. The common theme was love and very danceable grooves.

A trio of young women was waiting for Al at the break. As soon as the sound system flipped over to the soundtrack created to keep the crowd happy while the band rehydrated, they surrounded her. Al had seen them around town but didn't know them.

"Chief Jones, you have such a beautiful voice."

"I could listen to you sing anything."

"Can we take a selfie with you?"

Al wouldn't have been surprised if one of them pulled out a marker and wanted her to sign their cleavage. If she had to guess, she'd say that none of them had ever changed their own lightbulbs.

She let them take a selfie, then quickly excused herself and headed to the bathroom. She thought she had seen Elena duck in there, and Elena was the only woman she was interested in spending her short break with.

"You have quite the fan club, Chief Jones." Elena shook her wet hands in the sink and grabbed a paper towel.

Al cracked a grin. "Do I? I didn't notice."

Elena tossed the towel into the trash can. "Are you kidding? You live for that kind of attention."

Well, that kind of stung, although Al wasn't exactly sure why. A young woman came out of a stall. She watched Al and Elena in the mirror as she washed her hands, and then scooted out.

Once they were alone, Al continued. "Do I? Live for that?"

Elena exaggerated her eye roll. "You don't do this whole Chief Shiny Boots thing for nothing, do you?"

"Chief *what* now?"

"Shiny Boots."

"That's what I thought you said." Al straightened her shoulders.

"Oh my God." Elena leaned closer. "Are those *creases* in your T-shirt? Did you *iron* your T-shirt?"

Al took a step back to put some distance between herself and Elena and accidentally caught a glimpse of herself in the mirror. The creases did look a little extreme, especially with the urban casual vibe she had going on.

She looked back at Elena. "Maybe I do. What's wrong with wanting to look good?"

"There is a difference between looking good—" Elena waved her hands unsteadily down the length of her own body. "Voilá." She paused, and then waved her hands at Al. "—and being strung so tight Jess could use you to replace her G-string."

Then Elena started laughing hysterically.

"Jess is your guitar player."

Tears were coming out of her eyes and she was snorting.

"Get it? *Get it*? Her G-string!"

Al couldn't help herself from laughing, too.

"Elena, are you drunk?"

"I might be. A little. I've been here for a long time. With Hazel."

"I'm glad you're with Hazel. At least you have a built-in designated driver."

"I'm just drinking water now, Chief." Elena saluted. "I already cut myself off."

Al nodded. "Good."

"I never do this," Elena whispered.

"Drink too much?"

Elena's head wobbled a little while she nodded it enthusiastically. "Tonight's different."

"What is different about tonight?"

"Well, first of all, it's all about the power of threes, am I right?"

Al shook her head. She had zero idea what Elena was talking about.

"*Threes.* That's what Lace said. These things always happen in threes." Elena held out her hand and stuck her thumb up high.

"First, a big hole opens in front of my house and I have to live with my parents and then it takes forever to fix it and Casper spends a month hiding under my bed." She kept her thumb up high, and added a forefinger. "Second, there is a *fire* behind my house, and my grandmother almost dies."

"I don't think that's quite accurate," Al interjected because facts matter. "Your grandmother just had a panic attack. I mean, it was understandable. But it was definitely never life-threatening."

"Whatever." Elena added her middle finger. "And *third*, you kissed me." She immediately began shaking her head vigorously. "No, no, no. That's not what I meant to say. What I meant to say is, *THIRD*, we found *BONES* in an old mine, right behind my house, even though I've hiked that mountain more times than I can count."

"Third, huh?"

Elena nodded and held up three fingers.

"Third is that I kissed you?"

Elena shook her head. "Third is the *bones*. Besides, you didn't kiss me. I kissed you."

The door to the bathroom swung open and Dana stuck her head in. "Here you are, Al." Her eyes swung from Al to Elena and back again. "Um, we're about ready to go back on. If you have time for that, I mean." She grinned.

"I'll be right there."

"Yes, she'll be right there," Elena shouted unnecessarily, punching the air with an enthusiastic fist.

Dana nodded, waggling skeptical eyebrows, and backed out of the door.

"Listen," Al said. "We need to get you some more water."

"Aye aye, Chief."

Elena let Al lead her out of the bathroom and back over to Hazel's table.

"Hey, Chief." Hazel stood up and gave Al a hug. "I see you found our girl. She's been having a rough night. Took me by surprise. She hasn't really even had that much to drink. I think she's just a lightweight."

"I'm fine." Elena plopped down in her chair and waved Al away. "Go entertain your fans, Chief."

"I've got this, Al. It's water for the rest of the night." Hazel smiled.

Al looked at Elena. "You behave yourself."

Elena gave her a messy salute.

Then Al went to join the band.

Two hours later, the dancers had gone home, the band's equipment had all been loaded into trucks, Tessa was behind the bar breaking things down with Madison, and Hazel was helping Lace clear tables. Elena was sitting alone at the table with her head in her hands.

Al sat down across from her. "You feeling okay?"

Elena looked up. "I'm sober, if that's what you mean. But I think I have a headache coming on."

"I'm sorry to hear that."

Gray clouds swirled in Elena's eyes. "I'm sorry to have been such an ass to you earlier, Al."

Al grinned. "You mean, you're sorry to have been such an ass to Chief Shiny Boots."

Elena dropped her head. "Oh my God." But when she looked up at Al again, she was smiling.

"You didn't answer my text this morning," Al scolded her softly.

"I know."

"I really think we need to talk about that kiss." Al looked around and noticed that, even though everyone was keeping busy, they were very, very quiet. As if they were trying to hear every word. "And I think we should have that chat somewhere private."

Elena nodded. "How about my place?"

"Now?"

"Yes, now."

Chapter Twelve

Elena slipped out of the tasting room with a quick wave to the gang. Al stayed behind to thank Tessa for having the Fireballs play, and schedule their next gig. But Elena was frantic to get to her house before Al arrived.

Her head was spinning. Should she change clothes? Light some candles? Pour wine? Sparkling water?

Definitely water.

She was so thankful Hazel had cut her off when she did. It had been a long time since she was so sloshed. Every time she thought about her encounter with Al in the bathroom, a wave of embarrassment swept through her and she felt a little dizzy.

But who could blame her?

When Al strolled in at the beginning of the night, carrying that heavy drum, her muscles flexing, Elena thought she was going to lose it. Forget *talking* about that kiss. All Elena could think about was doing it again.

And when Al took the stage, grabbed her mic wearing that cropped T-shirt, showing off perfect abs, and opened her mouth to sing, the room lit up. So did Elena, who was pretty sure she wasn't the only person feeling the heat. It didn't help when, at the end of her first set, Al was mobbed by a group of women with more cleavage than Elena would dare show on the beach. It took everything in Elena's power not to charge up the middle, shoving them all out of the way, to grab Al and kiss her hard, right there in front of everyone.

Instead, heart racing, she dashed off to the bathroom so she didn't have to watch them flirt with the woman she planned to—

Planned to do what with, exactly?

What *was* her plan?

Casper was meowing in the kitchen.

"I already fed you twice today," Elena said, loud enough for him to hear.

She looked around the living room in a panic. It wasn't as much of a disaster as it was the last time Al was there, but it was still her studio. And things were everywhere. Although she was making new friends in town, it's not like she was entertaining. Having Grandma over for lunch didn't count. She did a quick calculation. If she hurried, she could use the empty boxes lying around, pile things into them, and move as much as she could into a closet in the hallway. After that was done, she took an old rag and dusted off the tables. From the kitchen, she grabbed a large bottle of sparkling water and two glasses, put a bunch of grapes on a plate, and filled a small dish with nuts. She put these on the coffee table in front of the couch and lit three votive candles, so she could dim the lights. Then she looked for music, scrolling through artists and genres, finally settling for a neo-soul playlist. Slow and sexy.

With her space nearly ready, she scooted into the bathroom to freshen up. First, she grabbed a brush in one hand and removed the band around her ponytail with the other, letting her hair loose. She watched herself in the mirror as she ran the brush through her waves. Leaving her hair down felt like the right move. Her makeup still looked fresh, despite an evening of overindulgence. She quickly brushed her teeth and added a dab of perfume. She looked pretty good, if a little freaked out.

Back in the living room, she took one last look around. The couch was clear. The table was set. Music was playing. But the rug?

"Casper, it looks like you shed all your fur right here on this carpet."

She looked at her watch, banking on having enough time, and pulled the old vacuum out of storage. As usual, as soon as she switched it on, Casper came running. Most cats would have fled in the opposite direction, but not this one. Elena quickly ran the vacuum back and forth across the rug, with Casper perched on top, enjoying the ride. She had just stuck the machine back in storage when there was a knock at the door.

She must not have heard Al's motorcycle over the noise of the vacuum. But that was okay. She was ready.

Well, she thought she was ready until she opened the door, pulling hard on it because it always stuck, and actually saw Al filling her doorway, wearing a leather jacket over that cropped tee, and a suggestive grin on her face.

"Hi."

"Hi." Elena was having trouble thinking of anything else to say.

"Are you going to let me in?"

Elena took a short step backward. "Oh. God. I'm sorry. Come in."

Could she have been more awkward?

Al stepped past Elena, gently brushing against her as she passed, sending a shiver down Elena's back, and Elena closed the door.

"Wow." Al elongated the syllable, like she didn't want Elena to miss the depth of her surprise, as she looked around the room. "I did not expect this."

"Which part? The candles? The music? The nuts?" Elena teased her.

Al smiled mischievously. "It looks like a different house than the last time I was here. Plus, you vacuumed."

"You can tell I vacuumed?"

"I heard it as I was coming up the stairs."

This was a silly thing to be embarrassed about. Didn't everyone clean up a little before they had people over? But for some reason it was like Al caught her sunbathing in her backyard in the nude. She knew her cheeks were pink. They were on fire.

"Okay, you caught me. I didn't know there was going to be another inspection. I just wanted the place to look nice when you came in. Is there something wrong with that?"

"Not at all, Elena." Al reached out and brushed Elena's cheek with the back of her hand. Then she swept her hand down Elena's neck and came up beneath her chin, tipping Elena's face upward, toward her own. "It's sweet."

Al's fingers gently squeezed Elena's chin, holding her face steady, so that Elena couldn't look away. It was a power move. And Elena's body didn't care what her brain *thought* about it, it was ready to surrender whatever Al wanted to take.

"So…" Al said slowly. "About that kiss."

Even if Elena had an answer to the question, she wouldn't have been able to form the words. An electric current, originating from the point where Al's fingers caressed her chin, flowed straight down through her core, grounding her to floor. She couldn't move. She couldn't speak.

"Um-mm." Whatever it was Elena was trying to say came out like a strangled groan.

A satisfied smile stretched leisurely across Al's face, and she mimicked the sound Elena had made. "I couldn't agree more."

Al's deep blue eyes were piercing. Her body hard and still. This was Al's moment and all Elena could do was be thankful that she was in it.

"I have been thinking about what this would be like, nonstop, since you stole that kiss from me yesterday." Al's voice was low and sexy.

Without letting go of Elena's chin, she leaned in and gently brushed Elena's cheek with her own. "You smell like vanilla…and citrus," Al whispered in her ear.

Elena wasn't sure she was going to be able to stand much longer. Her stomach was swirling, and her legs were weak. "You smell like leather," she whispered back. "And danger."

Al slid one hand behind Elena's waist and pulled her closer, while letting go of her chin to slide the other hand behind Elena's head. Heat radiated from her body. "Do I have your permission to kiss you, Elena? Or do we need to talk about it first?"

Elena's heart literally stopped beating and the room started spinning. Elena shook her head.

"No, I do not have permission to kiss you? Or no, we do not need to talk first?" Al's eyes sparkled and one corner of her mouth rose higher.

"I definitely do not want to be talking right now." Elena managed to choke out the words.

And that was that. Al bent down until their lips met. They were warm and soft and made Elena tingly all over, in all the best ways. Elena put her arms around Al's waist and moved her hips closer. They had been on this path since the day they met, in the middle of her street, beside a giant, mysterious, annoying hole. But too many things had distracted her from what she saw when she looked at Al through her camera, or when she watched Al at work, or every single time Al came to her rescue.

Why had she fought so hard not to see what everyone else seemed to see, including her own grandmother?

She's one of the good ones, Elena.

That was true. Elena could see that. She could from the beginning. Al was good. Reliable. Strong. Al would be there, no matter what Elena got herself into.

But the Al she wanted right in that moment wasn't good. Elena hoped she could also be just a little bad.

She wanted Al with every tingling inch of her body, and she wanted her now. When Al parted her lips with her tongue, Elena answered her, sparring with a ferocity that intensified everything that was happening, deep in her core.

She moved against Al with just enough force to push her against the door. Then she thrust her hands up under Al's jacket, to her shoulders, lifting and dropping the jacket to the floor. Al's kisses burned Elena's lips, as her hands dropped to Elena's hips, drawing her even closer. Flames leaped between them and Elena slid her hands under the bottom of Al's cropped tee, needing desperately to feel skin upon skin. Al's abs tightened under Elena's touch, spring-loaded, ready to discharge. Taking control, Al flipped them around, so that now Elena's back was pressed against the door, and Al's hips were hard against her. There were no words between them, just passion, which had been building for months, finally unleashed.

Elena pulled Al's T-shirt up over her head, exposing hardened nipples, and she knew she needed to have them in her mouth. She moaned as she clamped hot lips down around them, circling them with her tongue, feeling them grow even harder. Al sucked in her breath as Elena nibbled softly, and she grabbed the back of her head as the nibbles got a little harder. Al's willingness to be undressed, to let Elena take her in her mouth, was surprising. And intoxicating.

But it ended without warning. Al pulled away and bent down to scoop Elena off her feet. The mirror on a far wall gave Elena a glimpse of what was happening. Al in low, dropped cargo pants, Timbs on her feet, naked from the waist up, muscles rippling across her back and arms, holding Elena in her arms, as if she weighed no more than a large duffel bag. Elena remembered the way Al swung that chainsaw around like it was nothing. She could probably have carried equipment heavier than Elena up five flights of stairs.

In that moment, Elena would have gone wherever Al wanted to take her.

Al carried her across the room, lowered her gently onto the worn leather sofa, and lay on top of her, smashing her lips into Elena's until they found a rhythm that matched the soulful music. Slow, lingering kisses followed an insatiable need for more, as they explored each other with hungry, searching tongues.

Al lifted her up to help ease her out of her shirt. Her hands were rugged. Not rough, but strong, and they lit Elena's bare stomach on fire. Al reached behind her and, with one hand, set Elena free from her bra, tossing it on the floor without leaving Elena's lips even for a second.

Elena had never been with someone who had such physical control. The women Elena typically dated lived in their heads. Their bodies, no matter how beautiful Elena thought they were, were always problematic. They complained about how they were too big or too small or had the wrong proportions. They spent endless resources trying to reshape them, through fad diets, cosmetic surgery. But regardless of how much time and money they spent, they were never actually in control of their bodies. Their bodies, and all the insecurities they carried, controlled them. Elena would quickly learn what not to touch, where not to explore, what not to say, where not to look. It made sex tricky. It made Elena feel anxious. It made it all a lot less fun. And it created a barrier between them that Elena could never figure out how to overcome.

Al moved with such certainty and confidence. She didn't hesitate when Elena stripped off her shirt, or took her nipples in her mouth. She appeared to lack any self-consciousness about how she looked. All that seemed to matter was that what she was doing felt good, and that Elena felt good, too.

Al's hand was cupping Elena's breast, but she stopped kissing her so that she could look Elena in the eye, maybe sensing that Elena's mind was spinning as hard as her body was responding. "Are you doing okay?"

Elena laughed softly. "No."

Concern filled Al's eyes and she quickly pulled her hand away. "No? What's wrong? What can I do?"

Elena reached for Al's hand and put it back on her breast. "Nothing's wrong. You asked if I was okay. And I'm not. I'm on fire. You feel amazing."

Al squeezed Elena's breast and kissed her on the lips. "And here I thought I was the funny one."

"I can be funny, too."

Al smiled back. "I never know what to expect with you, Elena."

Elena opened her eyes wide. "What does that mean?"

Al used a finger to gently trace the shape of Elena's nose. "You're so feisty. Sometimes I think you're ready to jump in the ring with me."

"Like when you scold me in front of your crew?"

Al laughed softly. "Like that. Then, sometimes you're so patient. You pay attention to who people are and what they need. You make them feel seen. Like at the photo shoot."

"And?"

"And sometimes you're fainting in my arms."

Elena tilted her head back and looked at the ceiling. Al wasn't wrong.

"Does it make you crazy?"

"Sometimes."

Elena looked back at Al, whose eyes were full of kindness and warmth.

"But I know you love a challenge."

Al nodded. "Yes, I do. And I have never had a more beautiful one."

Al paused, as if considering what words to say next.

"Elena—I want you."

"Then, take me."

Al kicked off her boots, and got into a position to make it easier for her to lift Elena up and pull off her pants. That left her wearing just a thong. Al's eyes made their way slowly up and down the length of Elena's body with such intensity that she tingled everywhere Al's eyes touched her.

"You look hungry."

Al nodded slowly. "I am famished."

Elena reached over to the coffee table for a grape, and Al grabbed her wrist. Then she pulled Elena's hand toward her and sucked the grape and Elena's fingers into her mouth, setting off an explosion that started at Elena's belly button and blasted down through her center. With her eyes locked on Elena's, Al licked Elena's fingers while slowly chewing on the grape.

"I want to taste you."

Elena's breath hitched in her throat, and she raised her hips, letting Al know she wanted that too. Al used the opportunity to peel off the last remaining bit of clothing Elena was wearing, dropping her panties onto the floor.

"Take off your pants," Elena groaned. "I want to feel you against me."

Al stood up and did as requested, dropping her cargo pants to the floor. Dark red, silk hip huggers skimmed the bottom of Al's taut stomach, making it look like her muscular legs went on forever. Elena licked her lips, anticipating Al settling back down on top of her. Instead, Al reached for her hand, and pulled her up off the couch. She grabbed a blanket that was draped over the back of the chair, and spread it on the floor. Then she lay down and reached up for Elena, pulling her down on top of her.

"I thought you wanted to taste me."

"Oh, I do. And I will."

But first Al pulled Elena's lips to hers and kissed her deeply. Their lips parted and their tongues found each other again, softly at first, then darting playfully, and finally diving deeper as their desire heightened. Al tugged Elena's hair, gently pulling her head back to expose her neck. Her breath was warm on the side of Elena's neck as she looked for and found the tender spot just beneath Elena's ear. Elena's pulse quickened as Al gently bit her neck, shooting heat missiles through Elena's core.

"Oh my God, Al. I don't know how much more of this I can take," Elena gasped.

"That sounds like a good thing," Al said wickedly.

"It is," Elena moaned. "It's also a lot like our relationship."

"Our relationship?" Al stopped kissing and looked at her.

"You know, this thing we do. Where we start to get close, and then something happens or one of us says something that drives us apart."

"Like magnets with similar polarities, pushing each other away."

"That's very science-y of you." Elena laughed. "You think we're too similar?"

"I mean, maybe. We are alike in some ways."

"Like how, exactly?" Elena tried to think of a single thing.

"Our closets look alike."

"Okay. I can picture that, actually."

"We both like your grandmother."

Elena laughed. "She thinks you're the cat's meow."

"The what?"

"Nothing. What else? How are we alike in some way that matters?"

Al squinted and looked off in the distance, thinking. "Well, I think we're both sort of outsiders. You know?"

Elena opened her eyes wide. "Al Jones? An outsider?"

"In a way, yes. I've figured out how to manage it, over the years. How to be a chameleon, adapt to whatever situation I'm in. I don't hate it. I mean, I think it's made me a better person. But I've never been anywhere long enough to have roots. And...just *look* at me. I don't fit easily into any category that exists out there right now."

Elena nodded slowly. "And me?"

Al shrugged. "You tell me...ghost whisperer."

Elena laughed softly. "Okay. Fine. So you think that's why we've been doing this dance? Because we're too much alike?"

Al shrugged again. "I don't know. But I'll tell you what. It's been fun. I think I knew from the moment you tried to run me over that we would end up here."

"I did not try to run you over," Elena exclaimed.

Al laughed and traced the edges of Elena's face with her finger. "You are beautiful when you get all excited."

"I would like to be a little more excited, to be honest. Did anyone ever tell you that you talk a lot?"

"Maybe." Al raised her eyebrows. "I have an idea."

"Tell me."

"I think we should move this party to your bed."

"I like that idea."

Al rolled Elena off of her, hopped up, and reached for her hand. "Lead the way."

She blew out the candles, picked up their clothes, and followed Elena into the bedroom.

"This looks familiar." Al grinned, looking at the bed. "Come here."

She lay down and pulled Elena next to her.

"Can we do less talking now?" Elena pleaded.

Al just smiled and lifted Elena on top of her. "I like the way you feel here."

She squeezed and caressed Elena's ass, and then ran her hands up her back and down again, sending shock waves throughout Elena's body. Elena straddled one of Al's legs and started to grind against her hip bone as Al kissed and sucked on her neck. Al put her hands on Elena's waist and held her tight as Elena moved against her, finding a rhythm that made Elena want to explode.

"Uh-uh," Al commanded. "Not yet. I want you up here."

She pushed Elena upright, and then grabbed her hips, lifting her up and pulling her forward, until Elena was straddling Al's face.

"Right here, Elena. I want you to look at me as I lick you. I want you to see how this is making me feel."

Elena's body ached with the need for release. So there was no argument. She would have stood on her head if it meant that Al would finally finish her off.

Elena leaned forward against the headboard, keeping her eyes on Al's face below her.

Then Al gently parted Elena's lips with her fingers and began a delicate dance with her tongue, finding Elena's heat and wetness. Elena rocked with the rhythm of Al's tongue, which probed deep into Elena's folds, sliding along her opening and teasing her clit. A deep moan slipped from Elena's throat. "Please, Al. Don't stop."

Al's eyes never strayed from Elena's as she slid a finger deep inside her. Tongue and finger worked together, creating an irresistible pleasure, bringing Elena right to the edge. Then, Elena closed her eyes and let herself go. She groaned loudly as Al took her over the top.

Elena rode wave after wave as Al kissed and licked her, intensifying her orgasm until Elena thought it might never stop. When she was finally done, Al helped her down, and Elena lay tucked inside of Al's arms.

She had never felt more safe.

❖

A tiny, rough tongue and a loud purr directly in Al's ear woke her up. She was on her back with Elena in her arms. With her free hand, she reached up and scratched the top of Casper's head. He responded by head-butting Al's hand for more, but Casper was going to have to be satisfied with what he got. As if sensing that, the cat jumped off the bed with a whiny meow and a thud.

Al shifted her position, jostling Elena as little as possible, so that she could check the time on her watch. It was a little after midnight.

She had not meant to fall asleep.

And she certainly had no intention of staying the night.

But she resisted the impulse to roll away, grab her clothes, and slip out the front door.

It felt good to have Elena, with one arm draped over her waist, tucked up against her.

Really good.

Al was a first responder. Rescuing people was what she was trained to do. And she excelled at the job. There were few things that gave her more pleasure or made her feel more alive than being able to do that job. That rescuing impulse had gotten her into relationship trouble more often than not, though. She loved coming to the aid of a damsel in distress as much as the next knight in shining armor. But she wanted that damsel to be able to swing a sword, too, if she had to.

Over the past six months, Elena had proven that she was both soft and fierce, occasionally in need of rescuing but also strong enough to stand her ground.

Al closed her eyes and gently squeezed Elena's shoulder. Elena's breath was steady, and she was dead weight, asleep. Totally at peace inside Al's embrace.

Al was built to move. To ride. To run. To chase. To win. She had been doing it for as long as she could remember.

But the weight of Elena's body, and the sense that she was where she belonged, kept her from bolting. Al took a long, slow, deep breath, and let herself feel grounded. Her legs and arms and torso became heavy, and she relaxed deeply into the bed, feeling the strength and support of the earth beneath her.

Somehow, holding Elena made Al feel held.

Al opened her eyes and looked around the dimly lit room. Several of Elena's framed photographs hung on the walls, as well as a painting of Venice Beach that looked both contemporary and like it could have been fifty years old. The furnishings, including a long, low dresser and nightstands, were sleek and modern. They were probably new back in the fifties or sixties and were now antiques that would cost a fortune to replace, if you could even find them. No doubt they had come with the house. It had belonged to Elena's grandparents. But it felt very much like Elena, too, whose asymmetrical, color-blocked style was as classic as the furniture. The then and the now embraced each other in Elena's house. It was solid without being suffocating.

It could not have been more different than the sterile apartment and blank walls Al lived with.

Elena stirred in Al's arms, and let out a little moan. "You feel good."

Al kissed the top of Elena's head. "You do, too."

"What time is it?"

"Just after midnight."

Elena didn't move.

"I should probably get going," Al said. But she didn't make a move.

Underneath the blanket, Elena ran her hand up Al's belly, between her breasts, and back down again, resting right above Al's hips. Al's heart began beating faster, and everything below her hips began tingling again, as Elena's fingers teased lower. Al shifted, lifting her ass slightly, inviting Elena to explore further, which she seemed more than eager to do.

"You're not going to let me leave, are you?"

Elena shook her head. "I think we have some unfinished business."

Then she took Al's nipple in her mouth and slipped her fingers inside of Al's silk hip huggers. "These need to go."

Al lifted her ass and slipped them off as Elena continued exploring. Al moaned and rose to meet Elena's fingers as they slid open her lips, searching for Al's swollen clit. She let Elena circle it and felt herself open. It would have been fast and easy to come. But she didn't want to do this alone. She grabbed Elena's hand and stopped her.

Elena looked up, confused. "What's wrong?"

"I'm assuming your unicorn is all charged up?"

A smile stretched slowly across Elena's face as Al reached over to open the nightstand drawer. "And I'm assuming it's in here?"

Al pulled out the rainbow-colored unicorn and handed it to Elena. "I would love for you to show me what you like."

Elena took the vibrator and looked up, searching Al's eyes. "You want me to show you what I like?"

Al traced a line of freckles across her nose. "I do."

"I'm not sure about this."

"Remember when you told me that you don't take dares?"

Elena nodded.

"I believe you. But I've also seen you in action. Running toward that fire to get the shots you wanted. Diving into that mine to get the answers you needed."

Elena grinned. "Almost running you over with my car."

Al grinned back. "I thought you said you weren't trying to run me over."

Elena shrugged playfully.

"My point is, which Elena Murphy are you really? The one who says she doesn't take dares…or the one who dares to take what she wants?"

Elena paused, considering her answer, finally raising one eyebrow. "Yes."

And that is what made Elena Murphy so impossible to shake. She was all the things. The only predictable thing about her was how unpredictable she could be. If the creases in Al's clothing revealed a need to control every situation, in Elena's clothes they were fault lines that, at any moment, might shift, exposing another unexpected side of her, opening new depths.

Before Al knew what was happening, Elena was on top of her. She grabbed Al's hands, pinned them to the bed, and kissed her hard. Al's body responded all on its own, electricity rushing through her, insatiable need thrusting her pelvis upward.

"You are making me very wet."

"That's the plan," Elena said, her breath hot against Al's neck.

She released Al's hands, pushing herself up and reaching into the drawer for lube. Then she positioned herself between Al's legs, spreading them wide. She took her time applying lube up and down the dildo, and Al squirmed, eager for whatever Elena was planning, the need for release building within her. Once the toy was ready, Elena teased her own opening with it as Al watched, and slid her wet finger up and down Al's slit, digging deeper to tease Al's pulsing clit.

Al pushed her head back into the pillow and moaned softly.

Once Elena clicked on the toy and it began vibrating gently, she made an unexpected switch, pressing the tip of the toy firmly against Al's center. Al hesitated for a second—this was uncharted territory. But Elena was in charge now. Al had put her in command. And Elena had taken it.

Al pulled her knees up to give herself more leverage, feeling the toy hard and huge against her opening. Even without being inside her, the vibrations were making her swell almost to the point of no return. Finally, she couldn't take one more minute. She pushed hard against the toy and Elena drove it inside her, bringing every cell in her body to life.

"This isn't what I was imagining," Al gasped, clutching at the sheets, "when I told you to show me what you like."

Elena grinned wickedly and clicked the toy into a higher speed. "I have wanted to fuck you since the moment you marched into this house the first time, giving me orders."

Seeing Elena so completely in control, and so turned on doing it, was more than Al could take. She grabbed Elena's hips and lifted her from between her legs, bringing her down onto Al's leg, so that Elena was straddling it. "Kiss me while you fuck me," she commanded, pulling Elena's face toward her own.

Elena's tongue opened Al's lips as the toy opened her body, filling her. Al shoved a hand beneath Elena and slid inside of her, feeling her silky wetness coating her fingers.

As they kissed, Al thrust against the toy inside her, and Elena rode Al's fingers. Somehow, as if they had finally learned something from sparring and dancing together over all those months, they found a perfect rhythm. And when Elena found her release, for the second time that night, it took Al over the edge.

"You are something else Ms. Murphy," Al said as Elena set the toy on the nightstand and rolled off of her before tucking herself back inside of Al's arms.

"I told you, you can call me Elena," she teased her.

"I'd like to also be able to call you day or night—or whenever I want to do that again."

"It was good, huh?"

"Oh my God."

Elena propped herself up on one elbow. "I'd be okay with that."

"You mean, if I called you?"

"Yes. In fact, I think you should. Call me."

Al smiled. "I will absolutely do that."

Elena lay back down, her head on Al's chest, and Al held her, feeling grounded. Satisfied in a way she knew was different but didn't have words for. Elena was very still but not sleeping.

"You're thinking very loudly," Al said a little teasingly.

"Am I?"

"You are."

"I was just wondering…was that new for you?" Elena's voice was as soft as her skin. "The toy."

"It was."

"And what do you think?"

"I think that my previous thinking about what feels good has been way too limited."

Elena propped herself up again and looked at Al. "You really are a daredevil, aren't you?"

Al liked the way she looked in Elena's eyes.

"Is there anything you *are* afraid of?" Elena asked, stroking the skin between Al's breasts, right above Al's heart.

Al sighed. There were too many things to list. Failure. Rejection. Boredom.

"No," Al said.

Then Al laughed. And Elena joined her. No one sane was afraid of nothing.

Elena lay back down. "You know what I'm afraid of?"

"What are you afraid of, Elena?" Al gave her a gentle squeeze.

"I'm afraid that tomorrow I'll wake up and it will be like this never happened."

Al closed her eyes. She didn't want to think about tomorrow. "I'll remind you."

Elena got up to go to the bathroom while Al got dressed. Casper reemerged and head-butted her until she scratched his head.

"He likes you," Elena said, coming back into the room, wrapped in a cozy robe. Her eyes were soft. "I do, too."

Al didn't stand up. She just sat on the bed thinking about how much she really didn't want to leave. Which was totally weird. She dated Maria for two years and could count the number of times she had stayed the night on one, maybe two hands.

Finally, she got up.

"So...I'll call you."

Elena put her arms around Al's neck and pulled her close for a kiss.

In her ear, Elena whispered, "I'm counting on it."

CHAPTER THIRTEEN

Al called first thing Sunday morning, before Elena's feet even hit the floor.

"Did I wake you?"

Elena rolled over onto her back, cradling the phone against her ear, so she could keep petting Casper, who seemed especially needy after having been exiled from the bed until after Al was gone.

"Not exactly. Casper woke me up about an hour ago. But I haven't gotten out of bed yet." Elena paused. "Someone kept me up past my bedtime last night."

"Should I be sorry?"

"Absolutely not."

She could feel Al smiling through the phone.

"So, today is pretty booked for me. I'm meeting my mother for lunch in Tucson, and Dana invited me to have dinner with her family tonight. It's her grandson's birthday."

"That sounds like a fun day." Elena tried to hide her disappointment. She would have liked nothing more than to have spent a lazy Sunday together.

"How about having dinner with me tomorrow night? My place. I'll cook."

"You cook?"

"I had to learn quick at my first post. We were all on a rotation and, if you sucked at it, the guys at the house could make your life miserable."

Elena strained, trying to imagine Al as a new recruit and not in charge of anything.

"I would love to have dinner at your place. And tomorrow night works great. I'm looking forward to eating like a firefighter."

"I'm resisting making a crude joke right now."

"Thank you."

Al laughed. "You're no fun."

"That's not what you said last night."

Al's humor made Elena roll her eyes sometimes. But she loved the banter, even if she hated to admit it.

Al said she would text the address, told her she could bring a bottle of wine if she wanted to, and dared her to get through the next thirty-six hours without thinking about her.

Like that was going to happen.

She spent the day in the darkroom, had dinner with her family, and tossed and turned that night until she finally gave in and fired up the unicorn. Her dreams were filled with images of Al.

It was a relief when the yellow warblers that lived in the brush up on the hillside started singing.

On Monday morning, the phone started buzzing before her eyes were even open.

"Are you always such an early riser?"

"Good morning to you, too, Elena."

Elena stretched. "Hi."

"Bad night?"

"Let's just say someone kept me up too late, two nights in a row."

Al paused. "I dreamt about you, too. I'm looking forward to tonight."

Elena sighed. It was going to be another long day.

"What does your day look like?"

Elena turned onto her side and propped herself up on her elbow. "I'm meeting up with Knox to look at possible locations for my gallery."

"I only think about Knox as owning Banter & Brew," Al said. "I always forget that he's everybody's favorite Realtor."

"That's because you haven't started looking at houses to buy yet."

There was a pause on the other end and Elena heard what sounded like a drumming sound, like Al was tapping the table in front of her. "Not sure I'm the buying type. But it does sound like we'll have a lot to talk about tonight."

"I can't wait."

Al didn't bother daring her to get through the day without thinking about her. She had to know that was impossible.

There were several texts waiting for her when she got out of the shower. Her brothers whining about having to make a pickup that morning. Knox confirming their ten o'clock at Banter & Brew, so Elena could grab a coffee before they headed out to look at property. And one from Al.

Don't forget to come hungry tonight.

Oh, there was no problem there.

Elena responded with a devil emoji.

She pushed open the door to Banter & Brew at exactly nine fifty-nine. Knox greeted her with a latte, skim milk.

"You know me so well."

Owen Station was finally starting to feel like home.

Knox grinned. "Give me a minute to handle one last detail in the kitchen. Then we can head out. I've got three spaces to show you, if you're up for it. I'm thinking we start with one that's available right around the corner, and we can go from there."

It was less than a minute, so Elena took her coffee to go.

"We can walk there," Knox said, pushing open the door and letting Elena go ahead of him, out to the street. "I want you to see the space in the old Miners Bank building. I love the light."

It was only a few doors down and across the street, next to the library. Knox grabbed the lockbox, clicked it open, found the key, and opened the large glass doors. Elena's eyes were immediately drawn upward by the high ceilings. She felt overwhelmed, but not just because the space was so enormous.

She was actually taking the first step toward having her own gallery. Here. In her hometown.

"I think it would be fairly easy to diffuse the light, to protect the artwork, without sacrificing natural light," Knox offered. "I also love these original counters, and the mill work everywhere. The molding and trim, especially. They don't make things like this anymore. It's too hard to get timber, let alone find the craftspeople to pull it off."

"I love the idea of repurposing whatever we can, plus people love that. And you're right. This space is stunning."

"Check out this old vault." Knox led her deeper into the space. "I'm picturing special exhibits in here. And come see the bathrooms. Marble floors and counters. Even the urinals are marble."

"I love this, Knox. I think this space alone would be a draw, before I even have anything on the walls."

He nodded. "Are you thinking you would want to make any significant changes to the outside of the building?"

Elena shook her head. "The more I can help preserve the original architecture, the better."

"Good. That will make permitting a lot easier." He paused and smiled. "Are you ready to sign?"

Elena laughed. "Not so fast, my friend. What's next on the list?"

"I want to take you through a building in the old downtown. Let's go grab my truck."

Ten minutes later, they were parking in the middle of what used to be a completely abandoned stretch of four blocks. After the mines closed down, downtown emptied overnight, as if someone pulled a plug and everything went swirling down the drain. It happened more than a decade before Elena was even born. It would still be that way if it weren't for Hazel's fiancée, Sena. Sena's family had deep roots in the area, but she was new to town. She had come with a vision for turning the abandoned downtown into a tech park, where women innovators and entrepreneurs, in particular, could have the support they needed to thrive.

"I want you to see the old city hall. You wouldn't have the whole building, just a space within it," Knox said as they got out of his truck. "After a water main break, the building was flooded, but they've worked to restore it using as much original material as possible. They pulled all the woodwork from a demolition in Tombstone."

Knox led her through the front doors, past a small rotunda at the center of the building, to an intimate space with high ceilings. "This is quite a bit smaller than what you just looked at, but I think you could use the rotunda for special shows. You could set up a bar out there, and even have room for a band."

"I like the idea of a flexible space, that can expand or contract as I need it—I'm assuming that would also lower the cost."

Knox nodded. "One of the other upsides here is that this part of town will have lots of full-time residents before too long, versus the tourists who stream up and down Main Street. The people living here will be designing their spaces, and some of them will have money to spend. Lots of interesting things are going to be happening over here, including maybe a second location for Banter & Brew."

"That's exciting." Elena looked around. "Natural light. Flexibility. Proximity to clients. I like it. I also love that it has a historic vibe, but it's got a kind of edginess to it, too."

"How many businesses are in this building now?"

"It's about half full. Sena tells me there is a yoga studio moving in at the end of the hall next week, and a new ice cream shop. She expects the building to be eighty percent occupied by the beginning of next year."

"That feels like a long way away."

Knox smiled. "It's just six months. But it sounds like you want to move quicker than that?"

"I do. Once I made up my mind that I'm really going to do this, put my roots down as deep as they can go here in Owen Station, I feel pretty eager to get moving."

"Do you want to see another space? Or is this the one?" Knox glanced at his phone, which had been buzzing for the past minute, and then looked back at Elena. "We could go over to the old YWCA building. Sena is already working miracles over there. Again, this would be a totally different space from the two you've seen. But it would give you an idea of what's available."

"Let's do it."

They circled back toward Banter & Brew. The old Y was a few blocks off Main Street, in the opposite direction of the bank building. "This was one of Sena's first projects," Knox explained while driving. "It was built to house women who came looking for work in Owen Station back in the early nineteen hundreds. The Y sold it to the town, shortly after the mines closed. They couldn't afford it. But the city couldn't, either. It was condemned decades ago and has just been sitting here, rotting. Sena worked with a committee made up of some of the old Y ladies, who are still around, to preserve as much of the building as possible. Now it's a high-tech apartment building, designed to cater to women entrepreneurs."

"I know a little about the history of the YWCA. It sounds like Sena is taking a page right out of their book."

Knox nodded. "What Sena is doing hasn't been without controversy. It's hard to do this kind of development without stepping on toes. But honestly, the economy hasn't been this good since the mines were here. For the first time in decades, there are jobs—real jobs—in this town. Sena is committed to hiring local and supporting local businesses, and she's lobbying town leaders into creating policies that will support and protect affordable housing. Plus, all of these old buildings are being given new life."

Elena was stunned when she entered the large lobby. Although the building retained much of its original Art Deco exterior, the inside featured a multi-story opening, and the whole first floor was dedicated to public space. The original windows allowed lots of natural light, illuminating a sleek metal and glass interior structure. Modern leather sofas encouraged you to sit and hang out. There was a coffee bar, a concierge desk, and co-working spaces.

"What do you think? Pretty great right?"

Elena nodded, looking around, trying to take it all it. "It is. But I'm a little confused. I don't see anything that looks like gallery space. Or any retail space, for that matter."

"This space is a technological wonder."

Elena turned around to see Sena walking toward them. "State-of-the art." She hugged Elena and Knox, giving each a kiss on the cheek. "I have women calling me about bringing their tech start-up to Owen Station, just because they want to live in this building."

"I'm not surprised. It's stunning."

"Elena is wondering about how a gallery might work in this space, Sena."

"However you want it to. We'll print 3D walls, either permanent or temporary, whatever height and width you want them, and put them wherever you want. But you don't need to be limited by actual, physical walls. We have the technology to *project* your work— onto anything. Imagine a wall of fiber or silk. You could project holograms of your photos, too. Or use them to create 3D sculptures. The space is fully equipped with high-tech sound and lighting, too. The only limit to what you could do is your imagination."

Elena wasn't even sure what to say. "I've never seen anything like this, Sena. And I've never even considered projects like these. I actually still have a dark room." She shrugged apologetically.

"Old-school, huh?" Sena smiled. "I can appreciate that. But think about how you could combine the old and the new. For example, you could create a show that projects video of you *in* your darkroom, so people can literally join you inside the process. All kinds of things are possible here. You could put Owen Station on the map, as being a place where technology intersects art."

Elena could not wait to tell Al about everything she had seen and everything she was thinking, and she was buzzing with excitement when she got to Al's apartment that evening.

She pulled up in front of the house about ten minutes late. A stop at the Mujer Fuerte tasting room to pick up a bottle of wine took at little longer than she expected. Which was silly. Tessa and Lace were both there and wanted to hear all about her day with Knox... and her night with Al.

Everybody knew everything about everyone. When Elena was growing up, it was one of the things she hated about living there. But there was something settling about feeling so known, and so cared about. Especially after everything she had been through.

Both Lace and Tessa owned their own businesses, and they promised to be there for Elena as she took these next big steps, to help in whatever way they could. And they encouraged her to see where things went with Al.

That's what friends did. That's what a community looked like.

Elena never imagined those things would be hers, back in her Wednesday Addams days.

She climbed the stairs to reach Al's apartment on the second floor of the house, and she was grinning when Al opened the door.

"You look amazing." Al grinned back.

"You do, too." Al's jean overalls were rolled up to just above her vintage Doc Martins, and she was wearing a tight fitting cropped tank top underneath.

Al bent over so Elena could kiss her. She tasted like spearmint, and the kiss wasn't nearly long enough.

"I hope there is more where that came from." Elena handed her a bottle of rosé. "I stopped by the tasting room on my way over. Tessa said this should go with anything you're serving."

"Let's get some in a glass." Al led her down a narrow hallway into the kitchen, grabbed two glasses, opened the bottle, and poured for both of them.

Al raised her glass. "Cheers."

"To new opportunities."

"It was that good today, huh?" Al asked.

"I'm not even sure where to start."

"How about if I start by giving you a tour of my apartment?"

"I would love that."

"Okay. This is the kitchen." Al laughed.

"I like it. The cabinets look like they could survive the apocalypse. And I love the floors. They're original, I'm guessing?"

Al nodded. "Pine. All through the whole apartment."

"Anything in here you're especially proud of? Your mother's pots and pans? A coffee mug collection?" Elena looked around expectedly. Everybody had something in their kitchen that meant something to them.

"No. Not really."

"Come on," Elena said disbelievingly. "Nothing?"

Al shrugged. "Nothing in here is mine. It came with the apartment."

Elena took a second look around. She hadn't noticed at first. Everything was nice. Hotel suite nice. But impersonal. There wasn't even an inspirational magnet on the fridge.

"Wow. Okay. That must have made it easy to move."

"Exactly. Come on, let me show you the rest."

Al took her by the hand. "This is the hallway," she said, moving quickly through it, waving into each room as they passed by. "That's the living room. This is the bathroom. Nice claw foot tub in there. This is the spare room. I use it for my workout equipment. And this—" She stepped into the doorway and turned to face Elena. "This is my bedroom. Would you like to see it?"

Elena raised an eyebrow. "You did tell me I should come hungry."

"And are you?"

"I don't think I can hold on one second longer."

Al took her by the waist and pulled her in, covering her lips, her neck, her nose with kisses. She had both their clothes off within minutes. They fell onto the bed together, embracing, tongues entwined, greedily exploring each other's bodies. Elena was intoxicated by the feel and the sight and the smell of Al's body.

"I don't know why it took so long for us to do this," she said breathlessly.

Al was sucking on one nipple and kneading the other, but she paused to look up at Elena. "You were intimidated by my awesomeness?"

Elena laughed. "That's gotta be it."

Al kept sucking while she slipped a hand down Elena's belly, where her fingers began to wander.

"I think it's because you're so not my type. And it took me a minute to get past that."

Al released her nipple but didn't look up. "I'm everyone's type."

Then she shifted to the other breast and started sucking and licking again.

Elena grinned. "I see your point."

Al's fingers stopped moving and she looked up. "What is your type?"

"Oh, you know. Lawyers. Investors. Cerebral types."

"Are you saying I'm not smart?"

"No." Elena squeezed her shoulder.

Al went back to sucking, and her fingers resumed their roundabout path to Elena's very ready, very hot center.

"I'm saying that, in the past, I've mainly been with women who are all up in their heads. Pretty focused on themselves. Chasing things that don't matter."

"Shallow?" Al's voice was a little muffled because it was full of Elena's breast.

"And self-centered."

Al's fingers found their way to Elena's opening and, with expert precision, slipped right in. Elena shuddered and her pelvis jerked upward. Al moaned her appreciation and used Elena's reaction as an excuse to slide down between her legs. With her fingers still inside, Al used her tongue to split open Elena's lips. Elena grabbed the top of Al's head, pulling her closer. She drew her knees up and spread her legs even wider.

"You are dripping," Al murmured as she slid one more finger inside. Then she withdrew them and looked at Elena as she licked them, slowly, one at a time.

"You are killing me, Al."

"Okay, let me put you out of your misery." She slipped a finger back inside and began rocking it, as she circled Elena's pulsing clit, sucking and licking until Elena threw her head back and screamed.

"Come up here," Elena said, as soon as she was able. She pulled on Al's shoulders, urging her to lie on top of her, straddling her leg.

Al pressed one knee up against Elena's pussy, creating another soft wave to crest within her. Then Elena slid her hand in between Al's legs and quickly found what she was looking for. Al buried her face in Elena's neck, kissing and sucking, as Elena used her fingers to create a rhythm that made Al's body tense. She pressed her hips harder against Elena, and Elena moved faster and harder until Al's breath caught in her throat and Al grew still.

She lay there on top of Elena for a while, and her breath was warm against Elena's neck. Elena wrapped her arms around her. And Al let her.

Elena looked around Al's bedroom. A few personal items sat on the dresser. Al's badge. Her wallet. Lip balm. Otherwise, everything looked like it could belong to anyone. The walls were bare. No artwork. No family photos. Nothing. The space wasn't just organized and neat. Elena had expected that.

The space was barren.

Al was a protector. A rescuer. But she was also human. And from the way it appeared, a human adrift in the universe. Alone.

Al shifted to get more comfortable but didn't seem in a hurry to get up. And the longer she lay there, with Al in her arms, the more Elena's heart opened.

Finally, Al rolled over onto her side. "Are you still hungry? For dinner this time?"

"Famished." Elena smiled.

Al kissed her on the lips, jumped out of bed, and held out her hand for Elena to grab. "Let's go."

They quickly washed up, put their clothes back on, and headed to the kitchen. Al pointed to a stool at the island, and Elena sat down.

"Can I top off your glass?" Al said, already pouring. "I have everything prepped. I just need about fifteen minutes to pull it all together. Mind if I do that while we talk?"

"Not at all. I'm excited to watch you work. What's for dinner?"

Elena hadn't known what to expect. A big pot of chili, maybe? That sounded like a firefighter meal. Or maybe fish and chips, something her grandmother would have made.

"Well, we're going to start with a caprese salad. I've got some farmer's market tomatoes, fresh mozzarella from the co-op, and basil I clipped from one of the plants they have growing at the firehouse."

"My mouth is watering."

"We'll follow that with my famous chicken piccata, with a lemon pasta. And roasted asparagus on the side."

Elena shook her head in disbelief. "I'm sorry. You're telling me you learned to cook like this at the firehouse?"

"I might have left out the part where my last girlfriend was a chef."

"Okay, now it's making sense." Elena picked up her glass. She wasn't sure she wanted to go down this road, especially after such wonderful start to the evening. But she did anyway. "How long ago did you break up? If you don't mind me asking."

"Not at all. Two years ago. Right after I accepted the job here in Owen Station."

Elena took that in as she sipped on her wine. And when she didn't respond, Al looked up. "What are you thinking?" Tiny lines appeared between her brows.

Elena slowly shook her head. "Nothing."

Al went back to her cutting board.

But it wasn't nothing. It was something she remembered Al saying, six months ago, at Banter & Brew. About not being able to imagine getting stuck in one place for too long. An alarm bell was ringing somewhere in the back of her mind.

An alarm Elena chose to ignore.

"So, tell me about your day." Al took a sip of wine. "It sounds like you saw some possibilities out there?"

Elena took a breath and forced herself to refocus on the moment. She was in Al's kitchen. Al was making a beautiful meal. She was still feeling the warmth of an incredible orgasm. And she had taken her first step toward opening her own gallery.

How could life get any better?

"What I saw today sort of blew my mind."

Al looked up. "In what way?"

"There are so many good things happening here, Al. When I left ten years ago, I never planned to come back. For all kinds of reasons. But there was nothing to come back to, either. The town had been dying for decades. The tourist industry, as anemic as it was, kept it on life support. But there weren't enough jobs, none that paid well, anyway. Small businesses had a hard time keeping their doors open. My family was even talking about closing the funeral home—after a hundred years. That's how bad things were."

Elena took a breath and another sip. "But it doesn't feel that way anymore. Historic buildings that had been abandoned and ignored are being restored. The old downtown was empty, literally falling apart. A wildfire waiting to happen. Now, those spaces are being transformed into high-tech marvels."

"I met Sena Abrigo at Lace and Tessa's wedding. She's behind it all, right? She is a powerhouse."

"It's not just her. She's working with lots of people in town. And people like me are taking the plunge, opening businesses, everything from yoga studios to tech start-ups. Everybody is making it happen together. But you're right. It wouldn't be happening without Sena."

Al was still cooking, but her head was tilted in Elena's direction. It was clear that she was listening closely.

"I actually think that was the most powerful thing I learned today. That one person can make a big difference in a town like this." The realization came slowly, but when it finally emerged, fully formed, right there at Al's kitchen counter, it made her catch her breath. "I want to be part of what's happening here."

Al stopped moving and her eyes met Elena's.

"That's awesome, Elena. I'm happy for you."

After a beat, she turned toward the fridge and pulled out two chicken breasts. They had already been seasoned, wrapped in plastic, and gently tenderized. So all she had to do was sauté them. Once they were cooked, she removed them from the pan and added lemon juice, chicken broth, and some capers to make the sauce.

The meal was perfection.

Elena gave Al the rundown of the three spaces she had seen, listing the pros and cons of each.

"But you know what I'm most intrigued about? This idea of experimenting with *how* my work is shown. The opportunity to be part of the innovations happening, where art intersects with technology. I've always thought that art makes a difference. It tells a story and has the power to change the way people see things. Like the work I did with the fire department—"

"Those pictures have made a huge difference, Elena. In all kinds of ways—"

"I went to LA because I thought I could make a difference there. But the past several years…I don't know. So much changed. I guess I lost track of what I was doing. Or why I was doing it. I wasn't sure what would happen when I came back. But after today, I feel like things I do here, in Owen Station, could have an impact that goes beyond this town or even this state. Like it could be part of the change happening in the art world. And you know what they say…art changes the world."

Al got up and cleared the dishes, which had been wiped clean by both of them. Then she sat down, topped off their glasses again, and took a sip. "It sounds like you really drank the Owen Station Kool-Aid."

Elena's head snapped back. "What does that mean?"

"I don't know. I guess I just figured that, with all your talent, you'd eventually get tired of this little town. Go someplace where you would have a bigger audience. More opportunity."

Elena sat back and took a deep breath. "You don't always have to run away to find what you think you're looking for, Al."

"What does *that* mean?"

"I don't know. How long have you been here? In this town… in this apartment. Two years? It looks like you just moved in. Or maybe like you're already moving out."

"What's your point?"

"You told me yourself. You can't imagine being *stuck* anywhere for too long."

"Well, I can't. I've never known anything else."

"I get it. I do." Elena reached out and put her hand on Al's. "I get that you got yanked away from your grandparents and the only stable life you had ever known when you were a kid, and then dragged around the country from place to place. I get that you've never really *had* a home." Elena paused, her heart breaking just a little. "But that doesn't mean you can't have one."

"I'm not looking for a home, Elena. I've invested everything in my career. That's what matters to me. Work hard, reach your goals. That's my focus."

"Work hard, reach your goals. That sounds like a bumper sticker, or the tag line for a gym. Not a life."

"Being stuck here forever doesn't sound like much of a life, either."

Elena snatched her hand back as though Al's skin had suddenly caught on fire. "Tell me how you really feel, Al. I'm sure your crew would love to know how stuck you feel here in this shitty little town."

"It's not a shitty town. I didn't mean to make it sound that way. And I do care about my crew. I care about you—" Al paused, maybe as surprised as Elena was to hear her say that. "But I can't imagine being here forever. I've been working my ass off for years to get to this point. And I want to be a chief someday. My goal is to do that before I'm forty."

"Why? Why is that so important to you? Why are you in such a rush?"

"Why is opening a gallery so important to you? It's your purpose, right? It's what you were meant to do. Well, this is my purpose, Elena. Do you know how few women in this country have been fire chiefs? Not nearly enough. And even fewer have been women of color. The fire service is brutal on people like me. The discrimination. The hazing. Most of us drop out before we can even think about getting promoted, if we even make it through the academy. No, I take that back. We don't drop out. We get pushed out. I want to be part of changing what the fire service looks like. I want to be sure that little girls out there have role models so they can see what is possible, so they know that *anything* is possible, if they're willing to work hard enough at it. And I want to change the culture *inside* the service, so that, when those little girls grow up, and show up at the firehouse to report for duty, it's different than the one I first reported to fifteen years ago."

Al sat very still, except for her fingers, which she tapped rhythmically on the table in front of her. Finally, she picked up her wine glass. Looking over the rim at Elena, she searched her face, and then took a long sip of wine. When she put down the glass, Elena could feel that something had shifted in the room.

"I've been talking to a recruiter. They found me online, thanks to the photo you took. Then they did their research."

Elena's stomach dropped. "And?"

"I'm flying to Detroit on Thursday for an interview."

Elena stood up suddenly. "Excuse me. I need the bathroom."

Behind the closed door, Elena sat on the edge of the claw foot tub and put her head in her hands. She focused on breathing.

It was absurd to think that Al would stay in Owen Station even for more than a few years, much less forever. Elena knew that. And she knew she had no right to expect anything. Or ask for anything. They weren't even a couple. If anything, they were more like antagonists, who bantered and battled each other at almost every turn. And they had sex. Twice. Three times if you counted the first time twice. And now they were on a date. Sort of. Their first. If Al wanted to move to Detroit, Elena couldn't stop her. Didn't even know for sure if she wanted to.

She stood up, looked in the mirror, fixed her eye makeup, which had gotten a little smeared from unreleased tears, and straightened her back. Then she went back into the kitchen and sat down.

"Is it the chief's position? That you'll be interviewing for?"

"No. But it would be an important step in that direction."

"Tell me about it."

"It's a new position. They created it after going through an assessment of the department, which was their response to a series of complaints from firefighters. Sexism. Racism. Homophobia. They would be bringing me in to fix all of it. I would still be a deputy fire chief—so the same as I am now. But it's a much bigger department, so it would be like getting a promotion."

Elena closed her eyes for a second, to settle her heart and try to get her voice under control. "I'm happy for you, Al. I really am. That sounds important. And like a great opportunity."

Elena really was happy for her. Al was an inspiring leader. Elena had seen her in action. She saw the way the crew responded to her. She would do amazing things in Detroit, or wherever she ended up.

But the mood inside of Al's kitchen had definitely been broken, and it was clear their date was over. What was the point? It was obvious that wherever Al would end up, it wasn't going to be Owen Station.

And Owen Station was the place Elena called home.

CHAPTER FOURTEEN

Al clicked on the "book now" button. Mum had called early that morning to say she and Al's dad were planning a last-minute overnight to Owen Station, and they would be there by lunchtime.

She tried to convince them not to come.

"Honestly, this isn't a great time, Mum," Al had told her.

She was leaving the next day for her interview in Detroit, flying out of Phoenix first thing in the morning.

"That's fine, honey. We're not really coming to see you."

"That's nice, Mum."

"That's not what I mean, Al. Of course, we want to see you. And we're so looking forward to seeing your apartment. But Dad and I have been talking about taking a quick little romantic getaway, and we've heard Owen Station has some lovely galleries and places to eat. We might even take the Ghost Tour tonight."

"You're taking a romantic getaway?"

Mum snorted softly. "Don't sound so surprised."

"Have you *ever* taken a romantic get-away?"

Dad said something in the background that made Mum giggle. Again, with the giggling.

"So, can you find a nice little rental for us, for the night? We just thought, since you know the area…"

"Yes, I'll book something for you."

"Thank you, sweetie. We'll be there at noon. Text us the address."

Al forwarded the confirmation email for the rental to her mother. Sometimes, it was like she didn't even know her parents anymore.

Her desk was covered with spreadsheets. It was budget time, and she owed the chief a first draft at the end of next week. But it had been hard to concentrate since she agreed to the interview. A month from now, she could be sitting at a new desk, in a new department, in a new city, looking at a whole new set of spreadsheets. And what happened here, to the Owen Station Fire Department, would be somebody else's problem.

She shoved the spreadsheets aside with a sigh.

"I think I need coffee."

Firehouse coffee tasted like sludge, and Al preferred a nice hot tea, but it was better than nothing. And Al could use the extra jolt of caffeine. So she got up from her desk, stretched out her lower back muscles, and headed to the house next door.

No one was around when she pushed through the door, so she headed for the kitchen. As she moved down the hallway, she could hear them before she could see them—and before they could see her.

"There's no way she's leaving us," Bobby was saying. "She's only been here for two years."

Al stopped cold. And listened.

"You've seen all the attention she's getting online. Half the country wants to marry her." Sam sounded angry. "There's no way some department out there isn't going to come hunting."

"She means headhunting," Jess clarified.

"You heard she's taking time off this week, didn't you? She never does that. Two days. That wasn't on the schedule last week. This week, all of a sudden, she's taking two days off?"

"We think she's going for a job interview," Jess added, apparently playing the role of Sam's interpreter.

"No way. The chief loves it here."

"How do you know that, Bobby?"

"I know because she and my mom are best buds. She was at my nephew's birthday party last weekend. She loves playing in the band. You two know that better than anyone. And she loves this department. You see how much she does for us. How hard she's working to bring in great new recruits—Jess, *you're* here because of her—and how committed she is to building a good culture for us."

"It's a whole lot different here than when I was coming up," Bruce interjected. "It was pretty awful, even as a young, white guy. The hazing. The bullying. The macho bullshit. It was like a contest to see who could be the biggest asshole."

"I can't even imagine joining a department like that."

"Me, either, Sam," Bobby said.

"I was pissed when the chief hired her," Bruce said. "A lot of us old guys were. I figured, why didn't that job go to me? Or somebody else who came up through the ranks, right here in Owen Station? But you know what? It was the best decision the chief could have made. He knew that we needed her to come in and do what she's doing. And you know what? It's working. I'm almost gonna miss it when I finally retire next year."

"You're not gonna miss nothing once you have that fishing pole in your hand," Sam joked. And they all laughed.

Al thought about backing down the hallway and sneaking out before they knew she was there. But if they saw her leaving, she'd have a hard time explaining why she had been lurking in the hallway in the first place.

"Hey, isn't anybody working today?" she yelled in a jokey voice, hoping they would think she had just arrived and hadn't been standing outside the kitchen eavesdropping.

It worked.

"We're in here, Chief," Bobby yelled back.

They all greeted her with smiles and fist bumps.

Sam yanked a chair out. "Have a seat."

"Actually, I just came over for a cup of mud. I've got a desk full of spreadsheets that need my attention."

"Spreadsheets, huh? Is that real work?" Sam joked.

Al laughed. "Not half as real as what you guys and gals do every day."

She poured herself a cup, and dumped some powered cream and two heaping spoonfuls of sugar in it. "I think this might counteract the poison."

Bruce looked offended. "Hey now."

"Just kidding, Bruce." Al slapped him on the back. "I know no one has ever actually died drinking this stuff."

She headed back to her desk and pulled the spreadsheets back in front of her. Whether she was sitting in that desk chair next year or not, it mattered that Bobby and Sam and the rest of the crew had the equipment they needed to do their jobs. It mattered that they got paid enough to support themselves and their families. It mattered that there were enough people on the crew, and that they all knew what they were doing, so that no one was put in unnecessary danger. These men and women put their lives on the line every day to protect the people of Owen Station. They mattered.

Three and a half hours later, she realized she hadn't even looked up, and she had less than half an hour before her parents arrived. She cleared her desk and headed to Banter & Brew to grab three grilled cheese sandwiches, with a side of fruit, and a selection of Knox's fresh desserts to go. Her parents pulled up in front of the house at the same time Al did.

"Hi, Mum." She gave her mother a hug.

"What about me?" Her dad held out his arms with a big grin on his face, and Al gave him an awkward hug.

Who *were* these people?

Al led them up the stairs to her apartment and dropped the take-out bag on the kitchen counter.

"Oh my goodness, Al, this is beautiful." Mum wandered from room to room. "I love the floors...and that tub. This house must be...how old?"

"It was built more than a hundred years ago, when the town was growing like crazy because of the mines, and it was always a duplex."

"It's a nice place." Dad was looking out the front window.

"Well, I'm glad you're getting to see it. I'm not sure how much longer I'll be here." Al said that more sharply than she intended. It's not like she had ever even invited her parents to come for a visit.

Dad turned to look at her. "You thinking about buying something in town?"

"I'm thinking about moving."

Mum's eyebrows shot up. "Moving to another apartment?"

"Moving to another state."

Her parents exchanged a glance and then sat down on the couch next to each other. Al took a chair.

"What's going on, Al?" Mum asked.

"Well, you know that silly picture you saw on the internet? I guess it's gotten a lot of attention. A recruiter saw it, did some research on me, and reached out. I'm actually leaving for an interview in the morning."

Mum sat back into the couch. "But, Al. You haven't been here for more than a few years. Don't you like it here?"

That was a good question. One Al hadn't really asked herself before. The answer was yes. She did like it there. But what difference did that make?

"It doesn't really matter if I like it here, does it? This new job would be a great opportunity. It would get me one step closer to making chief."

Al's dad nodded. "I get that. But I can also tell you that moving around all the time isn't exactly the best way to live." He looked at Mum as he took her hand and held it. "There's more to life than running after that next promotion or chasing the next opportunity."

Al's heart started to race and she could hear it beating in her ears. "You know, I thought you two, of all people, would be proud of me."

"Allison, I *am* proud of you."

"You know I would prefer it if you didn't call me that, Dad." Al was really pissed now. "Excuse me. Lunch is on the kitchen counter. Help yourself. But I need to get some air."

Al's dad jumped up out of the couch and grabbed her by the elbow. "Alli—" He dropped her elbow and stood perfectly still.

"Al. Please don't go."

Al turned around to face him.

"I *am* proud of you, Al. I always have been. You don't have anything to prove to me, or to anyone. But I do worry about you. The way you jump from one position, one place, one relationship to another. I know why you do it, and where you learned it from. And I'm sorry. Living that way lost me the two things I love most in the world. Your mother. And you. It took awhile, but I got your mother back. I'd like to have you back, too. But even more than that, I just want you to be happy. I want you to stop feeling like you have to constantly be on the move, trying to prove yourself, looking for the next *whatever* that you think is going to make you happy. Happiness doesn't come because you chase it. It comes because you let it find you."

Al was trying to process everything her dad just said. She stared at him, wondering where the man had come from, and then glanced over at her mother. She was wiping her eyes with her sleeve.

Dad cleared his throat. "Can I give you a hug?"

Al paused and then nodded, and her dad put his arms around her. After a few seconds, she put hers around him, too.

"I love you, Al."

"I love you, too, Dad."

There was no smooth way to get out of this. Al had never seen either of her parents emotional, and she wasn't sure what to do next. Fortunately, her phone rang.

It was Dana.

"I'm sorry, but I really do need to take this call."

"Of course, honey," Mum said. "We'll just head into the kitchen."

Al nodded and answered the phone. "What's up?"

"We have a break in the case of Mystery Mine. It involves Elena's family. Her grandmother, in particular. I'm headed over there now. I just thought you might want to know."

"Is she in trouble?"

"I'm not sure yet."

Al hung up and hurried into the kitchen. "Dad. Mum. I need to go. I'm so sorry."

"Is it a fire?"

"No, it's a friend. Her family is in trouble—the chief of police is heading there now—and I need to be there for her."

"Her?"

"Yes, Mum."

"A girlfriend?"

That was complicated. And Al didn't have time for complicated.

"She is very special to me."

"Then go." Dad's eyes narrowed. "You go, Al. Nothing is more important than being there for the people you love."

Al nodded solemnly, looking at her dad. She knew she had gotten her work ethic from him, for better and for worse. Now he was teaching a different lesson and she was listening.

She kissed both her parents on the cheek and raced out the door.

Ten minutes later, she was parking her motorcycle just as Dana pulled up in front of the funeral home.

"They don't know I'm coming," Dana said. She was in uniform. And she looked serious.

"Thanks for giving me a heads-up. I'm going to see if Elena is in her office. If so, I'll bring her up. One way or another, I'll meet you upstairs."

Dana nodded and headed up the stairs to the family's apartment. Al sprinted into the funeral home and went looking for Elena. She found her sitting behind her desk.

"Al, this is a surprise. I wasn't sure if you were flying out today or tomorrow."

"Tomorrow. I'm here because Dana called me about ten minutes ago. She said she has information about what we found in the mine. And it has something to do with your family. With your grandma, specifically. That's all I know. But it sounded serious. Dana is on her way upstairs right now."

Elena stood up slowly. Al wasn't sure what she was expecting, but it wasn't deathly calm.

"Are you alright?"

Elena looked at her. "I had a feeling this had something to do with my grandmother. I mean, not *that* kind of feeling. She's just been acting so strange, whenever the subject of that mine has come up."

"I'm sure it's all going to be fine, Elena."

Elena nodded. "I'm going to go upstairs now."

"Okay," Al said.

"Would you come with me?"

"Of course."

There was no place Al wanted to be in that moment than right there. For Elena. And for her family.

Everyone was sitting in the living room when they got upstairs. Elena's brothers were there, and her parents, who sat on the couch, with Grandma between them. They had pulled a dining room chair in for Dana. Al grabbed one for Elena, who sat down, and Al stood behind her.

"I was just starting to tell Mrs. Murphy that we have recovered evidence from the mine, Elena," Dana explained. Then she turned back to the family.

"There was a small red purse found a bit deeper into the tunnel, as well as the remnants of what looked like an abandoned campsite. Old blankets, some clothing, some eating utensils. All of it was in very bad shape, so bad that recovering DNA samples would be difficult, if not impossible. The purse was also in a state of severe decomposition, and it was completely empty. The contents appeared to have been spilled on the floor of the mine. One of the items we recovered, beneath decades of dirt and decay, was an old metal name badge. It was badly tarnished, and it took some effort to identify its owner. She worked at Miners Bank from 1952 to 1954. Her name was Mary Lou."

Elena's grandmother gasped and fell back into the couch.

Everyone else just started looking at each other, as if someone in the room would understand what was happening. But each one seemed as confused as the next.

Except for Elena's dad, who sat perfectly still on the couch beside the distraught grandmother.

"Mary Lou was Grandma's twin sister."

"What?" Elena and her brothers all shrieked at the same time. "Grandma had a sister? A *twin* sister?"

Elena's father nodded his head.

Mrs. Murphy sat up and looked at her son. "How...how did you know?"

"Seriously, Mom? The kids in school all knew. Their parents talked. It was just you who never talked about it. No one in the family did. Eventually, no one else talked about her anymore, either. It was like she never existed. I've never even seen a picture of her."

"Okay, can someone please tell me what is happening here," Elena said sharply. "First, why are we just finding out about this now. And, second—oh my God." She looked at Dana. "Was that her? Her...body? In the mine?"

Dana shook her head. "The remains belonged to a male. Caucasian. Six feet tall. Mid-thirties. The remains are so degraded the coroner doesn't think we'll be able to extract a good DNA sample, although they're trying. But we do have a pretty good idea of who they belonged to."

"Bud," Elena's grandmother said quietly. "It's Bud. It must be him."

"Who is *Bud*?"

Elena was clearly agitated, and Al put a hand on her shoulder and squeezed it. Elena put her hand on Al's and squeezed her back.

"Bud was a horrible person," Mrs. Murphy snarled. "Horrible."

"Grandma, can you please explain all this?"

"Bud got my sister pregnant when she was eighteen. She never told me all the details, but the way she described it, it was not consensual. I never liked that man. Almost no one did. He was a drifter, much older than my sister, who drank too much and got mean when he did. But it was 1952. My parents made her marry that man. Even though she—"

Mrs. Murphy froze. "I've never said this to anyone. I don't know if I *should* say this. It's not my truth to tell."

Everyone was staring at her, wide-eyed, waiting.

She took a deep breath.

"My parents made Mary Lou marry Bud even though we all knew that she...didn't want to be married. To a man. No one ever talked about it. But I knew that my sister was already in love with someone else."

She folded and unfolded her hands and closed her eyes. When she opened them, she looked right at Elena.

"My sister was in love with her best friend. They worked together. At the bank."

Elena took in a sharp breath. "Grandma—"

"Let me finish. Mary Lou was gay. But in those days that wasn't a thing you did. They put women in mental hospitals for less. Especially here, in such a small town, in the middle of nowhere. It wasn't safe, and it certainly wasn't accepted. I never knew if my parents made her marry Bud because they were embarrassed of her or because they were afraid for her. Either way, they gave her no choice. And they made her stay married to him even after she miscarried. Even when she told them what he was doing to her. The way he treated her. *Mis*-treated her. She would come to see me, and I knew she was using makeup to cover the bruises. I wanted to kill him myself."

Dad glanced quickly at Dana, who was taking careful notes, and then held up his hand. "Mom. Don't say one more word."

"Oh hush up, now. I've been keeping all of this a secret for way too long. Your children have never ever heard my sister's name before today. Keeping secrets, especially this one, and shoving down all the emotions that went with it, has been like a toxin, seeping through this family. And I'm done with it."

Al shifted her weight from one leg to the other and cleared her throat. She wasn't sure what her role was in that moment, but she knew someone in the family needed to be thinking clearly. "That's understandable, Mrs. Murphy. But your son is right. It might be best for you not to say anything else." She glanced at Dana. "Until you have a lawyer with you."

Elena looked up at Al with deep lines between her brows. Her eyes were filled with both gratitude and fear.

"Chief Jones. I appreciate your concern. But I am ninety years old. I am not going to carry these secrets with me to the grave. It's time my family knew the truth. Besides, what are they going to do? Arrest me? Are you going to arrest me, Chief Garcia?"

"Honestly, ma'am, I don't know yet."

"Well, even if you do, what will happen to me? They'll lock me in the same nursing home my husband is in? The old idiot. Just open up a wing for the Murphy gang. We're a bunch of hardened criminals."

Al tried not to laugh. This was extremely serious. But Grandma was funny.

"Gran. What *happened*?" Elena gripped Al's hand, which was still on her shoulder, even harder.

"I honestly don't know, Elena. I wish I did. Here's what I do know. Mary Lou needed to get away from him. Things were getting worse. She and her friend, Bertie, made a plan. First, Mary Lou was going to escape. She needed to get out of that house. Bud was beginning to suspect something, and she was afraid he was going to kill her. She planned to hide in that old mine shaft for a week or so. And just let everyone think she had run away. She only told me so that she could say good-bye. She knew she would never be able to come back. Bertie was going to take care of her, bring her food and so on. And then, a few weeks later, Bertie was going to tell everyone that she was moving back east to live with a cousin. And the two of them would disappear forever. She didn't tell me the rest of the plan, so that I couldn't accidentally give her away. I gave her all the money I had and hugged her so hard. I have never cried so much in my whole life, not before and not after."

"But what did your parents do when Mary Lou disappeared?" Elena asked. "Weren't they worried?"

"Everyone was. Well, everyone except Bud. He didn't even report that she was missing. The bank president finally started asking around, after she didn't come to work for three days. Three days! Can you imagine?"

"Dana, you must have records on all this, right? A missing person? There have to be records." Al didn't know a lot about police protocol, but this seemed to make sense.

Dana nodded. "Mary Lou Brown, maiden name Murphy, was reported missing in April of 1954. Mr. Edward Brown, known as Bud, was the chief suspect in her disappearance. No body was ever recovered, but eventually, Mrs. Brown was presumed dead." Dana paused and looked at Elena's grandmother. "But she wasn't the only missing person that year, was she, Mrs. Murphy?"

Elena's grandmother shook her head. "Two weeks after Mary Lou disappeared, Bud went missing, too. And so did Bertie. It was the biggest scandal this town had ever seen."

Elena sat back in her chair, shaking her head. "I don't understand any of this."

Mrs. Murphy sighed loudly, wringing her hands. "When Bud and Bertie vanished at the same time, right after Mary Lou, everyone in town assumed the two of them were having an affair. Especially when the bank president remembered that he had recently seen Bertie and Bud having a passionate discussion outside the bank. People figured the pair of them must have killed Mary Lou, hidden her body somewhere, and then run away together. It was the only thing that made any sense."

"But how did Bud end up—"

"Dead? I don't know," Elena's grandmother snapped. "And frankly, I don't care."

"Mom, you are looking tired." Elena's mother put her hand on Mrs. Murphy's knee. "Chief Garcia, can we take a break, please?"

"Of course. Just one more question, if you don't mind. Mrs. Murphy, do you know where your sister is now?"

Mrs. Murphy shook her head sadly. "I know she survived this whole mess, Chief. I knew she wasn't dead. I could feel it. She was my twin. Her heart beat the same as mine. But I never saw her again. She never made contact with me or, as far as I know, anyone else in town. Then, a few years ago, maybe ten now, it stopped."

"What stopped?"

"Her heart. I don't know how I knew, but I knew."

Dana stood up. "Okay. Thank you, everyone. I'll let you know if I have any further questions."

"You're not going to arrest me?"

Dana smiled softly. "Not today, Mrs. Murphy. I don't see any evidence that you did anything wrong. And I'm sorry for your loss, ma'am. I know you loved your sister very much."

Mrs. Murphy's face contorted, as if she was fighting hard to hold back tears. "Thank you, Chief Garcia."

Dana turned to Al. "I'll give you a call later."

"I'll walk you out."

Elena stood up. "I'll come, too." She kissed her grandmother on the cheek. "I'll see you soon, Gran. Go get some rest."

Downstairs, Al and Elena walked Dana to her car, and Elena asked the question that hadn't been answered yet. "So, what do you think happened? In that mine."

Dana shook her head. "I don't know. We may never know."

"It does sound like nobody was sorry that guy was gone," Al said angrily.

"That's true, Al. But it's still my job to try to solve the crime."

"I know it had something to do with a fire," Elena said. "Maybe it wasn't a crime. Maybe it was an accident."

"Maybe it was karma," Al snapped.

Elena reached for Al's hand and held it. A warm, silent thank you.

Dana said good-bye and Al followed Elena back into her office.

"One thing I've been wondering is, how did you know all of this, Elena. You said you saw fire coming out of the hole and that something led you to that mine, so that we could find those bones. If that's true, who or what do you think was trying to tell you something?"

Al wasn't sure what to believe about all this, but it did seem like a lot of strange coincidences.

Elena sighed. "I've been wondering the same thing. I'm thinking that maybe there was just so much bad energy trapped inside that mine, it had to come out somehow, sometime. And when the tunnel collapsed outside my house, because of the snow melt and the heavy rains, everything that had been trapped inside just sort of blew."

Elena sat on the edge of her desk. One of the overhead lights flickered and died, casting a shadow on her face.

"You look exhausted."

"Thanks." She smiled sadly. "It was hard watching my grandmother go through that. Having to relive those days. What a horrible loss."

"Well, and how terrible, carrying that secret with her, alone, for all these years."

"It explains so much about my family. It sounds like, at some point, they all just stopped talking about Mary Lou. No pictures. No memories. I don't even know if there is a cemetery plot for her somewhere. If there is, I don't know where it is."

"And it sounds like there was never any truth telling. About her life. Or her marriage. Or her disappearance."

"Or about who she loved," Elena said softly. "No wonder my family is so awful at expressing real emotion. We have silence baked into our DNA."

Elena crossed her arms and looked away. The silence between them felt heavy. Finally, Al took a deep breath.

"Speaking of people we love. My parents came for lunch today."

"They did?" Elena looked as surprised as Al felt.

"It was totally spur-of-the-moment. They called this morning and said they were coming to town for a quote-unquote romantic getaway. I didn't even know what to do with that."

"Why?"

"Let's just say my parents have lived very separate lives. My dad put his career first, before everything. Now that he's retired, it sounds like he's trying to make up for that."

Elena sighed again and looked out the window.

"What? What are you thinking?"

Elena's eyes found Al's. "I was just wondering if you and your dad are alike in other ways, too. And if, one day, you'll be trying to make up for the choices you're making now."

"Ouch."

"I'm not trying to be mean. Actually, I take that back. I'm sorry I said it."

"You're not sorry you thought it, though."

"I am. I know you have your interview tomorrow. I hope it goes well. I really do. You deserve every opportunity to succeed."

The bell rang, indicating that someone had come in the building, and Conner popped his head into the office. "Oh, sorry. I didn't know you had Chief Shiny Boots in here."

"Conner," Elena said sharply. "Do you have a question?"

"Um, let's see. We just found out that we have a great-aunt we never knew about. That she was a lesbian who got pregnant and had to marry a monster, and she maybe killed him, and then escaped with her lover to God knows where, and was never seen again, but she's probably dead now. And that our grandmother knew all about it and never said anything to anyone. Nope. No questions at all."

Then, just as suddenly, he pulled his head back and disappeared.

"Well, that about sums it up," Elena said.

Al nodded. "It's been quite an afternoon."

"Yep."

"Are you going to be okay?"

Elena sighed more deeply. She would probably be doing that for a while.

"I honestly don't know, Al. But I do know this. I am happy for you. I really am. But I'm also sad. It meant the world to me that you came here this afternoon. Especially now that I know your parents are in town. It seems like, for the past six months, you have been here for me through one crisis after another. You've been *annoying* sometimes. But you've been here. You're the first person I think of when I get into trouble. God help me, you're the first person I think of when I want to share something good that happened, when I capture something special through my lens, when my brothers are driving me bananas, when I wake up in the morning. I have finally let myself admit how much I like that, the constant thinking about you, and how much I like *you*. And now—" She shook her head, shrugging. "Now, I just feel sad. But will I be okay? Sure."

Al wasn't sure what to say. If only Dana had been there to kick her under the table and shake some words loose. But she was on her own. And her heart hurt.

"This job interview isn't about you, Elena."

"I know that."

"I care about you, too. I care about your family. Well, maybe not Conner." Al tried to smile.

"I know that, too."

"I have to follow my dream, though."

Elena nodded. "Well, you should probably get going. I'm sure you have a lot to do before you leave tomorrow. And I have a pile on my desk that needs attention before I can call it a day. I think first I'll change that bulb, though," she said, looking up at the ceiling. "It'll be annoying if I don't."

She looked back at Al. "Let me know how everything goes with the interview tomorrow, okay? I'll be sending you positive vibes."

"Thank you, Elena." Al paused. "Is it okay if I hug you?"

Elena held out her arms. "Of course."

As Al drove home, she had three things on her mind.

How sad she felt for Elena's grandma, and how much she hoped Mary Lou and Bertie had escaped to live a wonderful life together somewhere.

That she was more like her father than she wanted to admit.

And that Elena Murphy changed her own light bulbs.

Chapter Fifteen

Elena spent most of the next day in an absolute daze. She got up, fed Casper, and went to the office. But she couldn't remember what, if anything, she accomplished there. Then she went home, pulled leftovers out of the freezer, heated them up, and sat at her kitchen table eating dinner alone, scrolling through social media, playing a mindless game on her phone, and reading random facts about Detroit. She spent a few hours in her darkroom before bed, but wasn't feeling even a little creative, so mostly she organized and cleaned. Except for the twenty minutes she just stood there, staring at the photo she had taken of Al holding a chainsaw.

That photo was what landed Al in a different time zone, interviewing for a new job.

But it was bound to happen eventually. Elena knew that. Al could go anywhere she wanted. She *would* go anywhere she wanted. Al was smart, confident, talented. She was the kind of leader any fire department, in any city in the country, would love to have on their team. And she was ambitious. It was foolish to have imagined, even for a second, that Al would stay in Owen Station one day longer than necessary to reach her goals.

Hazel and Tessa both texted a few times, to see if she needed anything. But she couldn't think of a thing. Knox stopped by on his way home to drop off a pie and, when she didn't answer the door, he left it on the porch.

By the time she dropped off to sleep, she hadn't heard a single word from Al. Given the three-hour time difference between Detroit and Arizona at that time of year, she knew that she probably wouldn't hear anything more that night. And she was right.

The first thing she did when she opened her eyes on Friday was check her phone. Hazel had texted about an hour earlier to say she was searching every database available to her, trying to track down her grandmother's sister, but no luck so far.

"Everyone needs a friend who is a librarian," she told Casper, while giving him morning scratches. He head-butted her hand, encouraging her to keep at it, so she responded to Hazel with one hand—a simple thumbs-up emoji.

Her phone buzzed a second later. She sat up in bed and answered it.

"Good morning, Hazel."

"Hi. I didn't want to call and wake you, but I just saw your text, so I knew you were up. Have you heard anything yet?"

Elena had sworn Hazel to secrecy. For obvious reasons, Al didn't want it widely known that she was interviewing. But Elena needed *someone* to talk to.

"No. Nothing."

"She's probably just really busy."

"Sure. That's probably it."

"I mean, you know how these things go. She got off the plane yesterday. Had her interview. They took her to dinner. They probably took her out on the town, you know. To show her around. This morning she was probably up early to get to the airport, and she's caught in the middle of travel hell."

"Uh-huh. You're probably right."

"I'm sure she'll text you or call the first chance she gets."

"Uh-huh."

"Do you want to meet me for breakfast? I could go for some of Knox's pancakes."

Elena sighed. "I don't think I'm ready for that yet. I know everyone is talking about what happened this week, with the mine and my grandmother and everything. I'm still processing it myself. I don't have any appointments, so I think I'm just going to spend the day at home. Maybe under my covers."

Hazel said she understood. News about Grandma's missing sister and the presumed identity of the Mystery Mine man had spread through town fast. The *Caller* was planning a front-page story on Sunday, and the Phoenix and Tucson papers had already reported the basics of the case.

"Elena?"

"Yes."

"You're not alone, you know."

And for the first time since this all began—leaving LA, coming back to Owen Station, her brothers, the hole, the fire, Grandma's panic attack, her gruesome discovery in the mine, family secrets, Assistant Fire Chief Al Jones swaggering into her life and stealing her heart—Elena released her tears.

"Are you there, Elena?"

Elena grabbed a tissue and wiped her nose. "Yes."

Casper climbed up onto Elena's lap, purring loudly.

"Is that your cat?"

Elena laughed. "Yes."

"He sounds human-sized."

"He is. You should come meet him some time."

"I would love that."

After they hung up, Elena padded into the kitchen feeling grateful for the community that was emerging around her. She made herself a latte and had a piece of Knox's pie for breakfast. She wanted to spend the morning working on her *Queer Work* show. With any luck, she would have a gallery to show it in before too long.

Around noon, there was a knock on her front door.

"Gran," Elena exclaimed when she saw her grandmother standing on her porch. "What are you doing here? Come in."

"May I sit down? The drive over here and the climb up the stairs really wiped me out." Grandma looked ten years older than she did just a day ago.

"Of course." Elena gave her a quick kiss on the cheek and then helped her to the kitchen table. "Would you like a cup of tea? Some coffee? I can put some on for you."

"Tea would be lovely. Thank you."

Elena put the kettle on and sat down. "How are you doing, Gran? I can't even imagine how you must be feeling. Or how difficult this has been for you over all these years."

Grandma sighed. "It hasn't been easy, Elena. But it hasn't been easy for any of us. I am sorry that giving my sister the freedom she wanted and needed has cost us all so much. I know it will take time to heal, to undo the damage that I helped cause. But at least there are no more secrets now. The silence is broken."

Elena reached out and took Grandma's hand. "I only hope that your sister was able to have the life she deserved. That she was able to be herself. And that her days were filled with love and hope and happiness."

"I hope so, too, my dear." Gran squeezed Elena's hand. "You know, that is the kind of life I wish for you, Elena."

Elena pulled her hand back, folded them in her lap, and studied them, as though they held answers to some question she hadn't yet known to ask.

"I see the way Chief Jones looks at you, Elena. And the way you look at her. I know that you mean something to each other."

Grandma let out a long breath. "But the other day, when you were both together, when we got the news about Mary Lou, something was off with you two. I could see it. I came over here today because I thought you might need someone to talk to."

Elena closed her eyes. She was literally surrounded by people who cared about her. Even Gran, in the middle of one of the worst times of her life, was looking out for her.

This, she thought, was what she had hoped to find when she moved back to Owen Station. She was home.

If only there wasn't an Al-sized hole in the middle of it.

"We do care about each other, Gran. But right now we're just moving in different directions. I'm making a life for myself here in Owen Station. I've started looking at spaces for my gallery. I have friends who really care about me. I have you, and the rest of our goofy family. I would love to have Al be part of it. But she is on a mission of her own. She is going places, not just because she is ambitious but because she really cares and wants to make a difference for the firefighters who come after her. I love that about her. The photographs I took helped put her on the radar of departments across the country, and it's just a matter of time before she moves on." Elena paused. "I would never do anything to come between her and the life that she wants and deserves."

Grandma nodded. "She is very lucky to have you in her life, Elena. Nothing is harder than letting go of the people you love—even when you know that is the only way they can really be happy. Believe me, I know."

Of course she did.

"You know, it might be a little early. But I think we need something stronger than tea." Elena got up, turned off the kettle, pulled a couple of glasses out of the cabinet, and smacked them down on the table in front of Gran. "And I think times like this call for the good stuff."

"Elena!" It sounded like she was scolding, but the wicked smile on her face told a different story. "I could hardly say no to my favorite granddaughter."

Elena rolled her eyes. "I'm your *only* granddaughter, Gran."

She poured them both one finger of a twelve-year-old single malt Irish whiskey that was one of Lace's favorites. Lace had pulled out a bottle one evening after closing time in the tasting room, the first time Elena was invited to hang out with the gang. And she was hooked, both on the gang and the whiskey. She added a single large cube to each glass.

Then she lifted her glass. "To breaking the silence."

Gran lifted hers. "To love."

"Oh my goodness. That is something." Gran grinned after her first sip. "Your mother would not approve."

Elena laughed. "No. She definitely would not."

Seeing Grandma lifted Elena's mood, and after she left, Elena dove into her work. She created another half dozen test prints in the darkroom before her stomach started growling. When she looked at the time, she was startled to realized it was well past dinner time. Her phone was vibrating on the kitchen table when she finally emerged.

She had missed three calls from Al.

She sat down, mostly to steady herself.

Al hadn't left a voice message.

Elena wasn't sure she was ready to hear whatever it was Al had to say, anyway. And she wasn't hungry anymore.

Casper was, though. He was prowling between her legs, meowing. She reached down and scratched his head. "What now, huh, Casper? I guess I have to call her back, right?" Casper head-butted her hand. "Okay, fine. You first."

She poured some kibble into his dish and he attacked it like she hadn't fed him in days.

Then she picked up her phone and clicked on Al's name. The phone didn't even ring. Al answered immediately.

"Hi, Al. I, um, saw your calls. I was in the darkroom most of the day. Are you home? I mean, in your apartment. Are you back from your trip?"

God, she sounded like a blabbering idiot.

"I am. I was actually calling you from the road as I was driving back from the airport. I'm home now."

"So, how did it go? In Detroit."

There was a long pause. Elena heard a familiar tapping sound. Whatever it was Al had to say, it was making her nervous.

"Detroit was pretty fantastic, actually. The job is an incredible opportunity. The whole experience was...clarifying. And I like the city, too. It is facing a lot of challenges, but there are exciting things happening there, too. Music, art, architecture, business. It would be an amazing place to live."

"I'm glad it was so good, Al." Elena meant it, too, even though her heart was slowly being deconstructed and the pieces rearranged into some shape Elena didn't recognize.

"I'd rather tell you about it in person, if you're willing."

"I'd like that." Actually, Elena wasn't sure she could breathe.

"Great. I need a day, though. I have some things I need to take care of. Will you give me a day?"

"Anything you need, Al."

They made a date, if you could call it that, for Sunday morning. Al asked Elena to meet at her apartment around ten.

She was there at nine fifty-five.

It had taken her a long time that morning to figure out what to wear but she ended up in a sleeveless, jersey, maxi dress with a high side slit and a large buckle belt that sat on her hips. She thought about wearing white sneakers but opted for her favorite open-toed ankle boots, something that would help her feel both grounded and a little sexy. Her large gold hoops were made by her favorite artist in town. And she kept her makeup simple. She felt put together. And she was going to need that in order to be able to show up for Al, in support of her dreams, even if her heart hurt at the thought of an Owen Station without Al in it.

She sat in her car looking up at the duplex, and was struck again at how impersonal it felt. The landlord obviously took good care of the place. The xeroscape design probably made that easy. But there was nothing on the outside of the house to make it look like anyone lived there. No yard art. No posters or stickers in the window. No sports equipment or personal belongings anywhere. Not even a grill. It looked like a place for people who kept one foot out the door.

Elena took a deep breath and got herself ready for good-bye.

Al opened the door before she could knock.

"Elena," she said breathlessly, taking her into her arms for a warm hug. "Thank you for coming."

"Are you okay? You seem out of breath."

"I've been very, very busy." Al grinned. "The bigger question is, are *you* doing okay?" Her face grew serious. "I've been thinking about you nonstop. I'm sorry I had to leave town right after the news you got. It must have devastated your grandmother. Is *she* okay?"

Elena nodded. As difficult as that whole situation with Grandma was, at the moment it wasn't the thing that was making Elena want to throw up. "Gran is doing okay. I saw her yesterday. Spunky as ever. Thanks for asking."

"Of course. You know I have a little crush on her."

That was the first thing that day to make Elena feel like smiling. "The feeling is mutual, Al. So…what has kept you so busy?"

"Come in. I want to show you."

Elena followed Al down the hallway, past the kitchen, into the living room. And Elena's mouth fell open.

The bland furniture, which would not have been out of place in a doctor's waiting room, had been completely replaced by a room full of eclectic pieces. A rustic leather sofa and two armchairs, that looked like they had been well-loved, created a feeling of warmth in the room. A vintage chest served as a coffee table, and two wrought iron end tables sat on either side of the couch. A framed photo of Al with her parents, that looked like it might have been taken when she graduated from the academy, sat on one of them, next to a candle that had been lit and smelled divine. Like chocolate chip cookies baking in the oven. The table lamps were made of vintage fire hose nozzles, and a collection of vintage firehouse signs were hung on the wall. But the centerpiece in the room was the photograph Elena had taken of the whole crew the day of the photo shoot—the one where everybody had their arms around each other, grinning like maniacs, and everyone was looking at the camera. Except for Al—who was looking at Elena.

The photo had been framed and was hanging right above the couch.

Elena looked at Al, who was standing in the middle of the room, beaming.

"What is this, Al? What is happening? I am so confused."

"I was tired of feeling like I was living in a hotel. I moved all the furniture out into the garage and spent a good part of my day yesterday scouring antique shops up and down Main Street. There is a lot of fire service memorabilia in this town, did you know that?" Al said in a low, excited voice. Then she waved her arms and spun around in a slow circle. "Well? What do you think?"

"I love it. But I still don't understand. What about Detroit? What about the job?"

Al took a deep breath. Then she held out her hand. "Come with me into the kitchen. We can talk while we eat."

In the kitchen, Al had already set the table.

"Oh my God, it smells amazing in here." Elena picked up a colorful, ceramic plate. "And what's this? You have all new dishes, too?"

"Everything is new." Al gave a lopsided smile. "New to me, anyway. I love the color, don't you?"

Al pulled a breakfast casserole out of the oven and served them each a portion. "I want to get my own, new set of pots and pans, but I'll need to order those. So I'm still using the ones that came with the house. But everything else in here now is mine."

Elena looked around. On the open shelf above the sink, Al had lined up a set of vintage toy fire engines. And there was a shopping list stuck to the refrigerator with an old Smokey the Bear magnet.

Elena couldn't even think about eating, no matter how good it looked and smelled. "Al." She said it sharply, to get her attention.

Al was just about to take a bite, but she put the fork down, and turned to look at Elena.

"What. Is. Happening? I came over here today, ready for you to tell me that you took the job and you're moving to Detroit and you're saying good-bye. Instead, you have toy fire engines in your kitchen."

Al closed her eyes and took a deep breath. When she opened them, they were sky blue, the blue of endless possibilities.

"I don't know if they were planning to offer me the job or not, Elena. I think they were but I can't be sure. It was an amazing experience. The department is a mess. But the leadership really wants to see things change. I would have all the support I need to turn things around. The pay is beyond what I was expecting, three times what I'm making now. Going into the interview, I was a little afraid they just wanted to make me their diversity poster child. That it was all a show. But I'm pretty sure I was wrong. I felt genuinely welcomed and appreciated. And whoever fills that position is going to make a huge difference."

"Whoever—?"

"It won't be me, Elena. I called and thanked them for the opportunity to interview, but told them that I'm not ready to leave my current position."

Elena felt unsteady on her seat, so she gripped the counter and tried to make her heart stop racing. She couldn't let Al do this.

"Al. Please. Listen to me. I can't let you—"

Al held up her hand. "I'm not ready to leave my crew, Elena. I feel like I've only just started to build a relationship with them, the kind that can be really transformative, you know? For them, and for me. The department is going to be going through a huge transition over the next few years as half our guys retire, and I want to be here to make sure that goes well. I want to continue building a department that is representative of the community, where young recruits who look like me have a place to learn. And I still have things to learn here, too. About how to mentor and recruit and train. About how to work through hard times and get to the other side." She paused thoughtfully. "That's something I've never had to do. You know, what I mean? When things got rough or I had a falling out with someone, it didn't matter, because I knew I wouldn't be there for long, anyway." She smiled at Elena. "I have a *lot* of things to learn."

"Plus!" Al almost jumped up and down in her seat. "I actually sort of love this quirky little town. Part of the reason I needed a day is because I wanted to spend time just *being* here. Walking around. Poking into shops. Talking to people. Madeline, at that funky little gallery on Second Street, framed my pictures for me. Did you know that she used to be a kindergarten teacher? And the two young men from the antique shop, Juanito and Jacob, helped me move all this stuff up here, and move the stuff that was up here into the garage. They're both attending community college. One wants to be a health tech and the other is a graphic designer. I spent the whole day sort of practicing what it would be like to actually live here. I've never done that anywhere before. Never imagined myself being planted somewhere. I wanted to be sure, before I made my final decision." Al leaned toward Elena. "I really kind of liked it," she said in a hushed tone.

Elena just sat there, trying to process everything she was hearing.

"Really? You're telling me that you aren't leaving? You're going to stay here. In Owen Station."

"I am for now, anyway. And maybe for a long time. I want to see what it feels like. To have a home." Al studied Elena's face. "Is that okay with you?"

"Oh my God, Al. That is more than okay." She stood up and took Al's face in her hands, kissing her deep and long. Al wrapped her arms around her waist and drew her close.

"I don't want to scare you, Elena. I know we are really still just figuring things out. But I'm not ready to leave you, either. I want to see where this is going. I like how I feel when I am with you. You are so good at letting yourself be cared for—and I really like being able to be here for you. But you also know how to take care of yourself. You're independent and strong and willing to get after whatever it is you want or need. That is very sexy. Plus," Al grinned, "as you know, I love your grandmother."

Elena laughed. "What's not to love?"

"So, what are your plans for the rest of the day? I have one more thing to show you, if you're willing."

"I can't even imagine saying no to that, no matter what my plans were for the day."

They took some bites of breakfast but didn't linger. Al was looking at her watch like she was late for a date.

"Let's take my bike." Al grabbed Elena's hand when they got outside and started to lead her to her parked motorcycle. "Oh, but wait. Can you ride wearing that? We're not going far but—"

Elena laughed. "Have you ever worn a dress, Al?"

Al shook her head with a crooked grin.

"Come on, I'll show you."

They put helmets on and Al threw her leg over the bike, stabilizing it for Elena to mount up next. Elena put her left foot on the footrest, hitched up her dress, and threw her right leg over. Then she tucked the bottom of her dress underneath her and settled in.

"That's how it is done."

"You're a master."

"One of these days, I'd like you to take me on a serious ride."

"Deal," Al said, firing up the bike. "There's a microphone inside the helmet so we can talk to each other."

They weren't going far, Al said about fifteen minutes on the other side of town.

"I spent an hour riding all through town yesterday morning," Al said through the mic. "Before I went shopping. I wanted to explore the neighborhoods."

"And what did you discover?"

"That Owen Station is beautiful."

Al slowed the bike in front of a bungalow with white siding and a gray metal roof. The window frames were the same gray, and the front door was a deep maroon. The porch looked like it needed some work.

And there was a for sale sign in the yard.

"Chief Jones!" A kid, maybe eight or nine years old, wearing a Phoenix Suns cap ran up to Al and threw their arms around her. "You're back."

"It's good to see you, too, Frankie."

An older man stepped out onto the porch next door and Al waved at him. "Hey there, Ed."

"Are you gonna let Frankie beat you at HORSE again, Chief?"

"I didn't *let* Frankie win yesterday. I lost fair and square."

"If you say so." The man grinned.

Frankie ran next door, grabbed a basketball, and dribbled it up the sidewalk toward Al, who immediately started trying to steal it.

"Too bad, so sad," Frankie laughed, spinning away and dribbling out of Al's reach.

Al laughed and turned to Elena. "I'm hoping these two will be my new—"

A horn honked behind them, and they turned to see Knox pulling up.

"Well, if it isn't our friendly neighborhood Realtor." Al gave him a big hug when he got out of the car, and then Knox came over to give Elena a kiss.

"How are you holding up?" Knox asked her quietly.

"I'm a little wobbly, to be honest. This has been a lot to process."

Knox nodded. "Well, it's not over yet. Let's get those keys, Al."

They all went onto the porch and Knox opened the lockbox. Then he tossed the keys to Al. "Why don't you do the honors?"

Al took the keys and unlocked the door. But before she opened it, she turned to Elena and dangled the keys in front of her. "See, this is how it's done."

And then Al laughed, warmly, gently, like all the tension she had been carrying around for decades had suddenly melted away. She leaned over and kissed Elena on the cheek. "I saw this house yesterday as I was riding through town. Frankie was outside playing and I stopped to say hello. We met that day at the hole. Then I noticed the for sale sign and I knew. This was the one. Knox couldn't show it to me yesterday and, besides, I was very busy." She grinned wider. "So I'm seeing the inside for the first time today. I'm really glad you're here to see it with me."

Elena literally had nothing to say. The Al she was looking at was still Al, for sure. Big, bold, fun. But she was looser. More relaxed. And if possible, even more herself. As if she had been existing inside a wax mold, which looked like her but wasn't her, and then someone cracked the mold open and peeled off the wax to set her free.

"Let's go." Al took Elena's hand, pushed open the door, and stepped across the threshold.

"Damn..." Al said, looking around. "It feels even bigger in here than I thought it would, Knox."

Knox nodded. "It's pretty special. Listen, you've read the specs, you know the details. I don't need to sell you on this. How about if you just wander around and see what you think. I'll be right outside if you have questions."

"Sounds good. And don't let Frankie fool you. They'll kick your ass at HORSE and take all your money."

"I've been warned." Knox laughed as he stepped outside, closing the door before him.

Al spun around toward Elena. "So? What do you think?"

"I love it, Al. The original floors, the built-in cabinets and bookcases, the molding, the beautiful stairway. It has good bones and really good energy."

"No ghosts hanging around?"

Elena laughed. "First, I don't really do ghosts. Second, it's Owen Station. We're in the southwest. Of course there are ghosts."

"Okay, fine. But seriously? Good energy? You like it?"

"I really do. Let's go check out the kitchen."

"I'd like to check out the bedroom." Al waggled her eyebrows mischievously.

"I'd like that, too, but I think I'll like it better when there is actually a bed in it."

"Fair point. I can wait."

Al wandered in and out of every room on her way to the kitchen and Elena followed.

"Check out this backyard," Al exclaimed.

Elena looked out the window. "It's huge."

"I can picture barbecues out there, can't you? With all our friends."

Elena squinted at Al, trying to figure out if what she was seeing was real. "You are really serious about this, aren't you?"

"I've never been more serious about anything."

"What changed, Al? Why are you really staying?"

"My dad said something to me the other day. When he and my mother were in town. He said, 'Happiness doesn't come because you chase it. It comes because you let it find you.'"

Al turned to Elena and held both her hands. "You know what? I hadn't even gotten to Detroit yet—I was still on the plane—when I realized that everything that makes me happy was behind me. It was right here. In this town. And nothing I experienced while I was in Detroit changed that. Honestly, I couldn't wait to get back here—I couldn't wait to get back to you."

Elena threw her arms around Al's neck and pulled her in for a kiss. "This makes me so happy, Al."

Knox stuck his head in the door. "You two doing okay? Any questions?"

Al took a deep breath. "Nope, no questions."

"Are you ready to head out? Do you want to look at a few more properties?"

Al shook her head. "This is the one, Knox. Tell them I'm making an offer. I'll give them their asking price. I'm ready."

Frankie came running over as they were putting their helmets back on. "Hey, Chief! So are we going to be neighbors, or what?"

"We are, Frankie."

"Awesome," Frankie yelled, punching the air. "That means I can beat your butt in HORSE every day!"

It was a little before noon when they got back to Al's apartment.

"So, I feel like we've gotten a lot accomplished so far. What should we do for the rest of the day?" Al said, her eyes sparkling.

"Oh, I'd like some of that, please. But I was thinking...how about taking me for that ride?"

"Now?"

"Why not?"

"Alright. You actually owe me a ride through the Chiricahuas."

"I do?"

Al nodded. "That's where I was headed the day you almost ran me over."

"I did not almost run you over." Elena laughed.

"I still haven't had a chance to do that ride, but I have been dying to. It's a good couple of hours. Can you handle it?"

"Are you doubting me?"

"Not even a little.

"Good. I need a change of clothes, though. Let's stop at my place."

Al packed up the makings of a gourmet cheese board and threw in a couple bottles of mineral water. Then they headed to Elena's, where she quickly changed into pants and boots, and grabbed her camera, which Al carefully stowed away in a saddle bag.

It was a perfect day, sunny with a bit of cloud cover. Al took the curves through the canyon like a pro, fast and low. But never once did Elena feel anxious or worried. She knew that, on the back of Al's bike, with her arms around Al's waist, she was as safe as she would be anywhere in the world.

Huge, other-worldly rock formations, that looked like they were out of an old Flintstones cartoon, blew by. When they entered the national monument, they made their way up winding Bonita Canyon Drive to Echo Canyon Trail. Al parked the bike and held it steady, so Elena could dismount first.

"I've never been here before," Elena said, taking in the natural beauty all around them.

"I love that, Elena. I love that you grew up in this area, but we can still find places that are new to both of us."

"I have a feeling I'm going to discover all kinds of new things with you, Al." Elena got up on her toes to kiss her.

Al grabbed their snacks and they hiked a short way to the grottoes, passing areas where the desert floor disappeared and all they could see were towering pines and hoodoos, rock formations of tall columns, pinnacles, and enormous boulders that appeared to be precariously balanced on each other. Wildflowers covered the ground.

They found a spot to put down a blanket and took their time enjoying the spread. It felt like the first time in months that they were together with no pressures, no crises, no drama.

"I could get used to this," Al said, spreading a bit of bleu cheese on a cracker.

Elena leaned over and kissed her on the cheek. "Used to what?"

"What it feels like to stop chasing happiness."

After a short break, they hiked out to the bike, packed up, and headed through the gates, back onto the highway. The sun was inching toward the horizon, and the sky was on fire as they headed back to Owen Station—to home. Rich tones of ochre, magenta, and eggplant created an explosive backdrop for the saguaro cacti that dotted the mountain.

Elena thought about asking Al to stop, so she could capture the view with her camera. But she didn't.

Instead, she just held tight to Al, and let happiness find her.

EPILOGUE

Nine Months Later

Al walked through the firehouse straightening pictures. She had a number of Elena's photos from the home hardening shoot framed and hung on the wall. The diverse faces looking back at her were her inspiration. But she had also hung photos Elena took for another project. This one was initiated by Al. It featured the older firefighters of Owen Station. In each photo, one of the guys was showing a younger firefighter the ropes. Maintaining hoses. Repairing an engine. Cooking a meal. It was a beautiful glimpse into life in a firehouse, especially one that was in a state of evolution. Those photos, and the fun little videos Sam and some of the other young firefighters were making, had accelerated and improved their recruitment efforts.

When she walked into the kitchen, everybody jumped out of their seats and snapped off salutes.

"Good morning, Chief," they yelled in unison, doing their best Marine Corps imitation.

"At ease, ladies and gentlemen," Al said with a laugh. "You know you do not have to do that every time I walk in here. It's ridiculous." And hysterical.

A new name had been installed on the fire chief's door last week—Chief Al Jones.

Not long after Al withdrew from the process in Detroit, her boss had a mild heart attack. He had just turned sixty and had thirty years in the service. He said he had been thinking about retiring, anyway. This helped him make up his mind.

"My wife wants to spend more time with the grandkids, and I want to spend more time with her. So, we'll all be spending a lot more time at Disneyland." He laughed when he told Al about his decision. "And I want you to apply for the job."

Al sat back in her chair. "You know it's been my goal to make chief somewhere before I turned forty. But this isn't the way I wanted to get it."

"I know that, Al. But I'm going to let you in on a little secret. This day is the reason I hired you in the first place."

"I don't understand."

"Do you remember when we had lunch together at Banter & Brew, that day you came to interview?"

Al nodded.

"Your smile lit that place up. I could see the way people responded to you. People like you, Al. You're a natural leader. And I knew that, when the time came for me to hang up my helmet, you would be the right person to take this office and make it your own. I didn't think it would be quite so soon. But I think you're ready."

"How did you know I'd last that long, though, Chief? You knew my record, the way I move around. You knew how ambitious I was. How'd you know I wouldn't bounce out of here the first chance I got?"

"Because I believe in this town, Al. And I knew that it wouldn't be long before you did, too."

Al hadn't finished decorating her office yet, but she did have one picture hanging on the wall facing her desk. Elena took it, behind her house. A single, yellow wildflower clinging to the side of a blackened hillside.

Al knew it would remind her, every day, of how important her work was, in support of the women and men of the Owen Station Fire Department.

"Are you seriously out of coffee in here?" Al picked up the empty pot, giving everyone in the kitchen side-eye.

"The machine broke this morning," Jess said.

"I am not very happy about it," Sam grumbled. It was almost noon, but she looked disheveled, like she hadn't had a very good night's sleep.

"Somebody woke up on the wrong side of the bed this morning." Bobby tipped his head in Sam's direction. "But I'm not naming names."

Al's phone rang and she stepped out of the kitchen to answer it.

"Is Chief Jones there?"

"Speaking." Al grinned.

"What are you wearing?" Elena asked in a sexy voice.

Al laughed. "My uniform, as always."

"Oh, my favorite. I can't wait to watch you slip out of it."

"You are silly."

"I am madly in love. I'm also hungry. I was thinking about heading over to Banter & Brew for an early lunch. Want to join me?"

"I can do that. How soon are you thinking?"

"I want to get one more test strip done. I think I'm close to being ready to finalize the show." Elena had signed a lease for her new gallery space inside the old YWCA a week ago, not long after Al's promotion was announced.

Al thought about the paperwork on her desk. It wasn't her favorite part of the job, but until she had a new assistant chief, she had twice as much of it. And it was important. She really needed to get moving on hiring somebody into that spot, and she was going to look inside the department to find them.

"How about half an hour?" Al asked.

"That's perfect. I will meet you there."

Al poked her head back into the kitchen. "What's cooking?" The aromas coming off the stove were inviting.

"Bruce is making his kick-ass chili. He's sharing his secret recipe with me today," Jess said proudly. "And I'm making a sourdough bread."

"Want to join us, Chief?" Bobby asked.

"I would. It smells irresistible. But I have a lunch date."

The room erupted in oohs and aahs.

"Let me guess," one yelled.

"No, let me guess," yelled another.

She didn't mind the ribbing they gave her about Elena. It was part of being a family. And that's what she was building. A firehouse where you could have a feeling once in a while, even a tender one, and be honest about it. Where your teammates really had your back, no matter what you were going through. Where everybody mattered.

"You're all very funny. I'm going to take off in about half an hour, and I shouldn't be gone long. I'm just going over to Banter and Brew."

"Hell yeah. Bring us back a pie, won't you, Chief? No one made dessert." Bobby's tongue was practically hanging out. Al couldn't blame him. Nothing tasted better than a pie from Knox Reynold's oven.

"You know what? You all deserve it after the work you've been doing around here. The pie's on me today."

They were still slapping each other on the back, proud of themselves for wrangling dessert out of the chief, when she headed back to her new office. She looked over her to-do list and squeezed in a few phone calls before she went to meet Elena. One of the calls was to the mayor, who was pushing back on the budget increase Al was asking for. Al made the case that her team deserved to be paid competitively, or it was going to be hard to keep talent in Owen Station. She thought she got through to him. She also talked to Dana, who had been such a help during Al's transition into the top job. Dana had been through that process before, and she was crushing it. Al was thankful to have such an experienced mentor. During their off hours at Camp Fury, Dana had helped Al put together some goals for her first year in the job. And Al had gotten Dana to commit to the next camp, too.

The Arizona papers had all run a story about how Owen Station now had two women of color at the top of their departments. One of the national nighttime talk shows had even made contact, asking if the two of them would be interested in appearing on the show together. They talked it over and agreed it would be a great opportunity to give people a chance to see what was possible, and that it would be fun to spend a few days in LA. Elena promised to take them to all of her favorite places.

It really was possible to have a positive impact, no matter where you called home.

She cleared her desk and headed out to meet Elena.

It was a prefect spring day, bright sunlight, crisp air. She rode through town with her windows down, noticing the progress they were making in fire remediation, smiling as she counted new metal roofs and cleared yards. Bobby was a genius. She was looking forward to promoting him.

Elena was already at a table, so Al just waved at Knox as she made her way through the dining room, stopping to greet folks along the way.

"You look great." She bent down and gave Elena a kiss of the cheek.

"Why, thank you, Chief Jones. I guess you did leave before I was up and dressed this morning."

"Actually, I think I left you in a very satisfied state of *un*dress this morning."

"Yes, you did." Elena's cheeks pinked up.

"How's your day going?" Al asked.

"So good. I can't believe how much things have changed in the past year. My brothers, thank God, finally seem to be growing up. They've entered the National Funeral Directors Association's annual Funeral Face-Off contest this year. And we've been nominated for the Pursuit of Excellence Award."

"Elena," Al said, reaching for her hand across the table, "that is wonderful. Congratulations."

Elena shook her head. "Two years ago, I never imagined it could actually be fun working with them. Something happened when all of our family secrets came spilling out. And once we could start learning how to be real with each other, it's like they didn't need to be such smart-asses anymore. They could just say what they were really thinking and feeling. Yesterday, I heard them strategizing about how to approach a pickup at the home of a man who had adult children from three different marriages. Potentially complicated, right? They were all over it. No insensitive jokes. Just, how do we do this in a way that will help everyone feel cared about? I could hardly believe it."

"You helped make it all happen, Elena. You know that, right?"

Elena nodded. "I'm happy I've been able to be here to help. But I'm ready to move on. This afternoon I'm going to be writing a job description to hire someone to take my place. I'm hoping one of my cousins applies. It would be nice to keep it in the family. But if not, we'll just build a team that *feels* like family, no matter who's on it. My goal is to be spending ninety percent of my time in my studio and gallery by the end of next year."

Al could see both excitement and nerves in Elena's eyes. "Amazing. Are your parents on board?"

"They are. Dad knew when he asked me to come back that it wasn't a permanent solution. We have gone over the numbers and things look good. I think we're all ready."

Knox came over to take their orders. "It's great to see you both. Do you know what you are having? Or should I guess?" So many of the town's regulars had standing orders, depending on the day of the week.

"I'm going to mix it up today and get the special, instead of my usual. And a piece of pie, of course."

Al looked up. "No way I'm passing up the special. It's always the best thing on the menu. Also, I need a whole rhubarb pie to go. I promised them back at the station I'd bring it back with me."

"Got it. I'll hold that in the back until you're ready to go. And I'll have those orders up in just a couple. Anything to drink?" Knox paused.

"Two ice teas please. And I'll take a pour over to go when you bring out that pie. The coffee machine broke this morning. It made mud anyway."

"Do you need one? I just replaced my old espresso maker with something bigger and fancier. How about if I make a donation to my favorite fire department?"

"That's a great offer, Knox. But you know what'll happen if Station One has an espresso machine? They're all going to want one."

Elena looked up. "Don't you have a discretionary fund, from all the calendars you've sold?"

Al's eyes popped open. "Love that idea. Okay, Knox. I'll take that machine."

"You got it." Knox turned and headed back to the kitchen.

The bell on the door jingled and Hazel walked in carrying her baby in one of those baby backpacks. She and Sena had named their little girl Catalina, after the mountain range north of town.

Hazel spied Al and Elena and headed straight for their table. She kissed both of them on the cheek.

"I'm so glad I caught you here, Elena. I was going to stop by your new gallery after work today. But since you're *here,* do you mind if I join you?"

Hazel was typically a pretty enthusiastic personality, but she was literally bouncing up and down on the tips of her toes. It looked like maybe she hadn't slept since the baby was born six months ago.

"Of course. Please. Join us." Al jumped up, pulled out a chair, and helped Hazel sit down. Then she got a high chair and Hazel tucked Lina in.

"How are you doing, Hazel? How's Sena? How is parenthood?"

"Oh my gosh. I'm so thankful that I can bring Lina to work for part of the day, until the daycare at Sena's office is up and running. Once that happens, she'll go with Sena each day." Hazel's mouth got all mushy and her eyes opened wide. "Sena is such a great mom."

Elena smiled, but there was something a little off about it. She looked nervous. "So, Hazel. Why were you coming to see me today?"

"As you know, I've been searching everywhere, trying to find your grandma's sister. Well, I don't know how to say this. I feel like I need a drum roll or something. But...I found them, Elena. Both Mary Lou and Bertie. I found them."

"You what? Where? Are they still alive?"

Hazel's mouth drooped a little. "Unfortunately, no. But here's the really amazing thing, Elena. They have a daughter. You have family in San Francisco."

"Oh my God. My grandmother is going to be beside herself."

Hazel filled her in on everything she had discovered and shared contact information for Mary Lou's daughter. They all got caught up on the town gossip, Hazel shared every detail of Lina's feeding schedule, and they finished up their lunch. Knox brought the check over and slipped into baby talk when he saw Lina. "I'm working on your coffee to go, Chief. I'll have your pie all packaged up wherever you're ready. And I'll put that espresso machine in your truck, if you want."

"That would be great, Knox. The team is going to be so excited."

Hazel pulled out her wallet to settle up.

Elena stopped her. "Hazel, please. Lunch is on me today. I am so thankful for the work you've done to bring closure for my family. You're a great friend."

Hazel packed up Lina and gave Elena and Al hugs.

"Good-bye, sweet one." Al kissed Lina on the head. "Don't give your mamas too much trouble."

"So, what are you going to do now? That was a lot of information Hazel just shared. How do you think Gran is going to react?" Al reached across the table and held Elena's hand. It was nice not to care whether or not they were front page news.

"I don't know. I think it will make her feel so much better, knowing that her sister was able to have the life she wanted. And that she has a daughter," Elena said, wide-eyed. "I hope it will help her know that, even though her secrets created all kinds of problems in our family, it also kept her sister safe, and helped make it possible for her to live a good life. I want to tell Gran as soon as possible. Can you come with me to dinner tonight at my parents? Gran loves you. And I would love for you to be there when I tell her."

"Of course. It would be my honor. But that means I better get going. I have a lot to do before I can take off for the day."

When Al got back to the firehouse, it was like she was carrying bags of gold. The pie would have been enough.

"An espresso machine?" Sam hooted and started a round of fist bumps and high fives in the kitchen.

Bruce was the only one scowling. "Coffee sludge is what holds these hard bodies together, Chief. You don't know what you're messing with here."

Al laughed and slapped him on the back. "This crew is tough, Bruce. I think they can survive a cappuccino."

The rest of the day flew by and she was just getting ready to pack things up when her phone rang.

"You still up for joining me and the fam for dinner?"

"Absolutely. I'm headed home to change clothes. Should I pick you up in about thirty?"

"Perfect. By the way, I was actually able to get a hold of my cousin today."

"Did it go well?

"Better than that. She wants to come meet her family."

"I can't wait to hear all about it. I'll see you in a bit."

Elena was ready when Al got to her house, and she jumped on the back of the bike. They were at her parents' before six thirty.

"Elena, I was so happy to hear you were coming to dinner. And in the middle of the week?" Elena's grandmother kissed her on the cheek and then she turned to Al. "I have a feeling you had something to do with this, Al."

"This is all Elena, Mrs. Murphy."

"Al Jones. You stop that right now. Please, call me Mary Ellen. That's my name."

"Will do, Mrs—Mary Ellen. Actually, though. I think I'd rather call you Gran. If that's okay with you."

"You're just trying to soften me up, missy. I see you." But Gran was grinning from ear to ear.

Al really did love Elena's grandmother. It made her miss her own. One day soon, she planned a trip across the pond to see them. They were going to absolutely fall in love with Elena, just as Al's parents already had.

"Dinner's ready," Elena's mom called from the kitchen. "There's wine on the table. Al, dear, would you pour some for everyone? Also, there are veggies and dip on the table, if you just can't wait."

The brothers were already in the dining room munching, each with a beer in hand. "Hey, sis. Hi, Al." They were used to seeing Al at their dining room table and treated her like one of the family.

Elena's mom came in carrying a pan of shepherd's pie. "This is Grandma's favorite," she rolled her eyes. "It's got too much butter, too much red meat, too much salt, and too much of everything that's bad for you. But she loves it."

"All that bad stuff is what makes it delicious," Gran said as she enthusiastically dug in.

Elena shifted uncomfortably in her chair. Al knew that, even though she had mostly good news to share, she was also going to have to confirm what her grandmother already knew, that her sister was gone. Scooting a little closer to her, Al pressed her leg against Elena's. She wanted Elena to know she wasn't alone.

Elena gave Al's knee a squeeze.

"Thanks for pulling this together so fast tonight, Mom. It tastes delicious..." Elena paused and took a sip of wine. "I asked you to do this so that I could share some news I got today."

Everyone stopped in mid-bite and looked at her. Al put her hand on top of the hand Elena had resting on her knee, and gave a little squeeze. Elena took a deep breath.

"As you know, Hazel has been using every search methodology she knows to try to track down your sister, Gran."

"What did you find out, Elena? Tell us." Gran looked even more frail than usual.

"Hazel actually found her by accident. After they ran away, Mary Lou and Bertie did a good job of disappearing. They dyed their hair, changed their names, and started a new life together in San Francisco. They were terrified of being tracked down by Bud. It doesn't sound like they ever knew what happened to him. They just knew that he found out about their plan to run away together, followed Bertie to the mine shaft where Mary Lou was hiding out, and attacked them. He must have had an accelerant or something with him, because he started a fire. Maybe planning to kill them. They took off running and never looked back."

"How...how in the world did Hazel find this all out?"

"She ran across an old series of videotapes, part of a series that a domestic violence shelter in San Francisco put together. The shelter is still there and it mainly serves the LGBTQ community.

Mary Lou was one of the people who told her story for the series, although she was using her new name, of course—Margaret. Hazel recognized parts of the story Margaret told, and had a hunch. She did some more digging and discovered that the woman in the video and your sister were the same person."

Gran was very still. "Is my sister—"

Elena shook her head. "You were right, Gran. She passed away about ten years ago."

"And Bertie?"

"Your sister and Bertie, or Betty as she was known there, lived happily for decades in San Francisco. That shelter? They actually started it together. They lived a really good life, Gran. And made an impact on a lot of people. Bertie passed away last year."

Al thought Gran might cry or something. But she held it together. That's where Elena got her toughness from.

"Elena, tell Gran the most exciting part." Al encouraged her to keep talking, to get the whole story out.

"Oh my God. I almost forgot." She turned to her grandmother. "Gran, your sister and Bertie had a daughter. Her name is Ellen. They named her after you."

And that's when the tears finally came. Elena got up to put her arms around Gran, and her brothers joined her.

"You should be so proud of what you helped make happen, Gran. You helped Mary Lou escape. And the two of them made a huge difference in their community. The shelter they started was the first of its kind in the country. They made it okay for the LGBTQ community to talk about domestic violence. To get help and not be ashamed. It is still one of the largest shelters of its kind in the country. Ellen is the CEO now. She took over about five years before Mary Lou passed away. She's doing a great job. And she's married." Elena paused. "She has two girls of her own."

Gran's eyes were wet. "I just don't know what to say. I can't believe it. They had a baby. I never would have dreamed that it would be possible for them to become parents."

"It wasn't easy, that's for sure. They were one of the first couples in California to do it. And only Bertie was able to legally adopt her at the time. It was hardly even possible for her to do it, as a single mother. That's how they classified her. It wasn't until much later, when they were finally able to get legally married, that they petitioned to have documents changed. That was right before your sister passed. They wanted to set the record straight. Ellen was *their* daughter. Together."

"You have a lot of information, Elena. Did Hazel tell you all of this?" Conner asked. A serious question. In a serious tone of voice. Without a goofy look on his face.

Elena was right. Things were changing in the Murphy family.

"I actually talked to Ellen on the phone today. She was so excited to hear from me. She always heard bits and pieces about how her moms came to California. But she never knew more than what Mary Lou shared in the video. She didn't know anything else or any of the details, and of course she respected her mothers' right to keep that information to themselves. She had no idea that she has a whole family here in Owen Station. And she can't wait to meet us. She's planning a trip here next month."

Elena's family was so grateful to have answers to the questions that had been hanging over them for months. Before they left, Gran gave Elena and then Al huge hugs.

"I am so grateful to live to see this day," she said. "My granddaughter has been able to find the happiness she deserves, with the woman she loves."

"I didn't find it, Gran," Elena smiled, looking at Al. "It found me."

"And me." Al smiled back.

Then she took Elena's hand and led her home.

About the Author

Writing duo Kelly and Tana Fireside love traveling, cooking great food, and making music around a campfire. They've been best friends for more than twenty-five years and are still madly in love after fifteen years of marriage. It took them a long time to find their way to each other, and now they're never letting go. After working for many years in public and community service, they are writing stories to help spark a revolutionary love of self and others. They spend most of their time on the road in Howie (their House On Wheels) with a frisky pup named Gabby and her best friend, Chip the cat.

Books Available from Bold Strokes Books

A Heart Divided by Angie Williams. Emmaline is the most beautiful woman Jack has ever seen, but being a veteran of the Confederate army that killed her husband isn't the only thing keeping them apart. (978-1-63679-537-9)

Adrift by Sam Ledel. Two women whose lives are anchored by guilt and obligation find romance amidst the tumultuous Prohibition movement in 1920s California. (978-1-63679-577-5)

Cabin Fever by Tagan Shepard. The longer Morgan and Shelby are stranded together, the more their feelings grow, but is it real, or just cabin fever? (978-1-63679-632-1)

Clean Kill by Anne Laughlin. When someone starts killing people she knows in the recovery world, former detective Nicky Sullivan must race to stop the killer and keep herself from being arrested for the crimes. (978-1-63679-634-5)

Only a Bridesmaid by Haley Donnell. A fake bridesmaid, a socially anxious bride, and an unexpected love—what could go wrong? (978-1-63679-642-0)

Primal Hunt by L.L. Raand. Anya, a young wolf warrior, finds herself paired with Rafe, one of the most powerful Vampires in the Americas, in an erotic union of blood and sex. (978-1-63679-561-4)

Puzzles Can Be Deadly by David S. Pederson. Skip loves a good puzzle. Little does he know that a simple phone call will lead him and his boyfriend Henry to the deadliest puzzle he's ever encountered. (978-1-63679-615-4)

Snake Charming by Genevieve McCluer. Playgirl vampire Freddie is on the run and a chance encounter with lamia Phoebe makes them both realize that they may have found the love they'd given up on. (978-1-63679-628-4)

Spirits and Sirens by Kelly and Tana Fireside. When rumored ghost whisperer Elena Murphy and very skeptical assistant fire chief Allison Jones have to work together to solve a 70-year-old mystery, sparks fly—will it be enough to melt the ice between them and let love ignite? (978-1-63679-607-9)

A Case for Discretion by Ashley Moore. Will Gwen, a prominent Atlanta attorney, choose Etta, the law student she's clandestinely dating, or is her political future too important to sacrifice? (978-1-63679-617-8)

Aubrey McFadden Is Never Getting Married by Georgia Beers. Aubrey McFadden is never getting married, but she does have five weddings to attend, and she'll be avoiding Monica Wallace, the woman who ruined her happily ever after, at every single one. (978-1-63679-613-0)

Flowers for Dead Girls by Abigail Collins. Isla might be just the right kind of girl to bring Astra out of her shell—and maybe more. The only problem? She's dead. (978-1-63679-584-3)

Good Bones by Aurora Rey. Designer and contractor Logan Barrow can give Kathleen Kenney the house of her dreams, but can she convince the cynical romance writer to take a chance on love? (978-1-63679-589-8)

Leather, Lace, and Locs by Anne Shade. Three friends, each on their own path in life, with one obstacle…finding room in their busy lives for a love that will give them their happily ever afters. (978-1-63679-529-4)

Rainbow Overalls by Maggie Fortuna. Arriving in Vermont for her first year of college, an introverted bookworm forms a friendship with an outgoing artist and finds what comes after the classic coming out story: a being out story. (978-1-63679-606-2)

Revisiting Summer Nights by Ashley Bartlett. PJ Addison and Wylie Parsons have been called back to film the most recent Dangerous Summer Nights installment. Only this time they're not in love and it's going to stay that way. (978-1-63679-551-5)

The Broken Lines of Us by Shia Woods. Charlie Dawson returns to the city she left behind and she meets an unexpected stranger on her first night back, discovering that coming home might not be as hard as she thought. (978-1-63679-585-0)

Triad Magic by 'Nathan Burgoine. Face-to-face against forces set in motion hundreds of years ago, Luc, Anders, and Curtis—vampire, demon, and wizard—must draw on the power of blood, soul, and magic to stop a killer. (978-1-63679-505-8)

All This Time by Sage Donnell. Erin and Jodi share a complicated past, but a very different present. Will they ever be able to make a future together work? (978-1-63679-622-2)

Crossing Bridges by Chelsey Lynford. When a one-night stand between a snowboard instructor and a business executive becomes more, one has to overcome her past, while the other must let go of her planned future. (978-1-63679-646-8)

Dancing Toward Stardust by Julia Underwood. Age has nothing to do with becoming the person you were meant to be, taking a chance, and finding love. (978-1-63679-588-1)

Evacuation to Love by CA Popovich. As a hurricane rips through Florida, so too are Joanne and Shanna's lives upended. It'll take a force of nature to show them the love it takes to rebuild. (978-1-63679-493-8)

Lean in to Love by Catherine Lane. Will badly behaving celebrities, erotic sex tapes, and steamy scandals prevent Rory and Ellis from leaning in to love? (978-1-63679-582-9)

Searching for Someday by Renee Roman. For loner Rayne Thomas, her only goal for working out is to build her confidence, but Maggie Flanders has another idea, and neither are prepared for the outcome. (978-1-63679-568-3)

The Romance Lovers Book Club by MA Binfield and Toni Logan. After their book club reads a romance about an American tourist falling in love with an English princess, Harper and her best friend, Alice, book an impulsive trip to London hoping they'll each fall for the women of their dreams. (978-1-63679-501-0)

Truly Home by J.J. Hale. Ruth and Olivia discover home is more than a four-letter word. (978-1-63679-579-9)

View from the Top by Morgan Adams. When it comes to love, sometimes the higher you climb, the harder you fall. (978-1-63679-604-8)

Blood Rage by Ileandra Young. A stolen artifact, a family in the dark, an entire city on edge. Can SPEAR agent Danika Karson juggle all three over a weekend with the "in-laws," while an unknown, malevolent entity lies in wait upon her very skin? (978-1-63679-539-3)

Ghost Town by R.E. Ward. Blair Wyndon and Leif Henderson are set to prove ghosts exist when the mystery suddenly turns deadly. Someone or something else is in Masonville, and if they don't find a way to escape, they might never leave. (978-1-63679-523-2)

Good Christian Girls by Elizabeth Bradshaw. In this heartfelt coming of age lesbian romance, Lacey and Jo help each other untangle who they are from who everyone says they're supposed to be. (978-1-63679-555-3)

Guide Us Home by CF Frizzell and Jesse J. Thoma. When acquisition of an abandoned lighthouse pits ambitious competitors Nancy and Sam against each other, it takes a WWII tale of two brave women to make them see the light. (978-1-63679-533-1)

Lost Harbor by Kimberly Cooper Griffin. For Alice and Bridget's love to survive, they must find a way to reconcile the most important passions in their lives—devotion to the church and each other. (978-1-63679-463-1)

Never a Bridesmaid by Spencer Greene. As her sister's wedding gets closer, Jessica finds that her hatred for the maid of honor is a bit more complicated than she thought. Could it be something more than hatred? (978-1-63679-559-1)

The Rewind by Nicole Stiling. For police detective Cami Lyons and crime reporter Alicia Flynn, some choices break hearts. Others leave a body count. (978-1-63679-572-0)

Turning Point by Cathy Dunnell. When Asha and her former high school bully Jody struggle to deny their growing attraction, can they move forward without going back? (978-1-63679-549-2)

When Tomorrow Comes by D. Jackson Leigh. Teague Maxwell, convinced she will die before she turns 41, hires animal rescue owner Baye Cobb to rehome her extensive menagerie. (978-1-63679-557-7)

You Had Me at Merlot by Melissa Brayden. Leighton and Jamie have all the ingredients to turn their attraction into love, but it's a recipe for disaster. (978-1-63679-543-0)